# THE JUDICIAL SYSTEM IS GUILTY

## THE RAPING OF LADY JUSTICE

### By: DAVID J. BROWN

COPYRIGHT © JUNE 1, 2022 DAVID J BROWN BOOKS

PUBLISHED BY
DAVID J. BROWN BOOKS, LLC
PRINTED IN THE
UNITED STATES OF AMERICA

# THE JUDICIAL SYSTEM IS GUILTY

### THE RAPING OF LADY JUSTICE

All Rights Reserved
Copyright © May 2022
DAVID J. BROWN BOOKS, LLC
www.davidjbrownbooks.com

Paperback ISBN:
Library of Congress Control Number:

PRINTED IN THE UNITED STATES OF AMERICA

*This book may not be reproduced, transmitted, or be stored in whole or in part by any means, including graphic, electronic, or mechanical without the express written consent of the publisher except in the case of brief quotations embodied in critical articles and reviews.*

This title is the seventh in a series by the author, David J. Brown.

Each of the author's seven books are stand-alone novels but run in a series with the primary characters moving through each book.

As in all of my other books, I am donating this book to the U.S. National Library Service (NLS) for the Blind and Physically Handicapped. This book can be listened to free of charge. Minnesota residents can order my voice recorded books from the "Minnesota Braille and Talking Book Library Catalog" through the Minnesota Department of Education.

GOD BLESS AMERICA

DAVID J. BROWN

Look for David's first two novels;

"Daddy Had to Say Goodbye" and "Flesh of a Fraud" in audiobook to be released in June of 2022 on his website, Davidjbrownbooks.com

This story is a work of fiction. It is inspired in part by true life events. In certain cases, locations, incidents, characters and timelines have been changed for dramatic purposes. Certain characters may be composites or entirely fictitious

## A note from your author:

Never let anyone tell you that you can't do it.
Never tell yourself that you can't do it.

Dreams are worth Dreaming my friends.
Dare to Dream and as always
Dream BIG!

Within all fiction, lies a bit of truth.
Within all truth, lies a bit of fiction.
Our perceptions are the deciding factors.

David J. Brown

DAVID J. BROWN

# INTRODUCTION

We have all had those special people in our lives who we knew we just couldn't live without ……until we had to.

Learning to live with the loss of someone we've loved is a lifelong journey and most oftentimes painful. We somehow get through it because we know that we have to. At times we may find ourselves bitter and angry. Nobody knows our pain as we do, but yet we think they should all understand, but they don't understand what our suffering feels like, so very few actually know or worse yet, even care.

My current truth Is that I hardly, if at all, care any longer. I've become hard edged. I don't like myself any longer. I know why I became this way, it is because of my need to survive, but I'm no longer surviving. There's a big part of my soul that has become quite darkened. I tell myself that living with dignity is more important than dying with dignity and yet I don't actually live that way any longer. I have to come back to grips with the fact that every truth that I'm not willing to admit, is another lie that I have to learn to live with. That's a lonely and empty place to be.

I Have suffered from PTSD way back to my earliest memories in life and throughout my many years as a Rescue Paramedic and a Police Officer, along with my own lousy life choices, have rendered me into a deep depression. I have struggled for the last several years to fight off using the term, PTSD because that term has been so badly bastardized and watered down. Now people get PTSD if they get caught in the rain without an umbrella or their kitty coughs up a hairball and you step on it in your bare feet. I guess what it really is that I'm just fed up with people. I've given more to them than I've given to myself and I feel empty. I no longer have the desire to evaluate and improve myself as I once did. I'll become just like some of those others, where I'm starting to evaluate and judge them rather than myself. Bitterness is a toxic poison. It's an acid that at some point will eat its own container. I'm not ready for that yet, but I don't know how to get out from underneath it. How much longer can I deny my own loneliness? I fully know that I've done this to myself. Yes, I carry a strong facade of okayness, it's the lie behind that lie that takes me to the darkness. It of course, is that damn fear, yet we all know fear does not prevent death, fear prevents life! There are times that I think I just want to disappear but in reality, what I truly want is to be found, found and respected.

    I fully know that I've set this up myself. There's a number of people who have claimed that I have helped them change their lives, that I brought them to a fresh awareness and they made a decision to improve and move on. For some reason I've telegraphed to them that I was not in need of any help or consideration and they owed me nothing and they were free to go on their way. I found myself angry that they didn't care enough to see through my facade and

I would take a hard line in silently declaring that, "Being a good person doesn't get you loved, what it does is, it gets you used!" Over the years I've learned that emotional cowards stupidly resent those who aren't.

I need to be ever mindful that actions prove who someone is, words just prove who they pretend to be. I have trained myself to ignore the many people who showed such doubt in my writing and even challenged whether or not it was truly my work. That even includes my own family and my few long-term friends. Success comes with a hefty price. I think it was JK Rowling in her book, "Half-Blood Prince" who wrote, "Greatness inspires envy, envy engenders spite, spite spawns lies."

That I can attest to, even my friend that I've known for more than fifty years and who I've given a free copy of each book to! We only live six miles apart so we have lunch a few times a month. He criticized one of my books because he claims that I misstated a common phrase. My response was a simple and level toned, "Fuck you pal, show me the books that you have written. Those that can't…criticize, pass the ketchup."

When I gave him a copy of, "#BeLikeEd" that was co-authored with my friend Christine Richie-Bomey his only comment was, "You had to have help from that woman!"

My response was again, a soft voiced comment. "You graduated college but your reading skills and comprehension is at a fourth-grade level.

This will be our final lunch together; I hope you choke on your jealousy."

My wife Heather is my grounding force. She always brings me back, right to where I need to be, as she reminds me of some of the words I've written and put in print in my last six novels. This morning she smiled as she said, "There are times that having a dream is every bit as important as realizing that dream. Dare to dream my friends!"

With a smile she further said, "Baby those are your words, printed in the books you wrote, that sit on the shelves with your other five books in the United States Library of Congress! I suggest you embrace your own counsel."

*Chapter 1*
# THE CREAM RISES TO THE TOP

It came in a brief email. It simply read, "I need to see you …. please?"
It's been close to a year since I've seen or even spoken to her but I think of her often because she's the kind of woman that you can't ever forget, nor would you want to! I have been feeling guilty for not staying in touch with her but at the same time I knew I had to leave her be. She is finding her way in life and her profession, with comfort and fondness I just have to say to myself, "It was a time that was, but now it has to be her time."

I couldn't help but giggle when thinking back to when we first met and the last time, I saw her. In a brief two-week span, she went from being a smart-ass punk kid, to a lovely, intelligent and sensitive young woman. I will always fondly remember our late-night flight back from Los Angeles when she laid her head on my shoulder and softly purred like a kitten as she slept. I will equally remember her drooling on my sport coat as she smeared her makeup on my best, white shirt collar. Listening to her breathing in her deep slumber was the prettiest music that I've ever heard. I remember wishing for that late night flight to never end. There is no question that I would be proud to call her my daughter. If there wasn't a forty-year age difference and if I didn't have Heather in my life she would be more, she would be a lot more.

It is that kind of purity of innocence that showed me my many blessings. When you do see it, you know what you're looking at and sadly, you know you may never see it again.

I had just finished my last novel, "Brothers of The Tattered Cloth" and sent it off for publication two days ago. I was still debating whether or not I wanted to start my seventh novel or just hang it up and walk away. I have nothing left to prove to anyone or even to myself for that matter.

So, I had the time and the interest of course, in seeing her. When I phoned her, she sounded a bit hesitant, perhaps awkward would be a better word. I knew there was something behind all this, it wasn't just a friendly, "Hey let's do lunch."

We met in the restaurant of the Corker Hotel. I was already seated at the table when she walked in. It seemed like the light's suddenly got brighter. What a lovely little creature she is. I stood and we had a warm embracing hug.

Me: Well sweetheart it's been almost a full year without any communication so I first have to ask you, are you, Rebecca or Reba, are you Val as in Valley girl, or are you perhaps still, Antsy Pants? Who the fuck are you today?

Val: Well, aren't you the same old sweetheart or are you the same old coarse son of a bitch that I left behind almost a year ago? God, I've missed you! I want to apologize for not reaching out to you earlier. I know about your loss of Father Martin and in part, what he meant to you. I wanted to be there for you but I felt like I'm in the outer circle of your life group. I didn't feel that I belonged there although I wanted to be. I hope you understand that?

Me: Yeah, I get that Babe, you're just fine but I've thought about you often, so what's the happs and why are you gracing me with your presence, this fine and sunny afternoon?

Val: I love it when you call me Val. When you say it, I hear a cautionary term of endearment. Well things have been going quite well for me, as a matter of fact this is the best my life has ever been. I'll run it down to you quickly. There were a few things that I left out when we spent our California time together. My family is quite well off. My grandfather, three uncles and my dad all run a very successful Law Practice. You're well aware that my end game is to become a Criminal Court Judge. I've just finished the two toughest parts of my quest. I volunteered at the Saint Louis County Prosecutor's Office for five months then I went on to the Saint Louis County Public

Defender's Office for five months. I wanted to get a read on the tempo and drive of those agencies. I don't understand the arrogance of people who think they are all powerful and mighty but work for government wages. Of course, my true goal was to fatten my resume for my hopeful judgeship appointment in the next couple of years. So, I've finished both of my what I will call, 'my internships'. But in all truth, I couldn't stomach them slimy fuckers any longer, not even for another minute.

I have done my very best to avoid going into the family law practice because of course, it's family and they want to be all up in my business. I don't want anyone in my business unless I ask them to join me. You, my lovely man, have an open invitation to be in all of my business, if you know what I mean and I believe you do!

I will practice criminal law in the meantime at the family practice. They have charged me with a daunting task. Although the law firm serves several counties in Minnesota and they have several divisions within the law firm, they want me to practice criminal defense.

They have given me my choice to pick any five cases to represent in different areas of crime. No one I know has the experience that you do. No one I know can and will call bullshit on me quicker than you do. There's no one, and I mean no one that I trust more than you. I'm here to propose an offer. I will pay you. I will pay you quite handsomely, if you'll interview each of the five top potential clients from a pool of twenty-three, "Applications for Representation" and tell me whether or not you think they're worth representing. I need you to help me prove that I have the right stuff to sit on the bench.

    Me:   On your feet baby, grab your purse and laptop, there are too many ears around here, we're going to my office and we will order lunch to be delivered.

    I of course couldn't help but notice how Val had filled out in the last year. When we first met, she had the body of a young woman that was cutting and starving for an upcoming bodybuilding event. Her hips were protruding so severely that I feared her flesh would tear open, I expected that she was severely malnourished which is common in bodybuilding competitions.

    Today I was looking at a full-bodied young lady with the confidence and composure of a woman beyond her years.

    Me:   Baby, it was an absolute pleasure to be walking behind you in the lobby. I see you have changed your cadence in the way you walk, I saw lady-like confidence and purpose. So, what happened?

    Val:   You were right to call me out on my childish posing behaviors and acting like a teen hooker. I hated going to CrossFit gyms but it helped me gain my self-confidence. Men only saw me as a piece of meat because I presented myself that way. I have only you to thank, I never let on that I was hanging on your every word, I guess I was too proud to admit it. I am no longer that arrogant little snot nosed kid that was lusting after you. Now I am a full-grown woman who still has the 'Hots' for you!

    Me:   So hot that you want to hire me? Am I going to be a 'kept man'?

    Val:   My sweet, sweet man. In another time and another place perhaps but currently my loins burn for your mind but if I need to strip and dance for you to reach your soul, put on some music!

    Me:   For some reason honey, AC/DC comes to mind with their hit song, "Highway to Hell." What the fuck do you want?

    Val:   Passion, I want your passion, I want it all big boy. Bring it hard, fast and dirty!

    Me:   Oh, that's real fucking cute. Tell me this baby doll face, what are you prepared to pay this nice man? I know of your family's law practice and I know how large they actually are and how wealthy the business actually is. In this world, my world, there ain't nothing for nothing sweetheart and you can write this up as your first lesson.

    The last few moments that we were together last year you became a cuddly purr kitty. You obviously want to change the game but don't trust for a moment that I'm going to pet you. I will talk and you will listen. I am going to remove your clothing and peel back several layers of your quivering flesh with my hands in my pockets. Listen tight little girl.

Do you remember what I wrote of my great distrust and distaste for lawyers in my first novel, "Daddy Had to Say Goodbye?" Baby, that was twelve years and six novels ago and nothing has changed other than lawyers have gotten worse, much worse!

Maybe you can explain to me why we have 17,000 pages in our law books? I will tell you why, it's because you and your law people cannot follow ten simple lines on a tablet carved in stone several centuries ago. Still love me, Babe?

Now let's get you mentally naked. You remind me of that little gal who had the pretty white anklets with rose petals on the folds with her new summer dress and shiny black patent leather shoes. You at the time had no idea of how wealthy your family was. You were just a kid and you took everything for granted but at the same time you knew that there were other little girls, even in your own school who didn't have what you had. How did you treat them? You were primed and groomed to be successful. I'm sure that you were on the debate team in junior high school or whenever the fuck they do that shit. You were assigned a pro or con of some certain argument. You competed with your opponent when you had no passion for the subject matter. You just wanted to win in everything you did. You have to understand that education is a setup and it sets the classes apart. You competed with your opponent to crush them. I don't fucking get any part of this bullshit of debate teams or student body councils and all the other crap of Prom King and Queen of the Senior Prom, whatever the fuck that is worth. That whole program is about you broadcasting to your lesser ones, "I am better than you."

For me, I was married in my junior year of high school and was divorcing in my Senior year. I didn't have the money for a Senior Class photo or to buy the yearbook or a class ring.

Then you roll into college without a second thought or worry of affording tuition, books, housing, meals or transportation while other people can't even entertain a dream of college and they're sunk because they don't have the financial backing and support of their families. You have to remember that I've spoken of that to you before. You know that I believe that we all poop and we are all going to die and when we do die, we are all going to go into the same size hole in the ground. I know you must find that extremely frightening because it'll be the one time in your life that you can't buy your way out of hell. Families like yours look down on all others simply because of what you have and others don't. I can only smile with the thought of a family such as yours, leaving their homes during the bitter cold months of winter to go play in the Bahamas and upon returning to find out that your furnace has puked. All the pipes in your house are frozen, the toilets are all lying in pieces with semi-frozen shit, four feet deep throughout the entire house. Suddenly you need help and you need help now and from the lowest form of human beings, you need an uneducated blue-collar worker, you need a plumber! But guess what sweetmeat, that plumber is busy and you're going to have to wait your turn. In the meantime, you're strolling through half frozen shit all throughout your home. Of course, because you have money, you can go to a hotel and live in the lap of luxury. That would be a very humbling experience for you. It's no different when your high-end Maserati breaks down and you have to call for a tow truck and have some greasy, dirty coveralled clown attending to your vehicle and hauling it to a dirty and dimly lit shop where it can be repaired by men with dirty hands. Of course, you needn't worry about the cost because well, you have money. Other people would have to rent a car or bum a ride or even ride the bus. But not you, because you have endless supplies of cash and credit, you've got enough money to pull you through most every dilemma that live delivers and in all honestly my dear, I resent the fuck out of people like you. And let's just back up for a moment. Where do lawyers obtain such great wealth and power and stature? From the little people like me, of course! Who really gives a fuck in the business of discovering guilt or innocence? It's all about how much I can hammer this poor fucking slob for. I'm sure that your family has sat around at the dinner table laughing about how you guys fucked some poor Jabroni while the client was thinking that you were fighting in their best interests when in fact, the opposing attorney is your tennis doubles partner! The judge of course is all part of the game. They are all members of the same Country Club; they all attend the same black-tie events and slap each other on the back while basking in their opulence and power. If I've enjoyed any one thing when I was a paramedic, it was knowing that no matter who you were, what you owned or who you thought you were, carried no weight with me or God. I have watched the wealthy beg and plead for me not to let them die. I always enjoyed watching them struggle to use the word, 'please' and actually mean it.

OK, enough of this dance for now, we're going to move on. People come to lawyers in most cases, because they're suffering some of the worst moments of their lives.

I'll give you a real-life example. My dear friend back in Colorado is divorcing. They own no property together, they've had no children together, they've been together for less than five years and are in full agreement with the separation of all household money and property. My friend actually wants nothing other than his clothes and a few mementos from his twenty-two years of military service. Suddenly she is working an angle. She has presented three different up-grades to her original lawyer drafted divorce papers by her lawyer. She has proven repeatedly that she is not trustworthy, either as a friend or spouse. She comes from a family of total scum, with her siblings all having lengthy jail and prison experience. Drug and alcohol addictions are a shared trait and they all bathe in the deep-end of the generational welfare pool. Few have ever worked. Their family motto is, "Give it to me or I will take it."

So, my friend went to an attorney, not trusting her or her prick-face lawyer and you know I can't stand fucking lawyers. Yes, my love, I fully know that you hold a law degree and you passed the bar exam the first time, which I understand is rather uncommon. My many experiences with testifying in court as a police officer along with my five divorces, I will always believe that lawyers are the scum of all scum as far as I'm concerned. Present company excluded of course. So, my Colorado friend saw a jerk-off lawyer that wants $3,500 up front as a retainer, $300 an hour or any part of an hour for his time, $230 an hour for his legal assistant, $300 for a phone call whether it's one minute or sixty minutes, $300 for every page written and the dollar numbers just keep rolling on. If you have any intentions of being that kind of lawyer you can simply rise from this table and spend the rest of your life fucking yourself.

Now tell me this sweetheart, does your firm knowingly represent guilty people? Because if you do, I don't want anything to do with you. I've seen all too often how defense attorneys twist shit and just flat out lie in court to get their client off the charge and the client goes back out and reoffends that very same day of release. Oftentimes these pukes of violent crimes will punish anyone who testified against them. I'm sure you won't enjoy this but you're going to sit here and listen to it because it's what the truth is.

Do you remember the O.J. Simpson trial in 1995 where O.J. Simpson was charged with the murders of Nicole Brown Simpson and Ron

Goldman? Does that ring a bell sweetie? Well Marsha Clark was the lead prosecutor in that case and she was not the fuck up that she wanted the world to believe she was. She made mistake, after mistake, after mistake, after mistake, and it was all by design. Do you remember the opening trial had to be set back a week because she was in the process of having her hair somehow fucking done and redone? The entire trial was televised. She played to the cameras like a cheap hooker would do in a porn video. It was fucking sickening to watch the way she pranced around the courtroom constantly posing. After she lost the trial, she developed a career as a big deal in TV and she claims she solely wrote some books which I doubt very much. She had to have a hell of a lot of help.

Do you remember the thing where Marsha Clark gave O.J. Simpson the glove that was blood soaked from the crime scene that had now been dried for several months and what happens when leather gets wet and then it dries? It shrinks from the chemicals in human blood that causes even greater shrinkage. So, the dummy of all lead prosecutor attorneys, had O.J. put on the glove and his lawyer chirped out, "If it don't fit, you must acquit!"

Honey every bit of that entire fucking deal was a setup, well-rehearsed and well executed. She was bought along with the judge, there's no other argument there as far as I'm concerned. Prosecutors and defense attorneys are bought all the time and you damn well know that! You may not want to hear or discuss it but you fucking must know that if any part of your agenda is to get a guilty person's case dismissed or the charges reduced, I don't want anything more to do with you, not just today but for fucking ever! If you're there to ensure they get a fair trial, as the same as I would expect if I were accused of a crime, then I think that's wonderful but if you get somebody off and they reoffend I think you should have to do the same amount of time they're going to have to do after they execute their next criminal escapade! *Kapish?*

Baby listen to me; I'm not going to buy any more of your bullshit. I don't believe that you want to run a chain of legal services offices any more than you want to slop hogs. I think I know and I think that you know, that I know, but now I want you to say it and remember, if I don't like the way it sounds, I'm not playing. Got it?

Val:   David, I prefer you call me Val, that is the most loving nickname I've ever had! Yes, you caught me already! So here is my end game. I want to take on five different types of criminal cases as directed by my grandfather and my dad. I want to and must win each of those cases. My Grandpa and Dad think I'm trying to prove my worth to come into the family practice. What I hope to do is garner their respect and support to assist me in my quest to be seated on the bench. I'm hoping you could and will help me to get there. I don't have to represent just anyone; they are allowing me to choose my five cases from a large stack of cases. I need you to vet those clients, I need you to sit with them and I need you to come back and tell me whether or not they're defendable, if they're not they can go somewhere else. I want to win; I must win all five of those cases and then I want to move on. I don't want to own a law office. What I'm going to do is I'm going to present them with a contract as to what they're going to do to help me to get to the bench. What do you think?

    Me: Baby you got monster balls and I love you for it. I don't know anything about your family nor do I care to know. I'm a little busy, if you don't remember, I'm actually a working writer and I write because that's what I do, because that's who I am. I don't like to play silly lil reindeer games but let me say this. I don't work for free, you've got a big money, high profile, high profit company and I want to be paid. I'm going to charge you $1,000 dollars a day for each case I review with a minimum of $10,000 per case. I'm going to spend no more than six hours a day on each case. That's right baby, my fee is $1,000 a day plus meals and $5.00 per mile. I'll be damned if I'm going to submit any kind of receipts. You will pay me what I tell you that you owe me.

    I will also assist you in jury selection. I can tell when good people lie as well as when liars lie. The last thing you want is a juror who lies during the prospective jury pool questionnaire sessions. Some people will lie just to sit on a jury. Some will lie to sit a case to get even with the accused because of their own unrelated life experience as a crime victim, then there are of course the pukes who live a life of slime and crime and will lobby other jurors to vote for the defendant to be found not guilty as a sign of some sort of twisted solidarity. You of course do know what a Rhino is? We have been dealing with those sons of bitches for the last thirty years in all government levels. Those fucking people that hold themselves up as Republicans to get elected and do nothing for the Republican party and everything for the Democratic Party. I think those fuckers should be hung. That in fact, should be a crime in and of itself, but who the fuck in this day and age charges any politician with a crime? I think Hillary Clinton said it best, "If I go down, I'll take half of Washington with me!"

There was a time that the FBI was solely established to fight organized crime. Today the Democratic party and the FBI have become organized crime.

I see you are getting antsy, sit still and listen; school is still in session. Once you come-to, you can no longer see the people of politics, entertainment, or celebrities as people to be envied or celebrated. Upon your awakening you will clearly see thieves, liars, fools, puppets and maniacal bullies. Our federal, state and local governments are nothing more than a well-orchestrated regime of Godless, Marxist fucks of all times. This by the way is nothing new. I think the greatest display of criminal immunity stems from the heirs of Walmart, Alice Walton. Sweet sister Alice is nothing more than a rich stumble drunk. She was convicted of four Drunk driving charges at different times. We will never know how many times she was stopped for suspected drunk driving when she played the, "Do you know who my daddy is?" card. The only fine she ever paid was $925 and she walked free. Her estimated wealth at that time was, 6.3 billion dollars, that's billion with a big fucking B! Five years after her latest conviction she was speeding in Fayetteville Arkansas while she struck and killed Aleida Harden, a 50-year-old cannery worker. Miss Walton was not even arrested or ticketed. She was let go on several drunk driving occasions because police and prosecutors feared repercussions from the wealth of the Walton family. One of her many DUI arrests took place in the Dallas/Fort Worth area. The Parker County prosecutor Fred Barker, told the Dallas/Fort Worth television affiliate, that he was going to allow the statute of limitations to expire even though they had video evidence of her sloppy fumbling gymnastics through her field sobriety test but the arresting trooper, Trooper Davis was unable to testify after he was mysteriously suspended last March and according to Trooper Davis's Barracks Commander, there was no blood alcohol testing ever conducted. Three weeks later, a Parker County judge granted a petition from Walton's lawyer to remove records of the arrest from the county's file system. How's that for power, babes?

 Now for a rather current case (or cases actually) in point;

 George Floyd was a celebrated career criminal who was void of any human value but highly honored by the lefties. That's as far as I want to go with that puke and his supporters.

Let's not forget about the supposed insurrection of the White House which was so badly and obviously contrived by the left for the sole purpose of burning President Donald Trump. Nancy Pelosi had the power to either shut it down or to promote it. Sweet sister Nancy didn't shut anything down but promoted all of it. There is another one who should have an X-ring on her forehead.

Next is that lying, repulsive piece of shit, Doctor Anthony Fauci. He claims that he is, "The Science." Yeah, he's the science all right, bought and paid for by whoever he has sold out to the highest bidders. His stock portfolio sits over ten million bucks with the bulk of his earnings from Chinese interests. Trust the science my ass, that's the most anti-science statement ever! Questioning science is how you do science and that is where the scientific findings come from, but not with that shit heel. He's just another one of the bottom feeders hanging from the puppeteer's control strings and who has done his utmost best to fuck everything and everyone for his own personal and political party pleasures. Every time I see him on television all I can see is a target X-ring on his forehead and I will rejoice on the day, if that in fact ever takes place. More locally, our illustrious governor shut down our state due to Covid to the point of bankruptcy while letting the cities in Minnesota burn, all to appease his voting base. Now, that the fuck-stick will not shut down the state when the rest of the adjoining states are shutting down because it's an election year and he is running for re-election. What a sweet fucking deal that is. Yes, he needs an X-ring too.

      The media, which of course is controlled by the liberals, has to be the greatest form of communistic behaviors ever witnessed on American soil. Let me run just a few of these matters down to you. Police officer Kim Potter accidentally shot a criminal who was resisting arrest and attempting to retrieve a firearm from inside his car, now she is in jail and on trial for her life, on the other hand Alec Baldwin "accidentally" shot and killed an innocent mother and he was never booked or charged and is now doing fucking talk show interviews! You don't think that we don't have a problem in our country? Better yet, the LA county prosecutor's office waited a full three weeks before they issued a warrant for his cell phone, then it took Baldwin another three full weeks to comply with the court order. This phony asshole along with a few of his liberal puke buddies actually filed a lawsuit against the NRA a few years ago. What's so fucking disgusting is that these anti-gun Hollywood hypocrite elitists have no problem strapping on a gun and shooting people to make millions of dollars! I'm guessing that Baldwin took several lessons from Hillary Clinton in her "Hammer and acid bath treatments" with her cell phones and laptops.

      Now we have the Wisconsin governor who in turn stands arm-locked with the Minnesota governor to fuck up everything in their respective states. They both allowed a large portion of their cities to be destroyed in the name of, 'mostly peaceful protests.'

And that, my darling child is where my personal hero comes into my thoughts, Mr. Kyle Rittenhouse. On August 25th, 2021 he shot three domestic terrorists (all convicted felons) and killed two of them in self-defense and he got two months in prison with a two-million-dollar bail before his trial. Then this asshole, eighteen-year-old high school shooter, Timothy Simpkins shot four children in a school and was captured and freed within 24 hours, his bail was $75,000. His attorneys claim that poor little Timothy shot those children because he had been bullied most of his life. If your firm runs games like that, I'm out! I think it's pretty evident and safe to say that white privilege is a total fucking myth.

    And let's not forget that Kyle Rittenhouse acted in self-defense in Kenosha Wisconsin. Meanwhile back in Wisconsin, Darrell Brooks Jr. a repeat felon with domestic violence, illegal possession of a weapon by a convicted felon and child sexual crimes is set loose on a $1,000 bail only then to plow into a crowd with his SUV and Waukesha, Wisconsin during a Christmas parade. The death count now stands at six but still has yet to be tallied. During a FOX news jailhouse interview with Darrell Brooks, he stated that he felt that he was being demonized. Yep, I guess that's just more white privilege, isn't it? That entire Kyle Rittenhouse trial just proved to the entire world that BLM are criminals, the media lies and Kyle acted in self-defense. Let's keep in mind boys and girls that if we are all disarmed, we have nothing to fight back with. Did we somehow forget about the German prison camps and gas chambers? The 'WOKE' liberals say if all guns were confiscated and it saved just one life, it would be worth it. Well for me, I think that if we deported all the illegal aliens and if that saves just one life, wouldn't that be worth it? Kyle was prosecuted to appease the liberal democratic machine and further their stance on gun control.

And lastly my dear heart, if anyone in your office or you yourself want to use the defense of incompetent or corrupt police officers, I will be out. The people that come to you to shout of their innocence, rarely are. Just because a very few don't have a criminal record does not mean that they have never committed a crime, it simply means that they have never been caught. Is there an off chance that the folks who want to defund the police may in fact, have a criminal history? Police officers find themselves saying on a rather regular basis, "We are here to provide and bring Justice but we fully know that there is little justice and then there is, 'just...... us'.

So, my darling child, now is the time to crack open that laptop. Here is a one-dollar bill. This dollar is my payment for your company's services. I am now a client of your corporation for the price of one dollar for a lifetime of representation. I am buying, 'Attorney/Client Privilege' for just a buck! What that does is it insures me that nobody in your establishment, including yourself, can testify against me or can you use me to testify in any legal proceedings, including depositions. None of your people can fuck me over like most lawyer's fuck everyone over, including their own clients. Now you're going to write the contract. I will have one of the ladies from the hotel front office dash up here with her notary pad and stamp and she will witness our signatures and make everything binding and legal. One final thing, I want payment every twenty days and I want cash. Don't give me that look, you people have plenty of petty cash that you don't declare. Well, I'm not declaring any income for my services, hence, bring me cash. I'm ready to get started. What I want from you is a listing of your clients who you've yet to accept for trial. I want booking photos and entire criminal histories. I want all the police reports and crime scene photos. Only I will decide who I choose to interview and no one else. If your firm holds back anything, I just may go to bat for the opposition. I'll tell you this much. If any of your clients are drug dealers or junkies or gang bangers, if they have tattooed necks or faces or are repeat offenders, I want nothing to do with them. Fuck them, I've got no time for people's bullshit. Now, you start typing and I'll order our lunch.

    The assistant manager for the hotel came up to my office and notarized Val's contract. As we were enjoying our lunch I looked over at Val and said, "Baby this contract here, along with this copy of my dollar bill is my ticket. It's kind of like buying a new car and paying cash for it and you receive the title of ownership. That's right little one, I now own you!

What's it feel like to be a piece of property? Still love me babe?"

Val:   I just lost my appetite. You're as fucking subtle as a coiled rattlesnake. I am looking forward to defending Heather when she drives a wooden stake through your Vampire heart.
Me:   You just burnt through two hours of my billable time. Keep talking and I will be able to buy the IFT Defiant Limited Master Competition pistols in both 10mm and 9mm that I have longed for, for a fair piece of time now.
Val snatched up her purse and laptop and all but sprinted to the elevator. I was doing a well pronounced slow gangster stroll to the elevator while giggling my ass off. The elevator door won't open automatically, it takes a key.
Val:   You bastard, I could charge you with false imprisonment!
Me:   You can't charge me for or with shit, you're not a cop any longer, the only thing that you can charge is with a credit card, if you're not over your limit!

We rode down the elevator together. As the elevator door opened, Tim the doorman was at the front desk, he started for the front door and I waved him off. I thought I would have some fun with the both of them.
Me:   Tim, I would like you to meet my friend Reba. She is an up-and-coming attorney, who loves

to defend 'dogs at large' cases, Tim please tell Reba about your dogs. Val started laughing as poor Tim looked like he was frozen in place. Val stepped forward and hugged Tim as she kissed him on the cheek. "Tim, it's so nice to finally meet you, this hug and kiss was originally meant for Mr. Brown but I think I like you better." Tim stood in absolute shock.

    Me:   Remember sweetheart, I want the complete files. None of that email bullshit or text stuff. I will start on those files today, I want them in one hour, one billable hour that is, now git!
    Val started to turn away and spun back to face me as she said, "Not without a hug, ya grizzled old coot!"
    The files arrived fifty-two minutes later.

## *Chapter 2*
# PICK AND CHOOSE

There must have been over a dozen folders in each of the two tightly packed, 'Banker Boxes'. I pulled the first file that had something to do with fleeing a police officer and a habitual reckless driving offender. Of course, I don't like anyone that flees from the police. People are killed every day in this country from some asshole who thinks they can outrun the cops and get away, and then crash into and severely injure or even kill someone. But of course, they thought they would give it a go.

The first thing I did was call the county sheriff and ask him what I needed to do to get clearance to visit inmates in the jail. He of course laughed and said, "Old son, I suspect that you still have that federal U.S. Marshal's badge, right? That's your ticket! You need not apply, just flash your shield and the facility is yours. When you come to visit your client, I'd like you to stop by my office for a few minutes. I have something I'd like to run by you, if you're not too busy."

# THE JUDICIAL SYSTEM IS GUILTY

Well, how could I ever be too busy to visit with the sheriff? Fair enough, I'll go to the jail, talk to the shithead and go off to visit with the sheriff. I read the case file from cover to cover twice. The following morning, I was at the jail at 08:00 am. The civilian clerk asked me to have a seat as she paged the jail captain. The captain came out of an employee door along with the Sheriff. I shook hands with them both, they had an amused look on their faces as the Sheriff said, "U.S. Deputy Marshal Brown," it's so nice to see you again, please follow me, I need a moment of your time. We sat in his office, he poured us three, each a cup of coffee with a grin and started to chuckle as he said, "So now you're going to save the world? That's quite admirable but the little asshole you asked to visit with this morning won't be able to see you, he is in solitary confinement until he is arraigned. Captain, you're up!

Captain Rice: Here's what took place late yesterday afternoon. His girlfriend came to visit but she never left, as a matter of fact she now has a cell of her own! It seemed that it was quite important that she slid him twelve Xanax bars during her visit. I believe she'll be with us for an extended period of time. You still want to represent that little bastard, maybe you want to do a 'two-fers'? You can defend them both at the same time!"

All I could do was laugh as I said, "Captain, I'm not defending anybody. I'm just here to find out whether or not this prick is defendable. Obviously not at this point. You just saved me a shit load of time, but you have to know that I'm paid by the hour so I'll take a financial hit with this case.

  Me:  With this in mind and if you fellas have the time, what do you say that we go to breakfast outside of this facility, you game gents? The sheriff grinned and said, "If you're buying, I'm game and there's someone else who would like to see you. Do you mind if the Chief of Police joins us? We both have something we want to discuss with you, strictly on the QT." The sheriff then said, "I'll drive but if you touch any of my emergency buttons, I'm going to break your fucking fingers, and don't be fucking with that shotgun rack either, just sit there and shut up."

  When we arrived at the restaurant there were two marked black and white, Duluth Police, squad cars and a rather obvious 'plain wrapper' with lights in the grill and back window with the trunk lid stuffed with antennas that made it look like a porcupine. Somehow, they think that if you don't put a shield on the side of the door no one will know it's a cop car, except of course for the spotlight on the driver's side door, what the fuck? The Chief and his three officers were leaning on their cars.

  As we parked, I opened my door but lingered getting out of the car waiting for the Sheriff to get out and to press the door lock button on his key fob. The moment I heard the lock click, I reached over and activated the emergency lights and siren and jumped out of the car, slamming the door closed. The Police Chief and three police officers were bent over in laughter as the Sheriff was fumbling in his pockets for his keys to open the doors of his squad to shut down the lights and siren as he was swearing a blue streak with something like, "Never trust a fucking Fed!"

Sitting in the restaurant was much like being in a hunting camp with your pals other than we had to watch our language. We certainly did enjoy each other's company. Other than that, I know how these pricks work. The Sheriff will set the trap, and the Chief of Police will bait the trap. One of the overused tactics with law enforcement administrators, is that they save the true topic of the meeting to keep their intended victim off guard before they spring the trap. I would normally say something snarky to upset their game-plan but I had a feeling that what was about to be spoken of, was quite serious in nature. Perhaps deadly serious! So, I knew I would have to come in soft to get the ball rolling.

I said, "Chief, obviously life has been good for you. It's nice to see you in full uniform. I think you might need a shirt size change however, larger perhaps? The Chief smiled back and said, "I've got four officers sitting around us and they would be more than a little bit happy to take you outside and dust you off. Are you ready to listen or you just want to keep busting my chops?"

We had finished our meals and the Sheriff nodded his head towards the front door of the restaurant. He said, "We will talk in my car and I'm putting your ass in the cage this time, I'll teach you not to fuck with my shit!" The Chief was laughing as he said, "Sheriff, you better handcuff him or he will light up a cigarette in your back seat!"

The Sheriff opened the back door for me and I slid onto the plastic seat and banged my knees on the heavy un-padded steel cage frame.

Me:   You better get to it boys before I start flipping off all these looky-loos around here.

Sheriff:   David I need your help. I have a nephew who I refer to as my son and I call him my son. He is actually my brother's son. My brother passed away at twenty-four years of age from testicular cancer. Shortly after my brother's funeral the boy's mother just disappeared without a trace or without a word. She just dropped him off when he was four years old and drove away.

My son is now twenty-three years old and he is a Police Officer in an adjoining city. David, I don't think he's right for the job. He's very passive. He listens and listens and listens to people whether they are victims or perpetrators. He gives everyone the benefit of the doubt. He greatly lacks situational awareness. He hesitates to draw his weapon in high-risk situations so as not to frighten anyone but that kind of behavior is going to get him hurt if not killed. He's been with his department now for a year and a half but he's not of the right material, he just doesn't have that edge. I'm sure that he became a cop to honor me, but he's not suited for the job. I don't think he believes he's actually suited for the job either, but he is afraid that he will hurt my feelings or somehow

let me down. I need somebody from law enforcement with whiskers, meaning you, my friend. I need you to sit with him and give him permission to find another line of employment. I don't think he has the heart to tell me that he'd like to lay down his badge. I'm hoping you can help him do that. He has a law degree, any openings in your company?
    Me:   Not my company pal, I'm just a contracted advisor.

    The Sheriff already had a sheet with all of his son's pertinent information. "You will want to talk to his boss first, he knows that you're going to do a law enforcement intervention."
    Me:   So, you shiny badge pricks, think you can schedule my time and give me assignments and now speak for me as well? Is that a direct order sirs?

    The three of us had a good laugh. I, of course, said that I'll be happy too, "He's got to be damn miserable. I'll call his boss this afternoon to try to set something up for his next shift."
    I got back to my office and I thought, well let's try another fucked up case.
    The next case looked quite interesting, it had to do with a murder for hire of a business partner. What was even more entertaining was that there was a suspected prior attempt on the same person by his loving wife. This looks like it should be fun. I read through the entire file and something wasn't feeling quite right. Yeah, it smelled like the good old days

when I sported a blue uniform, a badge and a gun belt. What my mind flashed back to was when I was writing police reports with questionable crime scenes or suspects and witnesses and I would write in capital letters, DNLR on the right top corner of the report, outside of the margin. DNLR is the first arriving officer's observations of a crime scene that, "Does Not Look Right." It was the officers' way to alert the investigators of the potential of a manipulated or staged crime scene. It was too late in the day to try to contact the homicide investigator who was building the case. Right after I do the shiny shield intervention tomorrow, I will call this officer. I might even just stop by the department.

    I met the young officer (Sheriff's Son) the following morning. He was very courteous and calm. Before he could sit down from our introduction and handshake, I just asked him straight up. "Do you like your job?" He looked puzzled as I said, "Let me rephrase my question. Do you love your job?" His facial expression told me everything I needed to know. In less than ten minutes he told me that he was only in law enforcement to honor his uncle for raising him and how he treated him like he was his own. "I can't take all the stress and sadness; all I can do is watch people destroy their lives and the lives of others."

    I told him to remain seated and I'd be right back. I went outside for a quick smoke and to call the Sheriff. I said, "Champ, haul your ass up to this Police Department, you're going to get to witness an honorable resignation. You pinned his badge on him and now you can take it off of him with dignity and honor and he can finally start to live his own life. He has an appointment Monday morning at the law office."

I was back in my office by 11:00 AM. I called the homicide detective who had this particular case and asked him if we could meet. He said, "Yeah sure we can, you're buying me lunch and I'll be at your fancy-ass hotel in twenty minutes. I am going to order off of the dinner menu, don't try to push off a lunch menu on me."

We had a nice conversation. He told me about the case and I asked him if he had anything other than what was not turned over to the DA's office or the defense attorney's office. He smiled as he said, "You're a slick one, you do know the game well. Here's the deal, we didn't have the manpower to investigate this level of a case at the time. There's three if not four principles involved in this nasty matter. We only have a three-person homicide division and when we're not busy we're working drug cases. A number of these drug cases where there's a death from an overdose, will oftentimes become a homicide case because of the drug dealer." I asked him if they had a "DNLR" program and he looked at me with a puzzled face. I explained the "DNLR" program. He laughed and said, "We are not as refined as you big city coppers." The detective grinned as he said, "We use the SAR program, "Shit Aint Right!"

Me: That's cute. I rather like that. So, was there some, "Shit Ain't Right" in this case?

Investigator: Yeah, but I didn't find it. The life insurance company Investigator came up with it and this is a fucking doozy! I've met with him three times now and I'd love to work with him. Maybe after I retire, I'll sign up with his outfit but this guy is golden and the real deal. Here's what he found out on behalf of his life insurance company. The victim of this homicide owned a painting contracting business. He painted mostly houses and small businesses, he had four other employees. He was a drunk, his entire crew were drunks and he accumulated a rather tall stack of small claim lawsuits for shoddy work and he missed several contracted start times by weeks and even months. He took down payments of 50% of the agreed contract price at the time of signing. Before I get ahead of myself, he was married to a gal who was a high functioning drunk who could not just say no, as a matter of fact, she always promoted saying yes. I think nymphomaniac is probably the best term. Her background is just a kick in the ass. She and her former husband worked for the same employer for eight years. She started out somewhere in the mailroom of this large auto parts shipping company which was a family-owned business. Her husband had an accounting degree and was slick smart. He was working as an internal auditor. He saw a deep weakness in his company with the shipping charges from their contracted delivery services. The husband went to the owner and suggested they buy their own fleet of twenty-six-foot-long box trucks. The owner knew that they were hemorrhaging money and told him that the company had to pay a premium for freight because they just put in a leading-edge product picking and scanning system and his credit lines were maxed out. The husband proposed that he would buy a starting fleet of twenty-four trucks and offered to lease his vehicles to the company as a cost savings so as to avoid some tax structures of some kind. The owner went for it and everybody was happy. The accountant's wife was promoted and it turned out that she was a super speed typist, with all but zero errors. She was promoted into the front office and shortly became a private secretary for the owner and his wife.

Well, that sweet gal who had four children with her husband, decided that she wanted to better her position in the company and in life, so she started sleeping with the owner of the company. I'm guessing that didn't last very long, because the owner's wife walked in on them. The accountant and his 'speed typing' wife were both fired and the company canceled the contract with leasing trucks. The husband and wife had to eat the lease contract for the twenty-four delivery trucks and had to file bankruptcy.

The husband was nobody's fool. He had an iron-clad prenup, he kept the children and the house and bounced her to the street. Did I mention that the private secretary was also a whiskey pig? She loved the bars and casinos. She was loud, obnoxious and lusted after most any man. She was a gorgeous woman and had a perfectly built frame and from several reports, she knew how to use it. Well, it wasn't long before she met her next husband, the victim of this homicide. I think they married in the first six weeks after meeting. This guy was a whiskey pig as well. There are reports that they would just get filthy drunk and act obnoxious everywhere they went. They were kicked out of a lot of different bars and casinos.

Stay with me on this, things are about to get interesting. They quarreled quite often in the bars and at home. Our department responded to eight domestic abuse calls to their home, reported by neighbors. They were put on notice by the police department that both of them would be jailed if there was another call for police service at their residence. The loving couple came up with a workable plan where they agreed that he would drink and gamble during the day, if he didn't have to work and she would drink and gamble at night to avoid conflict. Come to find out that she was banned from one casino because they had video of her having sex in a car in their parking lot on two different occasions. I guess that's one way to cover your gambling losses. Needless to say, they didn't pay many of their bills and were in arrears with most all of their creditors, including their mortgage company. The one bill that she did pay every month was his life insurance policy. He was insured for $750,000 and twice that amount if he died accidentally.

So, the new husband had four employees who were all heavy, 'on the job' drinkers other than a high school kid who was the prep man for the painters. The three painters along with the foreman and owner were usually all drunk well before noon, except for the one high school kid. The high school kid is our only reliable witness. I'll get back to him in a few minutes.

    The deceased only had one professional painter (his foreman) and the other two were paint slappers. His foreman would come to his house every morning to pick him up to go to work because our victim lost his driver's license about three DUIs ago. They would sit and enjoy Bloody Mary's for the first work hour of each day in the victim's home along with the victim's wife. So, the victim's wife decides that the foreman of the business is actually far more desirable than her husband. She devised a plan to poison her husband. Her laptop Google searches showed dozens of searches of, 'how to poison' and 'how to hire a hitman'.

    But wait, there's more! At some point the foreman agrees with the wife that the husband has to go, so they can live a life of joyful bliss together. The best way to get rid of him and cash in at the same time, is of course for the husband to die in a tragic industrial accident. Mr. Baldwin, the owner of the painting business is well insured and of course, his wife Rochelle Baldwin is the sole beneficiary. The owner/victim didn't like spending money on equipment. He didn't want to waste good money unless he was sitting in the bar. They had scaffolding which most painting contractors or any contractor for that matter, would probably have discarded and sold as scrap years ago. But Mr. Baldwin wouldn't replace it. Long story short, there were three ten-foot lengths stacked four high, of scaffolding set up for this job. Supposedly a locking pin pulled out of the base stabilizer foot plate and a support bar twisted and the entire scaffolding system collapsed and the owner fell twenty-eight feet and died on the spot.

    The incident, which I will not call an accident, took place on August 4th 2021. The police department was short staffed that afternoon as they were practicing for the "Guns and Hoses" ball game for the following day. It's a baseball game between Duluth Police and Duluth Fire departments. It is mostly just a good-hearted fundraising event but each team plays their guts out. There is a lot of pride in bringing home that trophy. The event it's well attended by non-playing officers, police family's, support staff and the public. So, the only two Police Officers that responded was a patrol sergeant who is an 'FTO' (Field training officer for rookies) and his trainee, fresh from the Police Academy who was a former sailor in the US Navy. Well, it was the rookie that caught it and he mentioned what he saw to the sergeant and the sergeant pretty much blew him off. There was no one available to photograph the scene so they used their cell phones and took only a few photos. The County Coroner arrived and simply said, "Yeah, his brains are bashed from the fall onto the concrete driveway."

    The scaffolding was scattered about like children's pick-up sticks. What the rookie noticed was that one bottom leg of the scaffold didn't have a foot plate (for stability) and was tied with a reef knot, on both legs, front and back using, '750' Paracord, which is the strongest cord available. You'll find those types of knots used in the navy, they are used for what's called reefing and furling sails. That type of knot is also used for macrame in the textile industry. Few painters would ever know of or use that particular kind of knot. Guess who was taught to use those knots? That's right, the foreman and our number one suspect (who is a navy veteran) Mr. Lanny Oaks!

    This would have been passed off as an industrial accident except for the rookie, he could not let go of it. Rookies are well trained and well warned in the Police Academy that you don't jump rank, regardless of any condition or situation. It's just not done, unless you want to go back to your old newspaper route. As you well know, it would be a career ending move. But the rookie was so driven with his observations that the following day he came into my office (on his day off) with a second report. It was the day of the annual, 'Guns and Hoses' baseball game. The rookie shared a second observation along with a startling opinion that his FTO failed to write in his report. The FTO and rookie were first on scene as they were only two blocks away on patrol, when they got the dispatch. Upon arrival they assisted the four painters with removing the collapsed scaffold from on top of Mr. Baldwin. The rookie observed that there were no scaffold pieces under the victim, just on top of him! Which told him and me that the victim could not have possibly been up on the scaffold but he was actually under it and at ground level, when it collapsed.

  Me: Sounds like a Police Sergeant needs to be immediately retired and a one-week-old rookie should be promoted!

  Investigator: Admittedly I kind of blew him off too. It was three hours before the baseball game and I wanted to go to Wheeler Field to shoot the shit with the guys and warm up. I was playing second base. From the minute the rookie left my office that damn cat tail started to swish in my belly. Just before the seventh inning stretch, I pulled off my cleats and jetted back to my office, still in my baseball uniform.

  I tape every in-person conversation and phone call in my office to make sure I don't miss anything and for future reference. Well, I never read the report that the rookie brought to me, I just listened to him and thanked him for his time. I sensed that there was something in that report that he had not spoken of. He was nervous as hell in knowing that he was jumping rank and the possible repercussions to shortly follow.

  Then I saw it, in his report he wrote that three of the paint crew members were working on the south side of the house. Our victim, Mr. Baldwin and the foreman were on the northside. When they heard the scaffolding crash, the south side painters ran to the accident. The painter's helper arrived first and saw the Forman cut the paracord from the base plate and roll it up along with the locking safety pin and stuff them into his jacket pocket. The Forman stood straight up with his arms akimbo with an, "Oh well" look on his face. The south side painters immediately started to lift the debris of the crashed scaffolding off of the victim as the foreman calmly watched as he called 911.

I ran into the dispatch center and had them spool-up the 911 call and record it for me. I took it back to my office and played it several times over. I could hear the painters grunting as they lifted the steel sections off of our victim and the steel clanging as they threw it off to the side into a pile while all the time shouting, "Phil, are you ok, are you ok?", repeatedly. That motherfucking foreman's voice with dispatch was calm and smooth, like he might have been examining his finger nails!

Now my guts were on fire! I typed up an arrest warrant for first degree murder for the foreman, Mr., Lanny Oaks. I called Judge Weaver who is a personal friend and my fishing buddy. He was at his cabin on Caribou Lake. I jumped in my car and raced the thirty-two miles to his cabin. The Judge laughed at me as he signed the warrant and remarked, "Nice costume, did you miss laundry day?"

As soon as the arrest warrant was signed, I drove back to the city code 3. I radioed for a full SWAT response to the suspect's home. As I arrived, they were walking Mr. Oaks out of his home and had him in cuffs. I had the officers stuff him into the cage in the back seat of my car. I delivered him to the St. Louis County Jail at precisely the stroke of midnight and still in my baseball uniform.

I somehow forgot to attach my prisoner's seatbelt while he sat in the backseat cage with his hands cuffed behind his back. Mr. Oaks called me several unsavory names prior to and during transport and made several threats of what he was going to do to my wife and children. I had to slam on my brakes several times in the four-mile drive to the jail. There seemed to have been a wildlife convention on the roadway that evening. My prisoner needed medical attention from his multiple face plants into the steel cage that somehow seemed to coincide with each of my prisoners' threats of harming my family.

Well that pretty much sums it up but here's a question. Why did the lovely Ms. Rochelle Baldwin (the decedent's wife) lawyer up before she even made funeral arrangements for her deceased husband, who tragically died in an industrial accident? Who the fuck does that in an accidental death? Mr. Lanny Oaks lawyered up through legal aid, hence I guess it was dropped in your lap. I guess it's going to be a 'Pro Bono' case, because that cat's got nothing but bar tabs and traffic tickets. The only person that we were able to interview was the high school kid, nobody else would speak to us. I think this high school kid has some level of knowledge about this dastardly deed of foul play.

I suspect as time goes on; more will be revealed but I think he's a big key to all of this. I don't think he was a part of it, but I think he witnessed someone either saying or doing something.

Deputy Marshall Brown, you're smart enough to know that all we are sitting on currently, is circumstantial evidence. As a matter of fact, if I don't get this case rolling in the next week, I'm afraid the DA or judge will release Mr. Oaks. Currently, our suspect Mr. Oaks, is in custody on the charge of felony child non-support and the murder warrant is in review with the State Attorney's Office, but we can't hold him on the non-support charge forever. Anything you can throw my way, I will deeply appreciate and yes, I understand that you're batting for the opposing team but I'm trusting that you're more cop than you are an adjudicator.

Me: We both know that if you don't pull out a confession, most prosecutions are based on circumstantial evidence. Eye witnesses are rarely reliable because of people's imaginations and their own prejudice, after all, most people watch crime shows so they know shit!

You paid me a rather flattering compliment earlier in this meeting, now I'd like to return the same compliment. You too sir, are a man of whiskers, you've been down the same block as I have, different cities perhaps but the same streets. So, I picked up a few words from the street. Yeah, the street still speaks with me. Word on the street has it that the "Princess Bride" (or in this case the, "Deadly Bride") Mrs. Baldwin had shared some conversations with a bar owner in reference to hiring a hitman. I'm guessing that would be for Mr. Oaks, since Mr. Oaks is nothing more than a mooching, sloppy drunk and she is coming into great financial prominence with a whole bunch of cash. She wants to step up her game and enter into high society. So, if she takes out poor old Mr. Oaks before he catches on that he is a scapegoat and burns her. Once he meets his untimely demise, she's free as a bird to spend all of her money on herself. Poor Mr. Oaks is in for a very rude awakening. Maybe you can get him to flip on her by introducing him to Ms. Baldwin's hitman?

Investigator: You do got game, old son. Yeah, we've picked up a few rumors here and there, as a matter of fact and between you and me (and I trust it will remain between you and me) we have an undercover agent from Minneapolis P.D. currently positioning himself to meet with who you like to refer to as the, "Princess Bride." Chances are, we could even go beyond the pending, "Complicity to Murder" charge. I'm hoping to write a "Murder for Hire" charge. I think that has a nice ring to it, what do you say?

I went home for a nap and to try to digest this massive meal just fed me by one of Duluth's finest. I couldn't sleep so I called Val and told her to clear her calendar for the next week or perhaps a bit longer. I called the Police Chief and asked if he had a file of photographs of homicide victims that we could look at in the morning. The chief told me he could do me one better. He said the County Coroner has a full photo library of every non-attended death in the entire county along with autopsy photos.

Me: Chief, I have a young lady who used to work for you, who is currently under my tutelage. I want her to see warm, fresh, wet running blood and steaming human gut piles. I'm going to take her to every major crash and crime scene. She only saw limited action in her small district during her ten-hour shift. Would you please direct your dispatchers to call me for every nasty event for the next thirty days?

Chief: I can only think that you are terrorizing my former police officer, Reba that you stole from me. You SOB, you spent six days with that lovely child and she resigned two days later. I do want to thank you for what you did for the Sheriff and his son, you do have some decency left in you, just not very much. I'll Talk to the Dispatch Captain. I guess you don't like sleeping at night!

I called Val back for an early morning, (5:00 a.m.) breakfast, before our secret (to her) visit to the morgue. This gal is sweet as hell and equally as smart but she greatly lacks hands-on experience. Val was a sworn Police Officer for three years but she was assigned to the evidence room. She only worked in uniform for parades and special events. I want to show her what a crime victim looks like, splayed out on an autopsy drain table. Yes, I am that kind of a bastard, I want Val to have a life lasting impression on a full stomach.

Me: Good morning, Sugar Britches. Do you remember back to our California trip when we were parked in that bowling alley parking lot, smoking cigarettes in the rental car and I told you to reach down and cinch up your seatbelt? Well sweetie, it's time for you to do it all over again. And yes, just like the last time, this ride is about to get bumpy. Let's order breakfast, it's going to be a long day and lunch will probably not be a consideration, you better order a heavy meal.

We had a nice conversation during our meal. Val did mention that the first two cases that I passed on were assigned to the newest attorneys in the office for plea deal assignments. I am getting the feeling that she might be catching on.

Me:   Honey it's time I bring you up to speed. Now you're not going to know a lot of this because I've never spoken of it, nor has anyone else ever spoken of it. Got it? As a matter of fact, we have never had this meeting or conversation. *Capish?*
I met with the lead detective of the homicide unit yesterday and he brought some things to light that you cannot possibly be aware of. You will find out everything that I know when this case gets to the Discovery phase of the trial and all you're really going to find out is that you don't have a defendable client or case! Not today, not fuckin ever!
You have been played, my lady. Who you may ask has been playing you? Well, it's time for you to grow up, baby doll. You've been hustled by your dad, your grandfather, your uncle's, your brothers and

everyone else who cares about you. They have been running a ruse on you. What their actions are speaking of, is of their deep love and a concern for you. In short, they are showing you that you're not cut from the same cloth that they are. You, my sweet child, are an empath. You feel, you feel for everyone, you feel as much for the suspect as you do the victim because you know at some point that the suspect was an innocent child and something went terribly wrong in the course of their lifetime that turned them into a dark and foreboding place. You don't have to agree with this but honey, there are some people that need to be put away and never see the light of day, ever again! Some just flat out need to be put to death!

    Evil walks amongst us and that evil displays itself in a multitude of cruel fashions that you can't even comprehend. Your family intentionally gave you loser cases trying to frustrate you to push you away from whatever fantasy of right and wrong you may believe in. Sweetheart, it's all a game. Everything in the upper levels of law enforcement and everything in Justice is a political game. They don't want you to be submerged in the muck and the mire of that filthy game. You are a kind and gentle soul, who doesn't belong on either side of the scale of Justice. It's ugly, it's damn ugly and they know it. Your loving family has had to deal with selling off their core values. That's how they make their livelihood. They know that you're better than that, but they had to show you rather than tell you because you're hard headed and strong willed so they had to show you.

The tears flowed as the lights came on behind her mascara and I saw her start to fold-up and tremble.

Me:   Baby, I'm going to help you fulfill your assignment because I want you to know that you're more than capable. But I believe you have a much higher calling but that's something you'll have to decide. As a matter of fact, I am canceling my plans with you for today. I was about to take you for a morbid and life changing jaunt into the guts (figuratively and literally) of crime victims. Our first stop was going to be at the Medical Examiner's office. Then on to the morgue, I wanted to slap you awake. You see the goodness in people whether it exists or not and oftentimes, it doesn't sweetheart.

I have made arrangements for you to view and assist in an autopsy today. The victim was killed in a head-on collision. The driver that caused the accident was drunk with a Breathalyzer reading of 3.8, Blood Alcohol. The victim is a twenty-eight-year-old female and the mother of three babies, ages four, two and four months old. I wanted you to see and feel the aftermath of what drunk drivers cause as they deliver their destruction and devastation to innocent people's lives. This is the sixth DUI arrest for this son of a bitch in four years. You best not try to tell me that this poor misunderstood son of a bitch might have a drinking problem and probably just needs to go to treatment and he'll be just fine after that. Fuck him, he needs to burn in hell and you know who's going to burn this piece of shit? His fellow inmates, because jail inmates have families on the outside and they don't like drunk drivers that kill women and children any more than they like pedophiles, he will live a very short life in lock up.

Do this baby doll, google Saint Louis County Sheriff's Department, 'Jail Roster'. You'll find approximately 190 inmates in the Duluth jail and as you scroll through looking at the mugshots with the charges listed, you will find that there is one great common denominator. Many inmates are on Department of Corrections holds for parole or probation violations along with their most current criminal charges. Which means they've been adjudicated for an earlier crime or crimes. They were put on probation because they're all fucking sweethearts who are just simply misunderstood children of God. You have to know that there was a Prosecutor, a Defense lawyer and a Judge not to mention probation office and parole board, involved in these fuck-faces being released back into our society. They don't learn because they don't want to learn because they are career criminals. We don't need to lock them up for punishment, we need to lock them up for us to remain safe. As far as I'm concerned, we should put them all in an oversized tree limb grinder and feed them to the fish. Fuck each and every one of them, good people don't go to jail and nobody goes to jail for singing too loud in church. You can't save fools from themselves, you gotta get that in your head!

Then, we we're going to view a few bodies, who are victims of domestic abuse. One victim was stabbed to death by her live-in boyfriend for not frying his eggs the way he liked them and the other woman was beaten to death because her pimp thought she was holding back his money. The common denominator was that both killers had extensive criminal records and you guessed it, both were on parole.

From there we we're going to go to two hospitals to the children's ward and you were to meet an emergency pediatric physician and a pediatric surgeon, who have treated young children with broken bones, children who've been scalded in a bathtub by a raging strung-out junkie parent. There are little kids who are disfigured for life from beatings and their multiple hospitalizations for broken bones with the parents shrugging their shoulders as they explain, "He must have fallen." I had plans of introducing you to families who have buried their junior and senior high school children from drug overdoses. These children were not junkies, they were thrill seekers. They just wanted to give it a whirl because it's the latest rage on campus, just to see what it's like. They ended up giving their life for no other reason other than peer group influences. So, you're going to be a defense attorney defending people that have done this to families of our community? How in the motherfucking hell can you possibly defend that kind of son of a bitch? You know you couldn't. I know you couldn't and your family knows that you couldn't. There's plenty of places to practice law but baby, you don't belong on a bench because both defense and prosecuting attorneys lie, they lie their asses off to pull out a win. I don't know how judges can live with themselves. But they've all been bought and paid for with either exotic vacations, gifts of memberships to exclusive country clubs and resorts and believe it or not, cash. Mother fucking cash!

Lawyers and their wife's attend high society, gala fund-raising events wearing clothes and jewelry worth thousands of dollars all in the name of raping, "Lady Justice!" I don't want you to be a part of that, I'm hoping you don't want to be a part of that.

Now, back to the industrial accident which is now a, 'Murder for hire' case. All that the police initially thought was that they were investigating an industrial accidental death. Everything else looked to be normal, just an unfortunate accident by a cheap asshole whose greed cost him his life. Right up until the point that the Life Insurance investigator swung by the Duluth Police Department and said, "I think we need to chat."

So, the foreman is now charged with 1st degree murder. The grieving wife will be charged soon with complicity but I don't think it's going to hold. All they currently have is evidence of her Googling 'how to poison your husband'. That's not against the law however, perhaps it should be. You are going to have to interview this asshole. I sat with him for less than twenty minutes and I wanted to kill him! He was nothing more than a completely fucking ignorant drunk. He's the kind of guy that if he didn't have to clean it up, he'd be spitting on the floor. Yup, he's a real dandy. Strange that he only has two DUI's and nothing domestic, nothing criminal, he's just a slimy drunk that thought he could kill his way into great wealth and hang out with a hot chick who would pay his way.

You do understand that the county prosecutor is retiring and he has three of his top assistant prosecutors on this case? They are all vying for the prosecutor's job and the grandstanding will be epic! Sorry babe, but you won't even be able to pull out a plea deal on either of these two cases, those cats are both fucked.

As we were talking, I was thumbing through the other cases on my desk. When Val says, "Well I'm sorry to disappoint you, but we got a fresh one that just came in last night. This one is probably right up your alley. Let me run It down to you. We have yet to meet with this client. We'll probably see him tomorrow sometime, but this guy has been on the radar with the ATF and the FBI and who knows what other government bodies that you like to refer to as, "The Alphabets." He was taken into custody last night after a thirty-one-hour police standoff. The search and arrest warrants had to do with the suspect having explosive booby traps all around his property and being in possession of six, armed Claymore mines which were placed along his driveway facing,

"Towards The Enemy" of course. It was suspected that he had an arsenal of military rifles with grenade launchers. He had made threats in the past that if anyone tried to come on his land that they would look upon "Ruby Ridge" as a day at the park. Obviously, he meant it. When arrested he did have several firearms strapped all over his body and explosives in a suicide vest. At this point I believe they've found sixteen hand grenades throughout his property and a shoulder held rocket launcher. David where the fuck do people get weapons like that. He's now cooling his jets in the Saint Louis County Jail without bond of course. He'll be arraigned in the next day or so. I thought you might want to get a jump start on it.

    Me:   OK, what's his name?

    Val:   Heck Wozniak.

I blinked several times and almost swallowed my face as I said, "Baby, I think I know this guy. I think I went to high school with him, send me a picture of him right now, I'll hold."

The picture came across and sure as shit, there's my old high school buddy, Heck. I graduated high school in 1968 and I haven't seen him since.

    Val:   Holy shit David, you actually know him? I mean, who the hell has a first name like Heck anyway?

    Me:   Shut up and listen. Get me an appointment for an interview with him, do it right fucking now, I want to see him today, like immediately, right fucking now and no, you may not come with me! Keep your office goons away from him. In the meantime, I'll write-up something to give you some background on Heck. This is going to be a wild ride and I am all in.

## *Chapter 3*
# COUNTRY BOY'S

I put on my coat and my boots and left my office. It was cold as hell and windy but I had to go for a walk. I just had to get this out of my head and try to make some sense of it.

Heck and I were school chums. We were in a 'Smith Hughes' printing class together. Its two-year trades class mostly for at-risk or failing students, to give them a trade to fall back on because college was most certainly not an option. We spent five hours each day in the print shop and only had one English class three times a week in the school. The print shop was in a standalone building. We did all the printing for the school district. We had several platen presses; some were auto feed and some were hand feed. We had only three small offset presses, two were Multi company and a new press, which was an AB Dick, model 360.

Heck was afraid of the hand feed platen presses. Understandably so, if you failed to pull your hand out in time your hand would be crushed. Heck mastered the set-ups and color separations on the offset presses.

Heck was a strange guy, not at all popular and most kids made fun of him.

I felt sorry for the kid, he was small and frail, he was always dirty looking with his hair matted to his head. His clothes were always dirty and grease covered.

The most outstanding memory I have of Heck was his smell. He always smelled like firewood, like a campfire but it had a certain scent to it like it was almost, I don't quite know how to describe it. He had a sweet-sour smell, almost like burnt fruit. I didn't think he bathed very often and he wore raggedy, threadbare flannel shirts with frayed collars and cuffs. His jeans all had patches on them, so that old term of 'raggedy poor' held true with Heck. He was quiet but likable. I liked him a lot actually. He came off like he might be a bit slow but I think he was a lot smarter than he let on. Some of the other guys made fun of him but Leo Johnson, whose first name was actually Francis, was quite fond and protective of Heck. Leo was a farm kid and bigger than any football player on the football team. When the guys kept talking shit to Heck, Leo would walk over to them and not say a word, he didn't have to, the guys got the message and slid away. Leo and Heck rode the school bus together to school each morning and back home each night. They lived down a dirt road just a few miles apart. Neither Leo's or Heck's family had a lot of property; they were just living in the country. They weren't actually farmers; they were just poor country folk.

# THE JUDICIAL SYSTEM IS GUILTY

It took Heck a while to warm up to me but eventually he started talking. It was mid-Winter and like every Minnesota Winter the winds howled and the temperatures were brutally cold. Any day that it was 0 degrees or above was a reason to celebrate. Most rural kids had a small wooden hut at the end of their driveway to sit in while waiting for the school bus. Leo told me that Heck didn't have a shelter to sit in, all he had was an old wooden fruit crate to sit on that was under a spruce tree. Heck didn't smoke but Leo and I did. Heck always joined us when we went out behind the print shop for a smoke.

One day Heck thanked us for being his friends with, "You two guys are the only friends I've ever had, in my whole life." Suddenly my past and current life's pains and disappointments all evaporated. One day Heck and Leo and I were sitting in the back of the print shop having lunch, when he told us that he wished he could go to a laundromat to clean his clothes, he said, "I know that I smell bad and all the other kids avoid me and they even make fun of me but I have to sleep every night in the chicken coup in the Winter to keep the kerosene heaters all going, so the laying chickens don't freeze to death. I have to wake up every two hours to check on the hogs too. So that's why I smell bad. We don't have any electricity or running water."

The next day Leo and I went to our print shop teacher, Art Verria and told him about Heck's living conditions. Our teacher told us to get in his car. Art drove to the goodwill store and paid $40.00 for nice used clothes for Heck. Back in the late 60's, $40.00 was a lot of money! Art set it up with the gym coach so Heck could shower every morning before class. Art was a good guy, he was Portuguese. We called him, "Geese" and he was ok with that. During rain or snow storms, Art would let us smoke just inside the backdoor of the print shop with the door propped partly open. I remember when my daughter died when I was a high school senior. Art, Leo and Heck attended my little girl's funeral. Heck had a fresh haircut and was wearing an obviously borrowed suit a few sizes too big for him, but he still wore a suit and tie to show his respect for my baby girl and me. Those guys handed me an envelope with a sympathy card and a fifty-dollar bill in it. The card was signed by all the guys (nine of them) in the print shop. Heck was the one that handed me the envelope with him saying, "This is for your baby's, Headstone."

I believe back then, that Heck said that they might have had eighty plus, young hogs in an old half brick-half wood, broken down barn. Heck told me more than I ever cared to know about hogs. The sows had two litters twice a year with the average of ten piglets for each birth. The piglets only live for six to eight months before slaughter. A sow can have litters for up to six years. Although a sow can live up to twenty years and weigh one hundred and twenty-five pounds, most all hog producers put them down as soon as they stop producing piglets. His dad raised the hogs strictly for slaughter. They had a big smokehouse and they smoked hams, bacon and pork ribs along with pork sausages.

There was another time when Leo, (knowing of the life out in the woods) asked Heck how in the world were they able to feed all those hogs and chickens when they didn't farm their 200 acres? Heck explained to us that his dad didn't want to clear the land because they needed the trees for future firewood for heat, cooking and the smoke houses. Heck's dad loaned him and his three brothers out to area farmers to work the fields from early planting to the very end of harvest. Heck was only paid $5 a week by his dad but the big pay came from crops. If you work on someone else's farm, they usually pay you in some type of crop. Heck was always helping with the corn planting, watering and harvest. They got four dump trucks full of corn every fall, from the farmers for his work. Leo and I both wondered what the hell they did with four semi-dump trucks loaded with corn. The other brothers were paid for their work with truckloads of potatoes, peas, soybeans, sugar beets, oats and barley. They sold some of those vegetables at a temporary vegetable stand at a vacant gas station in Hermantown.

Heck's three older brothers were greatly favored over him according to Leo. The brothers were paid for their work and got to ride with dad in the 'stake bed' farm truck to all the grocery stores in the area to pick up spoils of bakery goods, fruits, vegetables and packaged lunch meats as feed for the hogs.

Heck was a junior and Leo and I were both seniors. I think only a week passed by after graduation when Leo joined the Army. Leo was only in Vietnam for two months before he was killed in action. There's a memorial to him at the Vietnam veteran's memorial in Duluth down by the Leif Erikson Park.

I've always wondered how life would have been for Leo when he returned from the war. He was a great guy and I think he had a lot of promise. He was a kind, sensitive and sincere guy. I'm sure that we would have been lifelong buddies. Heck didn't return for his senior year of high school. All I heard was that he dropped out of school to help on the family farm. Over the years I've thought of Art, Leo and Heck more than just a few times. I always wondered where life may have taken Heck. I don't have to wonder any longer. This is so fucked up!

I'm not a walker, but this day I couldn't stop walking. I took an oath that day to Heck, with thinking, "I haven't seen you for more than 50 years but that's OK, we are still friends and I'll do all I can to help you."

## *Chapter 4*
# SCHOOL PALS

I got a call from the jail captain as I was still walking, he said I was clear to visit with my client at any time. I double timed it to get back to my car and sped off to the county jail. With the way I was driving, I was damn lucky not to be escorted to the county jail in the backseat of a squad car, if you know what I mean.

When I entered the Justice Center which is the front face for the jail, I presented my credentials to a very young-looking deputy. I told her I would need an escort to the Sally Port where I could secure my weapon. She had an alarmed look on her face and said, "You're carrying a gun right now, in this building?" I said with a smile, "I can carry a gun if I go to meet the President or the Pope." She gave me a shitty smile and said, "Your ID card isn't any good, there's no expiration date and you're too old to be an active agent and besides, anybody can get a U.S. Marshals badge off of eBay!" I smiled and told her that she better hit that panic button above her right knee and prepare to update her resume, as I dialed the Sheriff on my cell phone. I smiled a more sinister grin as I said, "Sweetheart, if you hit that panic button you will lock down this entire facility. All office doors will automatically lock, you better hope that your boss is not in the bathroom.

    The heavy sound of boot soles slapping the polished tiled floor caused me to giggle. She must have hit the fucking panic button!

    After the dust settled and the Undersheriff reviewed the tapes, they had the receptionist removed. I went through all of the preliminary check-in procedures with another person and I was brought to an interview room. There was a viewing window and a table with nothing but two chairs. One chair was obviously for the prisoner because it was bolted to the floor. There was a large eye-bolt in the center of the table top which was also bolted to the floor and a chair I would guess, for the visitors or the attorney. I wasn't seated for more than five minutes when the door opened. In walked two deputies with Heck in handcuffs with a belly band and leg shackles. Heck looked like warmed over dog crap. I could see the misery in his face and his posture. This poor guy had obviously taken a hard fall in life. One of the jailers asked if I wanted the cuffs off. I smiled with some of the memories of old when I said, "No, leave them on."

    Those memories of old, caused me to inwardly chuckle with all the memories of the times when I was both a paramedic and later a police officer, when I would bring an aggressive drunk or psych patient or a dangerous prisoner in custody, into the hospital emergency department, to be medically cleared before they could be jailed. On almost every occasion, either a nurse or the attending physician would demand that we remove the handcuffs from their patient and every time there was an argument. My canned response was something like this, "Folks, this is not your patient, he is my prisoner, let's get that straight!" Then they would refuse treatment if the handcuffs were not removed. I would smile as I would recite the condensed version of the, 'Hippocratic Oath'. Quickly followed with my having to remind them that I was a sworn Police Officer and my authority and power of arrest was statewide including this hospital. I usually would say, "All right, I'll remove the handcuffs but I assume no responsibility for damage to property or personnel." I would take off the handcuffs and step out of the room into the hallway and listen for the fight to start. I would have to guess that more than 50% of the time when I was ordered to remove the handcuffs by civilian medical people, their patient returned the favor by deftly issuing bloody noses, blackened eyes and a few fat and bloody lips! It was a good time, damn I hated those arrogant assholes!

    I didn't bring in a notepad or any pencils or pens, because those can be used as weapons. Check out a few John Wick movies where he killed three people with a fucking pencil! It has happened in court rooms all around the nation where the defendant has attacked witnesses, victims and their own attorneys with an ink pen left laying on a table.

    I don't know who Heck is anymore. I have fond memories of him but I can't and won't trust him, at least not now. I had a tape recorder that I took from my pocket, turned it on and put it on the table. I looked at Heck and asked him if he remembered me. He smiled as he said, "There's only one man with eyes like yours and a voice like yours, you're impossible to forget. Are you a lawyer now?"

    Me:   No Heck, I'm not a lawyer, I'm an investigator for a law firm, that law firm is going to represent you in this case. Lucky for you, you have drawn the very top criminal defense law firm in the state. I have some forms here that I want you to look at and take back to your cell when we complete our conversation. The actual attorneys representing you will be here in a few hours, that's when you'll sign the agreement of representation but you and I don't have to sign anything. As a matter of fact, you can say anything you'd like. Our conversation still falls under client/attorney privilege, our conversations cannot be listened to and cannot be used in any proceedings. I hope you have not said anything to anyone since you were taken into custody. But if that's the case, your lawyers will be able to take care of all that stuff. I want to give you a strong word of caution and you best remember this. Not one of these swinging dicks in here gives any part of a fuck about you. Do you currently have a cellmate?

Heck: You must have been who they were talking about out in a hallway before they unlocked my door. I heard someone say to a couple of other guys, "That they'd better be on their best behavior because the guy in the interview room is a personal friend of the sheriff and he's a former bad-ass big city cop and a retired U.S. Deputy Marshall. If anybody fucks with him, we're all going to be kicking rocks down the road before lunch time tomorrow!"

No, they have me in some kind of isolated place, it's a small room but not really a cell. It has a steel bed with a two-inch-thick pillow and mattress and an all-in-one sink and toilet. I've never been to jail before in all my life. This is a spooky place. David, I don't have any money to pay for a lawyer.

Me: You won't need any money after you fill out the financial/ability to pay forms. Let's get back to the words of caution. These lousy bastards (inmates) only want one thing and they don't care what they have to do to get it. They want to get free and they will use everything and everyone to get out of here. If you talk to them, they will manipulate and fabricate anything you say, so they can step forward and rat you out and get a reduced sentence or early release. These losers will claim to have heard you say all kinds of bullshit in a private conservation but they have never even seen or met you. Everyone here is your enemy, inmates and staff alike. Say nothing to no one and I mean no one!

The only people that currently give any part of a shit about you, are me and your lawyers. Don't lie to me or to them. If you do, we walk. Can you dig it?

Well pal, let's start from the very beginning. I haven't seen, spoken or heard of you in the last fifty years. Bring me up to date. You talk and I will sit and listen for as long as you need me to, so I can have a better understanding of what took place. I don't so much want to know why you were arrested. We'll get to that later. I want to know how you've been living. I wanna know from day one how you've been living so let's start at your earliest childhood memories.

Heck:   Jesus Christ David, oh my God, I don't even know where to start. No one has ever asked me to tell them about my life, but I'll do my best. My early childhood memories are about being cold, dirty and hungry. That was pretty much it. Every day I was cold, dirty and hungry. I mostly ate cold field corn and the burnt ends of the hams and dried out bacon that couldn't be sold. I'm sorry but everything is so fucked up in my head right now. I can still see those bright lights in my eyes and all those red dots bouncing off my chest from last night. I've never been so afraid in my life. I thought for sure that they were going to kill me. I couldn't tell if they were military or police but they had some nasty looking weapons.

Me:   OK sport, tell me this, why did you take thirty-one hours to surrender?

Heck:   I'm not sure, I was just so scared, I couldn't think. I didn't know what I did! I thought maybe I was cracking up, maybe there weren't any cops out there or maybe they were just some neighbors pissed off at me. Our neighbors and my family have been feuding since I was a little kid. Our whole area is full of pig farmers and yet we scored all of the grocery store spoils and throw-away's and they never got anything. They had to use restaurant leavings or pay for hog feed. They more than resented us. They hated us and threatened to burn us out several times. My dad and my older brothers had fist fights with the dad's and brothers or those families' boys. You know those were very scary times.

    Me:   Heck do you have any mental illness in your family or are you mentally ill, do you have a drug problem, were you high when they came last night, what's the deal?

    Heck:   No David I swear to you, I'm not crazy. Yes, there were times that I smoked marijuana and drank more than I should have but no, I'm not a drug addict and I've never done any hallucinogenic drugs. I guess I was just scared and my brain locked up. I spent most of those 31 hours crying and waiting to die. I just knew they were going to kill me and I didn't even know what for.

    Before this all started, I was sitting at my kitchen table cleaning my shotgun because I shot two rabbits that morning. I was watching an old, 'Wagon Train'
movie. All of a sudden, I heard a loudspeaker like it was next to my ears and a spotlight that lite-up the whole house!

Me: Did they hurt you? Do you have any injuries, do you need any medical attention?

Heck: No, when I decided to come out, they were actually really cool. They gave me very firm commands and said if I displayed any weapons or made any attempt to resist that they would shoot me. So, I complied with everything, there were nice guys. After they pulled me out of the snow bank that they tackled me in, they actually brushed the snow off my clothes and my hair after they cuffed me.

Me: Well, that's good news, yeah there's a lot of decent cops around, they have to be hard at times but they're not all brutal like the networks and liberal politicians want the world to believe. OK pal, let's get back to your childhood. I need everything you've got from the very beginning so let's have it.

Heck: Well, I dropped out of my senior year of high school because my dad needed help with the stills because two of my brothers went into the Navy and my other brother took a job at the Minntac mine in Mt. Iron. I think that's a big part of the reason why I'm here. We lived in Arnold which is now called, Rice Lake Township, we had two hundred acres that my grandpa homesteaded, just below Mud Lake. The headwaters of the Amity Creek runs through our property. It was just a trickle but it served our purpose quite well. Our big family secret was that my dad operated a large Moonshine still operation along with the smokehouse. The smoke from the smokehouse was a good cover for the moonshine stills smoke.

The used mash was sloppy, nasty stuff to handle but the pigs loved it. My mom dried it and used some of it as feed for the turkeys, ducks and chickens. We actually had three twenty-six-gallon copper stills and we made Whiskey, Vodka and Rum. Well, I tended to the stills and the smokehouse when I wasn't in school. That's why I always smelled so bad. A lot of people in our area raised hogs. As a matter of fact, hogs, I think, is the biggest meat producing industry in our part of the state. My dad had a lock on all the area grocery stores (there are several) to get their spoils to use for hog feed. The reason my dad scored all the spoils was that on the first of each month, he gave the store manager's, the receiving manager's and produce managers at each store, a 32-ounce mason jar of our latest batch of shine. I only tasted a few batches. I never really drank back then. My brothers drank all the time and dad couldn't trust them to manage the stills so that was my job. We didn't actually feed the pigs much of the fruit, most of that went into the mash. Dad sold a lot of hams, ribs and bacon. My dad would add pure virgin olive oil to the used mash and use it for a rub on the ham and pork bellies. That's the reason that he had such a strong following. Dad had a large customer base for the many different whiskies we made also. Dad made a shit-ton of money but we never saw any of it.

We don't know if he buried it in the ground or hid it in the walls. No one's ever been able to find the money but we're thinking it has to be in the thousands and hundreds of thousands of dollars. Perhaps even in the millions, who knows?

    Well, I met a gal at the Cove Nightclub in Superior when I was twenty-two years old. It was a strange thing because her family had a large farm but they didn't live on it. They lived in the city and they contracted with other farmers, kind of like a land lease or a share-crop project. Well, her and I hit it off right away but it was a strange deal, she was pretty and had a beautiful body and I looked like Goober from "Andy of Mayberry!" She seemed to be more interested in me than anything else in the world. It was almost like she was an actress. I found out later that she was an actress. It seemed like she wanted to marry me the first week that we met. Of course, the way that I lived out in the country, I had never even held a girls or woman's hand before her, so that was exciting. I spent five months tripping on my dick with her and then we got married. Believe it or not, I actually lost weight as skinny as I was. I lost even more weight from all the sex. I was in hog heaven, pardon the pun. Of course, I left the farm and we got an old but nice, two-bedroom house in the city on 27th avenue west and 12th street. I worked on the house every night after work and every weekend remodeling the house. We had four lots so I doubled its footprint. I turned it into a four bedroom and remodeled the entire interior. I put on a large two-sided deck, on the upper level the full width of the house, so we could enjoy the view of the bay of Lake Superior.

Me: Heck, I don't need a stroll down memory lane. Just the facts, sport, just the facts.

Heck: I'm sorry, it's just that it was the first time in my life that I had a dream and I went for it. I guess losing that house still hurts. I was lucky to work with a guy whose wife was a mortgage broker and she suggested that I roll the construction loan into the mortgage loan. My ex-wife got and sold the house the day after the divorce was final. She walked away with eighty-six thousand dollars, all from my sweat!

So, I was working for one of the big printing houses in Duluth, I was in charge of color production. They had some of the finest equipment in the printing business. I won a lot of awards from the Inland Press Association. I loved printing and worked there for forty years. I was very well paid.

My wife grew up in the taxi and limo business, her dad had a fleet of thirty taxis along with both limo town cars and stretch limos. Her name was Jill and Jill started out doing oil changes on the taxicabs in the garage when she was thirteen. She liked it but she didn't like being around the drivers because she thought they were all filthy, foul-mouthed pigs, but she actually liked them. At some point she graduated to learning how to dispatch taxicabs. That's when we met. She was good at it and she looked after the drivers to make sure no one got hurt by their fares. There were a lot of robberies and a lot of 'no pays' in a taxi business. She got bored with dispatching taxis. Back in those days It was a total street battle among the drivers and other taxi services to pick up fares but she made sure her company got their fair share. She even drove a taxi for a bit but she would only do the airport or hotel pick-ups. Then she went on to only drive a town-car limo with appointments. Most of those customers were, of course, wealthy people that were attending special events at the new 'Arena Auditorium and Convention Center' for events like concerts. She got to meet a lot of interesting people, who were mostly celebrities and movie stars. We were married when she was driving the town cars. I didn't realize that my wife was quite a flirt but she would come home and tell me about the nice police officers she met at the airport, hotels or the convention center, while waiting for a fare. She wore short shorts and halter tops and she had a body that was out of this world. I guess I was pretty stupid, I thought she was doing that just for me.

    My wife enjoyed the interactions with the police officers so much that she decided to become a police dispatcher and she was hired by an area police department. It didn't take long until she had to work overtime shifts and was called in when she was off duty to cover for another dispatcher. The problem was that I never saw the overtime on her paystub. She wasn't working on those times she was supposedly called in. She was dating cops and she had become a, "Badge Bunny." She wasn't even trying to hide it! After the divorce, I found out quite a bit about some of her antics. Word has it that she caused one cop to get fired and two others to get suspended and demoted because of her behaviors. She would make complaints to the department when she was done with them as to how she was being sexually harassed, when she was the one that instigated each situation. Well, I actually loved her and she did become my world and she's all I ever wanted and then this happened. I walked away from the house and retired from the printing business and went back to the farm and for the most part, I became a hermit.

I just couldn't ever take the chance of having my heart broken like that, ever again, it's just too painful.

David, do you remember coming to our house when you were a paramedic? My dad had a heart attack and you guys came and did CPR for a long time, but he didn't make it. I remember watching you guys working your ass off trying to revive him. I remember your uniforms. You had the identical uniforms as the county deputies wore. Tan slacks with brown stripes, brown applets and pocket flaps with silver badges and EMT patches on your shirt sleeves, man you looked cool as hell.

Me:  I'm sorry Heck, I don't remember that, we ran a lot of rural calls for heart attacks, I don't remember seeing you there.

Heck:  I kind of hid out in another room and just peeked through a couple of holes in the wall and watched from there. I guess I need to back up a little bit. My mom died when I was seventeen and that's the reason, I left high school to pick up her load with the stills and the hogs and the ducks and chickens. My mom would have to candle over eighty eggs every morning before dad took them to deliver to local Mom and Pop restaurants. So that became my job too, after she died.

    My parents didn't like me. My brothers told me that I was named Heck because when they found out mom was pregnant with me, they just looked at each other and said, "Heck, another mouth to feed." And that's pretty much how I was treated all of my life by them, I was just another mouth to feed. Well, I guess that's most all of my childhood, all I did was sleep in a chicken coop and tend to the hogs and work the stills. Outside of my brief stab with marriage and I have to tell you, do you know what actually ended the marriage beyond her being a cheating, lying, whore? Get a load of this shit, just as she walked out forever, she hollered back to me, "You son of a bitch, I was only with you to find out where your dad was hiding all of his money. What a wasted time in my life, you son of a bitch!"

    When we got to divorce court, the judge gave her everything. She got the house and all of the furnishings. I left with just my clothes and a few pictures. I was lucky that I had the old Homestead to return to and yes, I had to fire up the stills again. The house was falling down so I knocked it down to the foundation and rebuilt it. I didn't find any money but I had forgotten all about the false floor that we used to store plastic jugs of water for the still in the crawl space for when the creek froze-up in the winter. We had a well and pump head in the kitchen but dad didn't trust the well. We had an old pickup truck with plywood sides that were level with the top of the roof of the truck. Dad had a plywood top with a tarp covering it so no one could see inside. At night we would drive to London Road across from the water treatment plant. They had a drinking fountain for the tourists to enjoy sparkling fresh, clean Lake Superior water. There was also a stand pipe with a faucet so people could fill pails and bottles of water. We filled our plastic jugs, for the stills, pigs and poultry."

I Knew that I couldn't interrupt Heck as he rambled on. I was seeing something in his eyes and face, his eyes were changing color and his facial muscles were contorting. He actually was changing his facial structure as he talked! I've seen a lot of crazy people but this was like a horror movie kind of stuff. One moment he was calm and well spoken, the next moment he looked like a mad man. I was waiting for him to either lunge at me or to burst into flames. This was some spooky shit!

Heck continued;
I didn't have enough money to buy more hogs or to fire up the smoker. I just made moonshine. After the divorce I would only date a couple of women and never the same one in the same month. I wasn't going to let myself get trapped and have to start all over again. I never remarried and my wife and I never had any children. I guess that's one of God's blessings.
So, the only thing I have to be grateful for, is that my dad taught me how to run a still and he had a

large customer base who couldn't get enough of his blends. I was the only one in the family that had the recipes in my head.

No one else really knew the process so when I returned back to the farm house, it was game on. I've been a bootlegger ever since, I smoke a little marijuana every now and then, but not a lot. I drink a bit, but again not a lot. I know I have to keep my wits about me not to get caught. The Fed's don't really expect somebody to be running moonshine stills in northern Minnesota, that's pretty much a southern deal. Do you know where the term "Bootlegger" comes from David? It's the practice of farmers and frontiersmen carrying illegal bottles of liquor in their boot tops. I can tell you this, I've made as much as $4,000 a week with all three stills running. I also made quite a bit of money on selling the mash to the local farmers who dried and ground it up to use it for fertilizer, it's the best fertilizer that money can buy! My dad was making money on both ends, he was pretty slick. I wish to fuck I knew where the hell he hid all that money.

Me: OK Heck, now listen, I'm not comfortable with you sitting here in handcuffs, obviously neither are you. So, I'm going to have to ask you, do you need to be cuffed? Are you a danger to me or to others? State your case now, but I have to tell you, if you make a move on me, I will kill you right where you sit, fair enough?

I reached back and tapped on the wall and the door opened, in stepped two deputies. I said,

"Gentlemen, can we remove the hand cuffs from my client's belly band?" They looked at each other almost knowingly and said, "You do know that's at your own risk but if that's what you'd like, we'll be happy to." They unlocked the handcuffs from the belly band, I nodded and asked them to secure the cuffs to the eyebolt in the center of the table but to leave the leg irons on.

Heck went on to say that he got the old farm backhoe running and he dug two sizable ponds, diverted the creek and planted trout in one pond and walleyes in the other. They matured quite quickly and he started selling smoked fish as well. I looked at Heck and asked, "Did you go to college?" Heck laughed and said, "No, I knew that I wasn't smart enough for college." I said, "Sport you are well spoken and you know what's going on around the world, where did you pick all that up? Heck said, "Well it's the same reason I took to printing. I loved the pictures in National Geographic magazine. I love the exotic places both here and abroad. I wanted to earn enough money to travel the world, but it looks like that won't be happening now, does it? It feels like my life is going to end, right here. I smiled as I said to him, "Over my dead body, we'll get you taken care of and by the way your entire defense team is the best in the business and this is a pro-bono case, don't worry about money. Do as suggested by your attorneys, they are the only ones that have your best interest in mind and don't worry about what we've talked about, that stays between you and me. I cannot be brought into court or questioned about any of our conversations."

I told Heck that I was done for now with the questions and asked him if he had anything more that he wanted to say. He smiled and he said, "You and Leo and Art were the only three people that ever truly cared about me. Everyone else saw me as a project to use anyway they saw fit. You guys treated me like we were friends. I'll never forget that, never!"

Me: Heck when you guys came to my baby's funeral and you handed me the card with the $50 bill in it to help pay for my baby's headstone it locked you and Art and Leo into my heart forever. So, let's just call this whole thing that you're going through and my being with you, is just simply pal's being pals and I'll do all I possibly can to help you.

I need you to tell me the truth now. Partner, I can see it in your eyes but I need you to tell me about it. I asked you earlier and for some reason you had an embarrassed look on your face. Friend, there's no shame in suffering from mental illness, the only shame comes from not being treated for mental illness. So, sport tell me old friend, have you been diagnosed or treated for depression?

Heck: Yeah David, I've been taking lithium for oh, I don't know, I guess ever since my wife left me. Some doctors said I had chronic depression, others said I was bipolar. I don't know and I don't think they know either.

Me: When's the last time you took your lithium?

Heck: I don't know, maybe a few months ago, I just got tired of it. I just feel so damn depressed. I don't know, I just sit and sit and I look at nothing. I don't watch TV much, I don't read, I don't even listen to music anymore. My only joy comes from riding my snowmobile and ATV through the woods as I check on the deer and leave feed for them and the wild turkeys and a few grouse. Sometimes I'll drop their feed, ride away for a distance and then walk back quietly and just sit under a low hanging pine tree and watch them feed. It seems that it is the only time that I can find some peace in my heart and allow my head to rest. I guess I'm just ready to check out of this world.

I reached back and tapped on the wall and the door opened with the same two deputies.

Me: Gentlemen, would you mind so much bringing myself and my client a cup of black coffee please? And I need to see the jail nurse please, asap.

The jail nurse showed up and I almost busted a gut! It was really difficult not to start laughing, she was the identical twin sister of 'Nurse Ratched' from the movie, "One Flew Over the Cuckoo's Nest!" She had that same, severely swept hairstyle with a heavily starched white cap and dress like in the movie from 1975! I stepped out of the room to speak with her. I asked her if my client told her of his chronic depression during his intake interview. She said, "No, he denied any mental health issues."

Me: Well, he fibbed you and more than just a little bit, my client has a problem with chronic depression at the very least. Would you mind contacting his doctor for verification so we can get him back on his lithium. He's been off of it for about two months now and I'm guessing that's why we're sitting here today. She nodded her head and said, "Right away sir, I'll take care of it."

We were approaching our third hour of conversation in this tiny room and I was getting restless. I needed a smoke and I had to piss. I told Heck that I needed to attend a church service so I would have to leave but his attorneys will be here to see him shortly.

When I came out of the elevator, there sat Val and two other lads in overpriced three-piece suits with high dollar silk ties. The men came to their feet on Val's que. I hooked Val's arm and said, "Come with me, you need to go outside, your lads may come along." I couldn't wait to fire up a cigarette. Val introduced me to her two associates who both looked like they were still in high school. When I asked, "Anybody have any experience with defending a client with mental illness?" It was blank looks all around. "Well, here's the deal boys and girls, your client and my childhood friend has a severe level of mental illness. It has gone untreated for the last two months. Yeah, you better crack a few books and talk to a couple of doctors. He needs to have a professional mental health examination, not a jail intake nurse. I want you three to listen tight now. So, you two fellows have dedicated your life to the defense of the falsely accused? Bullshit! If an insurance company dangled a few extra bucks and gave you a windowed, corner office you would never look back. If you two, "Warriors for Justice" fuck this up you will answer directly to me and you'll answer with my boot heel on your throat are we clear? I suggest you bleeding hearts take a hard look at a few articles that I will send you and be assured that there will be a quiz! I'm sure you don't know the name Leonard Sipes because you're too busy to be bothered with facts. Mr. Sipes studies criminal cases that are hidden by defense lawyers as well as the justice system. I guess there is no money in the truth. Mr. Sipes wrote and published an article that was released on January 7th of 2022, just six days ago. His data came from 'The Bureau of Justice Standards' otherwise known as the BJS. The data came from 2016 but for some reason didn't find its way to publication, until just last week. Just six short years later! How fucking cute is that? You lads want some nice hard numbers? These are just two small examples of the bullshit of our justice system, "More than 40% of all prison inmates had 5-10 prior incarcerations and 78% of all inmates had at least one prior incarceration." You can dig out the rest. My point is, if you defend the innocent as aggressively as you do the guilty, we would all live in a safer world. You defend the guilty for fear of retribution and those candy-ass sentencing judges follow suit!

    This man is my friend and has a mental condition which he has been able to manage most of his life, up until now. He is now in trouble with his mind and of course the courts.

Val, call your dad, you'll need a heavy hitter in on this one. Have your dad make an emergency appointment with a judge. We've got to get Heck the hell out of jail. He needs to go to a secured mental health facility. Then find out who his doctor is and drag him into the judge's chambers along with your dad, yourself and these two young fellows. At this point your client and my friend, is in extreme danger of harming others or himself. Don't let that boyish face fool you, there could be a Hannibal Lecter hiding behind that face. I saw it several times when we were just talking. We did not discuss the charges or the case. I have a great deal of info on his past and lifestyle on this recorder. Val you can pick up a copy when you come for dinner tonight at the hotel at 6:00, sorry gents but you'll have to fend for yourselves. Heck is not a criminal; he is a sick and broken man.

Now kids, I've got a raging fucking headache and I'm well behind in my Folgers coffee consumption and nicotine levels, so I'm going to get the hell out of here.

He is handcuffed to an eyebolt on the table in the interview room, do not fuck with those. I'll tell you one more time, do not fuck with those restraints, he may have a problem with paranoia or schizophrenia as well as his depression, if those cuffs are removed and if he hurts anyone of you, you will be at fault! As a matter of fact, I'll have you three charged with inciting violence on an inmate! *Capeesh?*

As I got behind the wheel of my truck, I realized that I still had on my snow hiking boots and my feet were hot as hell. I just wanted to get on the freeway and bury the speedometer and drive as fast as I possibly could until I ran out of gas or blew the engine.... Or when I was done crying.

## *Chapter 5*
# **PREDATORY KINFOLK**

I was midway through my second pot of coffee with my feet up, watching the world go by on my back deck. Suddenly, out of nowhere, comes the shit storm. First was the call from the 'on scene' deputy sheriff who was leading the search team on Heck's property and gathering evidence, along with an ATF agent and a county prosecutor. The deputy said the crime scene was well taped off and secured. Suddenly, there were two women and a small child walking out of the main barn. They obviously entered the property through the woods. When the deputy challenged them, they said they were preparing to do a quick claim deed on the property and they were having to do an inventory. The deputy got their ID's, ran their backgrounds and released them with a stern warning not to come back onto this crime scene. The names of course were Heck's two brother's wives. I don't know what made me ask him but I just simply said, "You have something else, what is it?" The deputy started laughing. He said, "I'm pretty sure my

boss will have my back on this but just between you and I, we have been had! The six Claymore landmines are all inert. They are training dummies and couldn't have ever possibly been armed. The grenades that he had hanging from the front of his assault vest, we're dummies as well.
The Claymore's were so old that they were sun faded. The only functioning firearms we've found were a 20-gauge shotgun and a 30:06 hunting rifle with a cracked stock and a broken scope.

    I don't think we have a case here. But of course, the ATF agent is jumping up-and-down like a school child who just won a prize because he wants that still. He told me that he doesn't think his boss will pull a prosecution because it was such a low volume system and the still had more holes in it than it had copper. The copper oxide was on both the outer and inner surfaces. It doesn't look like it's been used for several years, it's nothing more than scrap. We looked for a water source but there was no piping anywhere. It looks like we and the feds will drop the charges."

    So next, I had to call the Register of Deeds for the county and ask for a speed search for ownership which would usually take up to thirty days. I didn't even think to ask Heck who actually owned the property. Well, I found out that Heck did own the property but he was only three weeks away from losing it to tax forfeiture.

I had another twenty minutes of bliss and finished my second pot of coffee before my phone rang. Well, it was Val and poor sweet sister Val, was pissed off. Or at least it seemed that way as she started the conversation with, "You prick!"

Me:   Hello Darling, how may I assist you?
Val:   I don't know who the hell you were sitting with a few hours back but I did not see that same man that you did. He scared the living shit out of us, he looked just like Anthony Hopkins in, "Silence of the Lambs!" I thought, "Here's a guy that needs a steel bite mask!" Son of a bitch he's scary! He glared at me and only grunted and ignored my every question. I asked him if one of the gentlemen in the room may ask him a question. He would only give them quick short answers. Obviously, he didn't like us. I tried to explain to him that we were there to help him. Heck said, "David Brown helps me and no one else!" He actually kicked us out of the interview room, and told us not to come back! What the fuck are we going to do?

Me:   Well, what the fuck you and your two faithful followers are going to do is you and they will hop in your buggies and race your ass down to the hotel. I'll meet you in the lobby. Call your top real estate attorney and drag him or her down here with you. Don't fuck around! It looks like they might release him and drop all charges. He's a sick man, we've got to help him, we can't let him get back to that property. My gut tells me that something very bad could and probably would take place. It's just a feeling I have, but I trust my gut. As far as dinner tonight, that's a no go. We will snack, we've got work to do and a whole shit load of it! *Capeesh?*

I called the jail captain and asked him that if they decide to release Heck, if they would please "Baker Act" him until I can shuffle through all the offices of social service to get him committed. "He will at least be safe on a seventy-two-hour mental health hold in a secure Mental Health Facility. I'm afraid he's going to harm himself or others if you release him." The captain told me that my firm had already issued a Mental Health hold and he was about to be transferred to a secured hospital ward. All I could do was inwardly smile and say to myself, "At least somebody's fucking listening to me!"

Val's legal team all arrived together. I wasn't comfortable with bringing strangers up to my office but I knew that this had to be away from all ears. I had security escort them up to my office. I didn't do my usual warm greetings as I announced that this is a working afternoon, probably going into the late evening, "If you need to call anybody to let them know you'll be home late, do it now, if not, let's get started."

I noticed that both the male lawyers made brief phone calls, Val did not, which told me she didn't have a special guy. I could see one of the young attorney's was puzzled as to who the fuck I was and how I got to carry the ball. He had an air about him that told me he wanted to challenge me. I didn't do anything to try to dissuade him, but I did let my suit coat fall open to show my custom Smith & Wesson 45 caliber acp in my shoulder holster, with a grin! I thought, "Sport, if you need to get knocked on your ass, I'm your man!"

We were probably an hour to an hour and a half into our conversations with a great deal of note taking when I got the call.

Just the caller ID in itself, told me that something was terribly wrong. I excused myself and went into the kitchen to take the call. It was the sheriff of the county. He said, "David we've had a situation here at the jail, your friend, Mr. Heck Wozniak has taken his life." The sheriff went on to give me a brief summation of what took place. I thanked him and wished him well and hung up.

I went into the master bedroom to gather myself. I called down to the front desk and told them that I wanted two security officers immediately to my suite. I waited for them in the hallway. I gave them a quick briefing on what I needed; they both nodded their heads in understanding. We walked into the office area where the three attorneys sat. I introduced the two security officers as two of Duluth's finest, retired Police Officers. The looks on the lawyer's faces were almost humorous but this is not the time for humor.

Me:   Did each of you take notes while interviewing Heck? (Three head nods) Hand me your notepads. Now I want you guys to place your briefcases over here on this table. Val, your purse goes on the table too. Now, these two officers are going to search each of you and they will be removing everything from your pockets. Go along with what I have instructed them to do and no harm shall fall to you.

    The two lawyers looked over at Val as if to ask, "What the fuck?" Val's only comment was, "You'll do as Mr. Brown has instructed you to do and I will do the same."

    After each person was searched, I sent them to the kitchen. When all three were searched, one of the officers joined them in the kitchen and closed the door. I walked over and grabbed a lined trash can for the other officer to dispense of all the writing instruments from the body searches. I then had him start with Val's purse removing all writing instruments and then on to the three briefcases on the table. When the search was complete, I went to the kitchen and poured myself a cup of coffee, without saying a word other than telling them to return to the couch in the living area.

    Me:   I have instructed these officers to remove all and any writing instruments and to place them in this trash can for a reason that you may never completely comprehend. At some point, you may even want to thank me.

    I don't give a fuck if it's a prized ink pen, a pencil, a fucking marker, or even a goddamn crayon, anything that can be written with must go in this trash can. Several times I saw some apprehensive looks and the other two lawyers were looking to Val for some kind of guidance. She just kept shaking her head slowly as a silent cautionary statement as if to say; "Don't get involved with this."

I handed the trash can with the notepads and pens to one of the security officers and said, "These go directly to the incinerator, now! Everything in this container goes into the incinerator now. Are we clear?" One of the officers, who I have known for several years said, "Yes Sir Mr. Brown, we are crystal clear. The officers left the office and I had the three lawyers sit on the couch. Now was the time that I had to level with them and it gave me no pleasure.

Me: My friend and your client, Mr. Heck Wozniak took his own life in his cell an hour ago. He is no longer with us. I don't have a lot of specifics but I do know he repeatedly stabbed himself in the neck and throat with some type of writing instrument. That's why I confiscated all of your writing instruments. So now, no one has a missing pen, pencil, marker, or crayon. It's the same as they do with a prison firing squad, where at least two of the guns are loaded with blanks, so no one knows who actually shot the deceased.

As I expected, there sat three youthful attorneys with the shock of their life on their faces and with noticeably deep emotional sobbing. They knew that one of them had played a part in Heck's suicide. My only comeback was, "I believe that Heck was bent on taking his own life, long before he met with me or you three. All he did was find an avenue to his desired end goal. What's so fucking tragic is that I somehow knew he was going to do it! He never said it but he kept having a look on his face that would come and go quite quickly. That's when I suspected that he had some mental health issues. Although I knew that look, I couldn't quite identify it at the time. That look is the look of total resignation. That look is one that says, "I am done with this life and it's time I go to my fate." I know that look because I've seen it many times, those were the times that I've looked into my own mirror. The look says, "This is it for me, I'm done, I'm done with it all."

  I know that you're all adults and you're big and strong with a ton of life experience but I greatly doubt if you have ever had this kind of experience. Here's what I suggest for tonight. I would like you three to be guests of the Corker Hotel tonight. If you have family or someone close to you, you may want to invite them to join you. If you have children, we have bathing suits and plenty of towels for them to enjoy swimming in the heated pool. I don't want anyone going home tonight alone. Val, dial up your dad and hand me your phone. Val's father answered and I walked away into the kitchen. We had a brief chat and her dad said, "Her mother and I will be right down!"

  I strolled back to the living area and said, "Kids, I'm sure that some of those writing instruments may have been gifts of congratulations or some kind of a family heirloom but I don't think any of you want to know what instrument my friend Heck used to end his life. So now that we're all clear in understanding that, some things are best to never be known and need to be left alone.

## Chapter 6
# HARD TRUTHS

It was not more than twenty minutes before there were several visitors. It was of course, Val's dad and her mother and the other two lawyers' families. There was one set of parents, one wife and a wife with two small children. A few moments later, in walked my wife, Heather. I looked at her and her eyes told me that she already knew.

I looked over at Val and asked, "Is this your handiwork?" Val said, "You're the one that's always taking care of everyone else and you never take care of yourself. So, I guess I took charge and if you don't like it, deal with it!" Heather came into my arms and held me close.

Once everyone got settled, I called down for snacks, sodas, juices and cocktails. A waitress from the lounge came up and took drink orders and dropped off several children's snack packs along with coloring books and crayons. Everyone seemed to be very nice people and I was happy for those three to have the support of their families.

I walked over to Val's dad (Clifford) and spoke loud enough for everyone else to hear me, as I said, "Cliff, these three will need a bit of help to exit from the bowels of hell that they fell into a few short hours ago. There will of course be a private Coroner's Inquest in the morning. I have been assured that the coroner's findings and any evidence will be sealed for the next one hundred years. I guess what we're looking at with these three young people, is now a team of Defense Attorneys with experience beyond that of most any others. What do you think dad, you got room for a three-person team that will never be separated?"

The hotel manager brought up room keys for suites for the three attorneys and their guests and I needed to go home. I left my car at the hotel and Heather drove us home. She said, "You look like you need some deck time, I'll put on a fresh pot of coffee."

As always Heather knows exactly what I need and when I need it. I hadn't finished my first cup of fresh coffee and it came to me; I knew what I had to do. I went into the kitchen, poured a travel mug of coffee, went to the gun room, pulled out four of my favorite 45 acp's and grabbed my range bag and a couple ammo cans. I went back into the kitchen, gave Heather a hug and said, "I need to go make some noise!" She knew exactly what I was talking about. She said, "Baby, normally I would come with you but I think this has to be your time right now, and I agree, go make some noise and make it rain! Sweetheart, I want you to dirty those gorgeous guns of yours. It

seems that when you clean guns you always find your center. I'll be right here when you get back."
There is something almost romantic at least for me with the smell of freshly spent gunpowder, and hearing the ejected brass hit the floor or the ground. The gun noise is minimal because I have adjustable noise canceling shooting ear muffs.

I shot until my wrist and elbows got sore. It seemed like every time I dropped and reloaded another magazine another level of stress and sorrow was leaving me. On the way home I called the deputy in charge of the search team and asked if he and I could visit the search site just after daylight tomorrow morning. He said, "You've got your credentials, you can go on that site any time you'd like.

Me: No, I would like a guided tour. I want to see what you're seeing through your eyes. He said, "Great, I'll meet you there at 5:30 AM." Of course, I had to ask for the address.

We strolled through the entire acreage, all of the outbuildings and lastly the house, which finished telling me the story. There was a snowmobile with a sled trailer that had several five-gallon pails of corn and some other grains, so I knew in-part that Heck was telling me the truth, at least about feeding the animals. But as we walked the property, I saw no tracks from turkeys. Turkey's fly only a short distance, most of their life is spent sitting in trees and walking on the ground. There were still a few small piles of deer feed along with plenty of deer tracks. Some looked to be rather large animals by the size of their tracks. I was surprised but certainly not shocked to not find either of the two ponds that Heck told me about. We went into one of the garage areas where I found a cluttered desk with new packages of Hydraulic Hoses and hydraulic fluid for the backhoe. There were also fuel filters and oil filters there that were obviously made to fit the backhoe. I didn't want to spend the time trying to put it all together in my mind as I wanted to observe more than think. We entered the old farmhouse last. There were very few furnishings, then again how much do you need for just one person? There were several strikingly beautiful framed photographs from this local area. I would have to suspect that Heck probably printed those while at work. I looked at the deputy and asked, "Have these been inventoried?" The deputy said, "No, we didn't see any need for that, so I guess you're thinking you want to take some of these with you?"

Me: I love the way you think, deputy! Yes, I would, as a memento from the days of old.

I called the coroner's office and asked if the death notices had gone out to Heck's family members. The coroner said, "The family has already been here to claim your friend's personal property. I told them that Mr. Wozniak's property is being held by the Sheriff's Office. They were not at all happy. The two surviving brothers were adamant about not claiming the body and repeatedly stated that they would not assume any financial responsibility for Mr. Wozniak's body or internment.

I asked if I could claim the body for a proper burial. He said that he had no problem with a man giving his friend a proper burial, "There is no honor in dumping a human body into a pauper's grave. Dignity and human decency are obviously not a strong suit when it comes to Mr. Wozniak's family."

I immediately drove to the mortuary. I asked what the parameters were for a burial for an unclaimed body. I was told they were usually cremated and put in a pauper's grave.

Me:   Bullshit that will not happen, since no one has claimed the body, the coroner has given me possession of my friend's (Mr. Heck Wozniak's) body. I will pay for his funeral service and burial.

The Mortician was more than happy to take my order. I ordered a better-to-best casket, along with four sprays of flowers. I also ordered a closed casket memorial service, a head stone and a burial plot. Well, I doubt very much if his own brothers were going to attend his funeral, but I would be there!

I went home and laid down for a nap. I had not slept for very long before I was awoken by a thought. I attended three AA meetings a week before Covid shut everything down. Each group has a phone list for its members to be able to contact someone if they were troubled and needed someone to talk to. I called eight of my closest AA friends and briefly told them about Heck and his empty funeral service in three days from now. I invited them to attend Heck's funeral and for them to in turn, to please contact other AA members and invite them.

I left Heather a note that said, "Gone fishin, will be home shortly after dark." I grabbed a folding chair, my ice auger and my fishing gear. I caught more than twenty trout but released them all as they were only lip hooked. I needed that time to process what had been dancing in my head for the last few days. Now it became clear what Heck was doing for those few hours that we sat together. Heck wasn't lying to me, yes, he exaggerated about the ponds and about the working stills and probably about the money in the walls and the bank. I think what he was talking to me about was that he had a dream but he just didn't have the heart to admit that he never got to realize his dream. Just the new parts for the backhoe told the story, all by themselves.

Depression is a cruel Mistress; I know her all too well. Depression steals our dreams and crushes our hopes. I'm sure that Heck had every intention of having what he claimed to have but he just didn't have the internal strength of heart, the strength of mind and the strength of soul that so many others take for granted. I think he made three if not four different statements alluding to his life being over, during our brief talk. As I think of it now, it appears that Heck was planning to commit, "Suicide by cop" with the standoff but his heart would not allow it.

Suddenly, Heck's, Claymore mines and combat vest with the dummy grenades hanging off the front of his vest, made sense. He wanted to die but he couldn't go through with it, knowing that his causing law enforcement to shoot him would destroy their and their families' lives.

That was what he was really telling me! I think that's where those strange looks came from when his eyes would turn colors. A part of me understands, actually a large part of me understands why Heck took his life. I'm grateful that his heartbreaking internal battle is finally over for him.

On the day of Heck's funeral service there were more than forty people in attendance. I was pleasantly surprised to see all three of Heck's Attorneys were in attendance as well. There were all of my eight AA buddies and several people that I have seen in AA meetings from around the area. These were people who all knew how close to death they were, at some point of their lives. They understood hopelessness, depression, anxiety and suicidal ideations.

I, of course, did Heck's eulogy and I spoke no different than I do when I'm in an AA meeting. Other than the three attorneys, no one in the room had ever met Heck but before the twenty minutes was over, they all knew Heck as well as they knew themselves. Not in a physical sense of course, but in the mental, emotional and spiritual sense. We alcoholics have all teetered with our toes over the edge of that cliff. That is the greatest commonality of alcoholism. "Heck is not just a dead man lying in this box, Heck is you…and Heck is… me. But for the grace of God go we."

## Chapter 7
# THE LOVE OF MANKIND

The funeral luncheon was held at one of our local AA clubrooms, the group of mourners from the funeral parlor increased from the approximated 40 to now 65 or perhaps even 70 people and I was fine with that. Some people can't go into a mortuary or attend a funeral for various reasons and I get that. But they still want to show respect to the life and memory of the deceased. There was one face that stood out as I had dealt with him before. He was quite a likable fella; he was a reporter for one of the local TV stations. Actually, he's done two interviews with me. The interviews (of course) were based on my books. The first time we met was for a joint interview with the Duluth Police Chief and myself. The interview was spawned from an article I wrote in an area social website the week before Christmas in 2020. The interview was held at the police department and county sheriff's justice center. I arrived fifteen minutes early which is my customary show-up time for any

# THE JUDICIAL SYSTEM IS GUILTY

meeting I attend, even if it's just for coffee with a friend. To me, it's a simple matter of respect.

As I entered the Justice Center lobby, I saw a mid to late twenties, young man seated in the waiting area with a large hard case and camera tripod, as I walked past to sign in with the receptionist. I approached the fledgling young reporter and introduced myself. Duluth has become the shallow end of the pool for beginners in the media industry due to the drastic loss of retail businesses, manufacturing and the collapse of the mining industry in the last twenty years. Our population has gone from 120 thousand to well under 80 thousand people. Anyone with a college degree gets the hell out of here in a hurry. It's much the same for the local media. There are five affiliate TV stations in Duluth and their advertisers are few and they pay very little for commercial air time. None of the area networks have a weekend news show. Reporters who are fresh out of school and hungry for their first job come to Duluth as the revolving door is always in hyper speed. Most don't stay for more than six months with the average pay scale being that of a fast-food worker. Sadly, the local newspaper followed suit. What used to be a two paper a day program with a morning News Tribune and afternoon Herald, seven days a week, is now a twice a week condensed paper that is no longer delivered but mailed.

I have seen this reporter in a few newscasts in the last few months. His name was John and he came from California. John was a recent graduate of San

Diego State University where he studied Humanities and Social Sciences. John was quite engaging and well spoken. He told me that he attended the 'Edward R. Murrow school of Broadcasting' shortly after college graduation.

The Police Chief was running a bit late so I asked John about his career goals. He didn't hold back with his love of humanity and all of mankind along with his hope for all. I grinned as I said, "You sound much like the Roman emperor, Marcus Aurelius from AD 161 to 180 and his "Stoic Precepts."

I think John might have peed himself a little bit with excitement, as he squirmed in his seat with obvious joy of finding a fellow believer.

I smiled as I said, "I'm not as learned as you, my friend. I'm a generalist, I know a little about a lot of things but not a lot, about any one thing."

Lucky for me, the Chief's secretary appeared and escorted us to the Chief's office. The reason for the interview was the chief wanted to personally and publicly thank me for humanizing the badge with my brief Facebook post that read:

"Dedicated to the current and past Police Officers of the Duluth, Minnesota Police Department. Your predecessors have left a legacy that few of you know of.
In 1957 a 9-year-old- boy was going to take his own life on Christmas Eve. The kindness and generosity of your entire department turned that little boy away from his darkness. I am that little boy.

David J. Brown
Goodspeed my friends."

    The joint interview was very pleasurable and I clearly saw the Chief as a 'Cops, Cop'.
    The next time I sat with John was due to a local post I wrote on Facebook on April 6th, 2021. I was leaps and bounds beyond pissed off! The entire month of April is nationally recognized as, "Child Abuse Awareness Month" but the entire media either didn't care or were busy with some gardening or high school sports bullshit! My ass was in flames and I wanted to share the fire. My post was answered by hundreds of area people who were as disgusted as I was and they turned up the heat. John came to my home for the interview, as Covid and our governor had closed their studios and offices. That interview was of course, about the hidden secrets of families and parents abusing their children. John did an excellent job with an in-depth special report. I was just a small part of his fifteen minute long, special report. Yes, I dig John and who he is as both a man and a reporter. I walked over to John with a warm smile and a firm handshake.

    Me:   Tell me Scribe, what is a human-interest news reporter/philosopher doing hanging out with a bunch of washed-up drunks on this fine day? Are you sniffing out a story my friend? He smiled and said, "Yes in part, but I am also here to support you in your loss. I'm intrigued, not with the situation but with you, when I contacted the jail about the suicide, they referred me to you, with the title of, Deputy U.S. Marshall Brown! I was flabbergasted, you never told me that you are a U.S. Marshall. I thought you were a long-time retired police officer. So now I finally get it, that's why you and the Chief got along so well! You were both smiling with your ploy to keep me in the dark but I get it. You wanted to focus on cops and not on yourself! I find that remarkably commendable.

    Well, I get around a bit too David and I got wind of you taking care of and paying for all the arrangements for your friend, Mr. Wozniak. And I know there's just more than a story to all this. I would like to interview you when the time is right, not today of course. So, in part, I'm here to support you because you're a very unique and likable man but I'm also a news hound and special interest freak, as you well know.
I don't have that full of an appointment calendar so, anytime, anyplace."

    Me:   You're on, let's do it on Thursday of this week, bring your checkbook, you're buying lunch.

    I next moved over to the table filled with Val and her family and her fellow lawyers and their families and I just couldn't help myself. I put my left hand on Val and my right hand on her father's shoulder with a wide grin.

    Me:   Hello Cliff and company! What's this? You high dollar solicitor/barrister types can't afford lunch, so you cruze funerals every day to score a free meal?

I heard a collective sigh as they were silently saying, "I think he will be OK." Of course, I full well knew that they were there to support me and that's quite admirable in my book. Dad stood, shook my hand and asked if I had a moment. Of course, I did, I needed a cigarette! We stepped outside of the building where I could have a cigarette and we could have a private conversation.

Me: Well, how's she holding up? I am sure that she is blaming herself.
Cliff: David she's terribly rattled. She didn't realize how sick some people can be and with no one knowing it. You have a very uncanny way of teaching. It's no different than when you took her on with the Cold Case homicide files. You knew that she was not a seasoned investigator, you drove her hard, damn hard but you didn't try to break her. However, you sure brought her home with saddle sores and a few spur burns on her flanks. When you two returned from California, you brought my wife and I back an adult woman. How in the world did you develop those skills?
Me: Oh, you mean the part where your daughter sat in on a Cold Case file investigation team and held herself up as a homicide detective, when in fact, she worked in the evidence room?

Cliff: Yeah, I set that up. I put it in your lap to see where it would take her and man you took her to the moon and back! You helped her to see and realize that not everything is bouquets and pinwheels by showing her what life and the world is truly all about. She's been greatly protected by her mother and I. We both have realized that we have done her no favors in that area. Now I'm wondering if she should practice law.

Me: So now what dad, you want me to vet her to see if she's capable or willing to dive into the family business? You want me to interview your daughter and to report back to you? That's not going to happen. I do agree that she's not cut out for the blood and gore end of it, come on sport, neither of us have any questions in that area, correct?

Cliff: David, I'm asking you, do you think she should go through with the defense of any of these five cases she selects? Or should we just turn her away?

Me: No, dumping her I think that would be a massive mistake. She needs to keep her feet in the water if she's going to learn to swim like a duck. I still want to help her identify those five defendable cases but it's not looking good my friend. I know that part of your license to practice law requires that every lawyer must give fifty hours of free time each year, or as you enlightened folks like to call, "Pro Bono" legal work each year. You have sixty-seven lawyers in your outfit. So, you need to burn 3,350 hours to keep your staff in compliance with the bar. You are dumping the office trash on top of her like she's a four-year-old in a fuckin leaf pile. Why don't you give her a pair of safety scissors that they have in daycare and tell her to cut your lawn! Maybe you could follow that up with giving her a measuring spoon to shovel snow from your driveway. You mistakenly think that if you overwhelm her with loser cases that she will walk away. Cliff, wake the fuck up and grow some balls, maybe even a full set! Sit down with her and tell her the truth, don't set her up to fail, allow her to win or lose on her own merits. What you and your wife are doing, is trying to settle your guilt for you both trying to keep her in a bubble.

When we were sitting with the property master at the movie studio, she actually vomited with the mere thought of a person planning my murder. Yeah, that was quite a clue all right. You guys need to take a breath and step back. If it were up to you two, you'd probably still have her in denim and corduroy jumpers with knee highs along with a training bra and wrapped in bubble wrap. She is a woman, she's not your child, she's your daughter.

One more thing, just so you know sport, it wasn't her ink pen that killed my friend, but then again, I'll say that to the other two attorneys and their families as well. It was no one's pen. Have a nice day!

I went back into the AA clubroom to thank everyone for attending. Cliff was sitting next to his wife and looked like his little ass was still red from his spanking. I kissed Val on the cheek as I announced,

"You three little darlings will be at the, "Lemon Drop Restaurant" at 7:00 AM tomorrow. Bring your laptops and your briefcases, we've got work to do and a lot of it. And Cliff, yes today is a billable day, that's right six hours at my rate! I need a nap. See you around kids."

I had no intention of going for a nap although I needed one. I knew I had more work to do and I didn't want anyone to know it. I had a strong suspicion that Heck had set up his standoff. I went to the 911 dispatch center and spoke with the actual dispatcher that took the original call. I asked her If she would let me hear the tape but before that I asked her what source that phone call came in on. She told me it was one of those convenient store cell phones that are untraceable. They couldn't even pull up a locator ping off of a cell tower in that area. She said, "The chief investigator asked me almost the same questions, is there a problem?" I said, "No, not a problem, I'm just looking for a part of an answer." Continuing our conversation I asked her, "What did the caller's voice sound like? Was he calm, frightened, agitated, or hostile? Was it muffled, was he throwing his voice, did he have a bucket over his head, how did his voice sound?" She said, "Well now that I think of it, he knew more about the layout of that property then a common caller would. He was very explicit in describing the weapons and the party involved."

She then played the 911 call, we listened to it five times. I smiled over at her as I said, "You almost got to witness a suicide by cop. That was most certainly Heck's voice that called. And you are right about the property description and weapons involved. The caller knew too much. Yes, I recognize his voice, he wanted to commit suicide but he was afraid to, so he thought he would use the police to reach his desired end. I'm sure this is not your first experience with issues like this." She sat there quietly, lowered her head and wept as she said softly, "No sir this is not my first experience but it just breaks my heart, "Why can't they just say they need help? I don't want to kill myself."

If they could just say that, someone could have reached out to him and stopped him. This didn't have to happen!"

I reached over and took her hand as I said, "Well, as my friend saw it, it did have to happen and no, there are no answers, there never are, there are only victims."

I thanked her for her time. She all but bolted from her chair and threw her arms around me and thanked me for understanding her pain.

I knew that there would be no peace on the drive home or once I arrived home. Those, 'what if's' were already kicking my ass as they were slamming around in my skull. It could be a bit of a reach, but I have to wonder what his two surviving brothers' voices sound like. Could they have called 911 and set Heck up to be killed by the cops? Where did Heck get these dummy grenades and Claymore landmines? Did they give them to him? Is there a deeper, more sinister plot afoot? He had three brothers, obviously one died. What did he die from? Heck's two sisters-in-law were there doing a physical inventory of the property the morning Heck was taken into custody. Did they have plans to snap up the property when he died and before it went into tax foreclosure? Did Heck out fox them, with his knowing that if he died before the foreclosure that everything would go to probate and the bank? Heck was certainly nobody's fool!

## Chapter 8
# THE WARRING TRIBE

I knew I was lying to myself about trying to catch a nap, even before I started my truck and headed home. I knew I had to go through those files. Before I did that, I contacted Cliff (Val's dad) and my buddy Lief Erikson who owns the local newspaper. I told Cliff that I wanted four of his best and brightest research analysts for a lengthy period of time. I told Lief that I wanted all but full, 'ownership papers' on that mouthy Nobel Peace Prize Candidate, Missy, for an undetermined amount of time with the promise that I would make him and her famous beyond his wildest dreams.

As always, I arrived at the Lemon Drop restaurant fifteen minutes early. There was only one person sitting there waiting for me and that was Val. I said, "Baby, fifteen minutes early doesn't mean that you're actually early, it just means that you're not late. Where's those other two clowns?"

Val had a sheepish look on her face and said, "I waved them off, I need an hour or so of your time, just you and me time." Of course, I jumped her ass and said, "Baby this is my show, you don't run anything, you don't change times and you don't break or set up my agenda. If this is your attempt at a power grab you just failed. I have food at my house, I don't need to fucking sit here and listen to your bullshit."

Val was at the edge of tears as she said, "David please, it's nothing like that at all, I just need your time, I just need your attention, I just need to be alone with you!"

Me:   Oh well, here you are alone with me, in a restaurant with what, 40, 50, 60 other people? You gotta feel so alone because it's just us in this big ole empty restaurant. What the fuck do you want?

Val:   David please, this is important! I'm having trouble breathing. I feel like one of those goldfish or a guppy in a fishbowl with just constantly moving but going nowhere and with my mouth popping trying to catch my breath. I feel like I'm having a nervous breakdown or something. Can we go back to California like we did before everything blew-up?

Me:   Baby, understand that you can never go back. Everything has changed, because you have changed. Nothing will ever be the same. We could do exactly the same things and go to all the same places but it won't be the same, it can't be the same.

You are an adult now and your vision has changed, your entire structure has changed. Your mind, your heart and your soul have matured.

Val: I want to go back to the Poseidon Paddle and Surf Shop in Santa Monica. I will pay for everything. I will pay for a swimsuit for you and me. I just wanna lay in that warm white sand and walk the beach like we did before. It just cleansed me so nicely. I want to go back to that 'Stinking Rose' restaurant and order every item on their menu. I wanna go to that nightclub you took me to, where you let me look for movie stars. I want to watch the adoring way people fall all over you, like you're carrying some kind of a magic potion.

Me: So, you're a romantic junkie, hooked on love and you need your feel-good fix?

Val: I want to go to the beach. I just need to breathe for a little while. I need sun, white sand and surf, I need to feel alive again.

Me: Have you ever seen a firefighter sit down on the tail board of a pumper truck, light up a smoke and drink a cup of coffee as the apartment building in front of them is well engulfed with flames and smoke with people hanging out of the windows begging for help with the flames licking at their feet and clothing? Have you ever seen or heard a firefighter just say, "I gotta take a break, I'm going to sit down here to catch my breath because I am uncomfortable?" Of fucking course not!

You want to reward yourself before you even start the project? No honey, we rest at the end, not in the beginning, not in the middle, just at the end. There will be times that even at the end of a case, there will be no cause for celebration, because some days you will lose. It is imperative that you do your very best with each and every case. And yes, my love, there will be times that your best won't be good enough and you will just have to eat it because there will be another client right behind them who desperately needs your help. Their freedom and their life are at stake!

So, what time did you schedule those other two monkey asses?

Val: I told them to be at the hotel lobby at 8:30.

Me: So now you're scheduling my time and breaking it down to thirty-minute increments? Who the fuck do you think you are? I know your daddy's little girl but you are not my little girl or my boss, you don't set anything for me, you better draw yourself up tight girl. I don't need your money and I don't give a fuck about those people in the Banker Boxes. So, what I'm hearing is that you showed up just to sabotage yourself? You need to fail so you can do what, feel sorry for yourself? I think it's time you grow up, my child and you're already out of time, actually. So, you're going to show your family that you're weak, you're not up to the task, and you are a poor choice and they should have never trusted you? I'm surprised your name isn't in one of those folders in the

Banker Box, you're about as fucked up as most of those people!

    Call your HR director or office manager, I don't know who the fuck you need to talk to, but I want both of those two swinging dicks personnel files on my desk and I want them in the next hour.

    Val:   We don't open the offices for another eighty minutes.

    Me:   I don't give a fuck about your office hours or your company's protocol, call them at home and tell them to shag their asses to the office, they can do their hair and make-up on company time. I want those fucking files! I'm leaving now, enjoy your breakfast.

    At 8:00am there were three young people sitting in the lobby of the Corker Hotel with puzzled looks on their faces. Those fancy suits didn't do a thing to hide their apprehension. When I approached them, they all stood up and bid me good morning, rather sheepishly. I took them into the small conference room and I said, "Well gentlemen, I'm sure you got word from your supervisor here, that she got your shit in hot water.

    I will tell you gentlemen just once; you don't take orders from anyone in your office when it comes to me and my orders. I'm the boss, no one else and if anyone wants to come up against me, we'll just call it all good. I'll walk away and I'll go fishing and you'll have the rest of your careers to wonder why your life is so fucking screwed up. Now gentlemen, you're each going to write down for me; where you grew up.

I want every home address you have ever had, every school you've attended, every social, political and service organizations you've been a member of and every vacation you've ever been on and what locations, both as a child and as an adult. I want your mother's maiden names and all relatives names and birthplaces and birthdates going back three generations. I have your personnel files here and I suspect that most of that is bullshit. So, this is your one golden moment for the two of you. I don't care what family structure you came from, what University you attended or campus fraternity you pledged to. What I want to know is how you have behaved from your earliest childhood. I want to know what you've experienced within your family structure and your school structures.

    I have people, gentlemen. I have people that know people, that have other people that have even more people, if you're trying to hide anything from me, I'll shove it right up your youthful asses. I know what you gifted folks are all about, you think that you're protected and nobody can get to you. You think that you're all better than everyone else and you're infallible with your law degrees. Boys you couldn't be more wrong. I have watched pricks like you two, mistreat and challenge good people's character and integrity in court for many years. You shout at witnesses in court to intimidate them and the shit head judges go along with it because you are all members of the same country club. You clowns get away with shit in court that if you were on the street, you would get your asses stomped into a mud hole. I don't have any reason to dislike either of you personally but I greatly despise what you stand for. And don't either of you give me any of your bullshit about how you stand for justice and the American way of life. You use the law of the land to intimidate and manipulate people for your own means. Your life is about and only about, personal wealth and prestige. Which one of you is Clark and when did you graduate college?

    The young man with a well-trimmed beard and thick eyebrows raised his hand and said, "I did my undergrad work at Carleton College in Northfield, Mn. and I received my law degree at William Mitchell College of Law in Saint Paul, Minnesota. I graduated in 2018."

    Me:   Clark, I know all of that already. I also know that you either stole or lost eleven law books from William Mitchell library. You owe several hundreds of dollars in library fines and penalties that you've been dodging for well over five years. Pull out your billfold, you're going to make that right as we sit here. You will also write a letter of apology to the Board of Regents for you being a deadbeat. Put your cell phone on speaker, call the library and make the apology and pay your fucking bill, do it now! Ain't that a bitch? Hell kids, I haven't even released the hounds yet!

I turned to the other lawyer who somehow looked like one of my dogs who tried to melt into the couch when it's her turn for a bath.

Me: Well Stanley, that leaves you and you're fucked! You are well behind in your student loans, it seems you greatly prefer the nightlife rather than you standing for your financial responsibilities. You asked for the student loan, you promised to pay it back, so pay it fucking back! I won't tolerate your generation's demands to forgive your student loans because you pissed that money away on booze, drugs and your backpacking and hostel stays while smoking dope in hookah bar visits all across Europe.

Your brother cosigned for a car for you six years ago, you went bad on the loan twice and each time your brother, who had three small kids at the time and who drives a trash truck had to make it right by paying for your past due payments and re-writing your loan with interest and penalties twice and he still let you drive the fuckin car! I have to guess that you now earn six to eight times his wages? Man, you don't at all mind who you fuck over! Make that right with him. You damaged his credit rating and took money from his family but worse than all that, you broke the bond of family. He believed in you and you straight up fucked him. Still think you're some kind of a big deal? You better check your heavy drinking or quit drinking altogether.

Well gents, what would your big boss say about your antics? Would you still have a job?

We listened to Clark make his apology to the library manager and give his credit card numbers. He actually owed more than I thought. Much more!

Me:  I can't look at either one of you any longer. Val, I understand that your firm has a personal loan program with payroll deductions. Take these guys to get them the money they need to clean up their messes.
Stanley, I want you to bring your brother the cash you owe him, along with six years of interest or don't come back tomorrow. I expect a receipt signed by your brother with his personal cell number and you can bet your ass that I'm going to call him! If you are not at the Lemon Drop restaurant at 7:00am tomorrow, you have effectively resigned from the law firm.

## Chapter 9
# SALVATION

    While thumbing through the file of 'loser cases' I saw a name that jumped out at me a few days ago when I opened the heavily loaded Banker Box. It was a name and face familiar to me. At the time, I didn't give it much thought because that person is a local whack-job, that I don't personally know but she is all over local social media as well as a frequent flier on the Saint Louis County Jail Roster. I decided to use her and most of the other cases in the Bankers Box as my test dummies, if you will.

    This young woman, (early thirties), like so many others, lives on a balance beam between drug addiction and mental illness. You can never really tell which side they teeter on. If you remove the drugs and do a complete detox program will this same problematic person have the same problems or will they clear up? In some cases, people use alcohol along with prescribed and street drugs to mask their mental illness. Once they are completely clean you may have one very sick, mentally ill individual. Nobody's challenged any of that. If somebody appears to be out of control doctors give them more medications and call it good. I've seen that going on for years, as a matter of fact there's a group home right next door to mine. It houses four mature, mentally ill females. Group homes are the thing these days ever since Bill Clinton and his sweetheart politicians got together and said, "We're closing all state hospitals to balance the budget and we'll make it the state's problems and not the federal governments." Of course, the federal budget allocated at that time to state hospitals seemed to somehow have simply disappeared. The states never had the ability or the money, so the states closed down those hospitals and today those people that need daily care are released into the communities. Then the state smiles (as the feds did) by saying to the city's, "Now that's your problem, you deal with it!"

    Nobody is dealing with anything; Duluth has become nothing more than a human warehouse of broken souls. Our homeless population is huge and growing daily. We are the county seat with non-profits tripping over each other offering all but identical services all on the taxpayer's dime. These program directors pay themselves quite well. It's like a monster employment program for social workers. Our city has warming shelters, mobile showers, food kitchens and overnight sleeping facilities, with several church groups offering similar services. The churches are also doubling as "Sanctuary" shelters for criminals and illegal aliens. There are several food and clothing banks as well. Street people come from all over the country because our Governor and Mayor are so liberal with the laws. Our police department has their hands tied and are told only to make felony arrests and release the people with misdemeanor warrants or are committing 'on view' crimes. So, a cop has to write a ticket to the offender to promise to appear in court for people that have a stack of warrants for not appearing in court!

    Many of the street people can't go to the shelters if they are acting violent, stoned or drunk, so on subzero nights, they fill up the hospitals. On any given day we see three different pharmacy delivery cars come to that 'House' next to our house. The residents aren't a problem but they move around like zombies. These group homes are privately owned but government financed and are a big profit center for that treatment homeowner. Of course, traffic up-and-down the street is constant with social workers visiting as well as God knows who else. Of course, the house is staffed twenty-four hours a day. Employees are leaving constantly and arriving. It's like a beehive of humanity. In my opinion these group homes are no different than the pharmaceutical manufacturers. They don't exist to cure, they exist for a continuum to treat, treat through sales and of course for great profits. And of course, it is a very high cost to the taxpayers. These group homes that are smattered all throughout the city (excluding the wealthy neighborhoods) are a business, make no mistake in knowing that, but what products do they deliver? What are their services, what are their goals? Who are they actually helping other than themselves? The biggest question in all of this is, who do they report to?

  Getting back to that particular young lady; she has ongoing posts on Facebook about her life's tragedies, either real or imagined. She reports that her brother beats her up or the neighbor beats her up or her buddy down the street beats her up, everyone steals her money and her cell phones and she has nothing to eat. It's one constant report with a litany of tragedies. She is quite adept at stealing outgoing mail from businesses and homes. She takes return payment envelopes and acid washes the checks and makes the checks out to herself, along with her shoplifting escapades that have her banned from most every retail and convenience store, hence her many jail visits. The question that must at some point be asked is; is she mentally ill or has her drug addiction taken over her life, and how well could she be if she were detoxed and properly treated? I know that goes against the goals of keeping her dependent not only on drugs but on the treatment services because again, that's where the money is.

  My mind raced most of the night but I had a solid plan before I even started my shower for the morning breakfast meeting. When I spoke to the two bosses of the people I wanted to be involved with this merry little band, I told them to have them at the Lemon Drop restaurant at 6:45am so I could brief them prior to the arrival of my crew.

    Well, those three lawyers are rather quick studies and they were already seated with their briefcases and laptops on the floor at their feet. I introduced the five new players in the game.

    Me:  We are going to go around the table and each of you will introduce yourselves and speak for ten minutes on what makes each of you the right choice for this new team and project.

    It went quite nicely and there was a great deal of humility being practiced (which pleased me greatly) as people were describing themselves and their successes. Val and Missy caught on rather quickly. I just sat and grinned nodding my head but mostly I said very few words. I told Val to whip out her corporate credit card and take care of the meal and get everyone down to the hotel. "We're going to meet in the conference room in twenty minutes. I don't want any lagers; you lag behind and you will be left behind!"

    Once everyone was seated in the conference room, I lifted the Banker Box on top of the table and posed the question. "Does anyone know what this box represents?" Of course, the three legal beagles piped up to those files are to be reviewed to be assigned and defended. I smiled and I said, "Not anymore, at least not in the way you're thinking. You people better get up to speed, your way behind here. Listen tight, I don't have time to repeat myself."

# THE JUDICIAL SYSTEM IS GUILTY

Me:   What is about to take place is all but epic, perhaps even history making. But first understand this, I run this show, I solely run this show. I'm the coach and I'm the owner of this lovely little dream team and we shall not fail. A few of you may, but you'll be gone and replaced quickly. Here it is in a very large nutshell, boys and girls. We, as in, 'We the People' in this room, have equal power. Nobody's the boss of anyone other than myself. You will support each other but nobody is to direct or criticize anyone's efforts. I will ride everyone's ass equally. I want results, I want them hard, fast and dirty. Here's what we're gonna do kids.

We The People in this room, the people of Duluth, Minnesota, in the next thirty days, are going to develop and serve, legal briefs, indictments and arrest warrants for gross misconduct and dereliction of duties against the city of Duluth, Saint Louis County, the State of Minnesota along with the all-powerful federal government of the United States of America. Not just by each office but by each name in each office.

Follow along closely. Within each of these case file folders in this box, there is one common denominator that is shared across-the-board. What is that common denominator you may ask? Now keep in mind that these are all criminal cases but what we are looking at but not recognizing, are abused mental health cases. The agencies have committed the crimes, not the accused. The agencies have failed to deliver the services that are directed by their own charter and a litany of both state and federal laws. We will be designing and developing the shit show of the century.

A case in point:
You may or may not remember a retail store in downtown Duluth named, "The Last Place on Earth." It started out as a record shop and morphed into the number one top selling head shop in the entire nation! I remember seeing the lines of screwed-up dopers on the sidewalk that went to the end if not wrapped around the block, waiting to get into the store. The owner, Mr. Jim Carlson, bragged to the media that he had over a thousand customers in his store each day. Those were all cash customers.

Carlson sold addictive and deadly synthetic drugs that were smoked and were much more powerful than marijuana. They were branded as bath salts, incense and spices which caused many users to spend time in the emergency room or even die from drug overdoses, that stuff was pure poison and made people act crazy. Well, that's where it all started. Everyday drug users came from all over the country to be able to buy and use those products without breaking any laws. The reason being is that we didn't have any laws that applied to labeling and selling synthetic drugs at the time. The long lines in front of the store from opening to closing, caused four other retail stores on that same side of the block to have to close their businesses because their customers were constantly harassed by the slimeball junkies in line. Police calls for assaults amongst that crowd were a daily occurrence. Many of the assault victims were everyday people just trying to go to work or shop in that area. Ambulance calls for unconscious persons and assault victims averaged four calls a day. Do you want your mom or grandma to have to step over and around these shitheads, passed out in the doorways and sidewalks just to go shopping?

It was so bad, that the Duluth Police Department had to station four, off-duty officers and pay them overtime wages for fourteen hours every day, seven days a week, rather than have on-duty police officers having to leave their patrol districts, to respond to a radio call to break up fights and other people being abused up-and-down the blocks. Supposedly the city billed the head shop for the officer's time and use of police vehicles. Shoplifting skyrocketed along with vehicle break-ins in that area.

In a special session the City of Duluth asked a county judge to shut down the controversial business. The city argued that the downtown head shop has created a public nuisance by selling synthetic marijuana. The president of The Duluth Chamber of Commerce, Mr. David Ross, organized a group of about fifty downtown business owners to show their opposition to the, "Last Place on Earth" during that meeting.

Jim Carlson, not to be outdone, organized his own group of supporters (his junkie customers) that attended that meeting along with his puke lawyer,

Randall Tigue. Tigue argued that the state's nuisance statute was unconstitutionally vague. He went on to say, "Giving to the city and giving to the courts the power to shut down anything that a minority of people decide offends their morals, comfort and repose, that power is a far greater threat to society than synthetic marijuana will ever be."

"The minority of People"....... bullshit! The citizens of the city were fed up also, not just the business owners. Kids, attorney Randall Tigue is what defines a shit box! The county judge Loki appeared skeptical of the city's request because at that point, there was still no state or federal law to shut it down.

The feds finally put some teeth into new laws against selling synthetic drugs and did a raid on, "The last place on earth." in 2012. The police seized 2.8 million dollars from Carlson's business bank accounts and a year later they did another drug raid at his home and recovered $750,000 in cash and several firearms. We of course, will never know just how much money Carlson took in as it was a cash only business. It's estimated that he has millions of dollars of cash hidden in multiple locations. It's been reported that this puke supposedly had multiple IDs and passports in different people's names and owned several homes, not just in several states but also in several countries. When it became apparent that he was ready to run is when he was taken into custody and held for trial. Carlson was touted as the number one synthetic drug seller in the entire United States. I believe he was found guilty on fifty-one of the fifty-five counts lodged against him.

Gordon Ramsay, the police chief at the time, had asked Carlson to stop selling his poison because he was damaging neighboring businesses and the way he and his products were impacting people's lives. Carlson was sentenced to seventeen and a half years in a federal prison, in Malin, Michigan. Some speculate he won't come out alive, I sure as fuck hope he doesn't. Of course, he held himself up as being the king of curing all illnesses as he claimed that he was helping people with their suffering by supplying those drugs. On the initial raid of the retail store two of his employees were found to have active warrants. Oh my, how interesting. Carlson admitted to using his employees to test new drugs, before he sold them to the public. Aint that fuckin rich! Guess he wanted to protect his customers from any ill effects, after all, employees cost money but paying customers spend money. Hell, I guess you can hire new employees after your current employees die from an overdose. Carlson was quoted saying that he felt like a "medicine man", helping certain people with their ailments. Of course, the chief of police response was that Carlson was totally out of touch with reality, "That's the biggest bunch of garbage I've ever heard!"

Now you want to hear some real sickness with this asshole Carlson? He was doing a local TV interview from prison. Saying "Well you know, not to compare myself to Nelson Mandela but he spent twenty-seven years in prison. He went in as a terrorist and came out and became president!" That silly bastard Carlson ran under the Grassroots Party in 2012 for the Presidency of the United States!

    Carlson's defense attorney, Randall Tigue is as much a freak as Carlson. At sentencing, Tigue described the sentencing guidelines as 'draconian' saying his client's sentence was similar to one given to Colombian drug lord, Pablo Escobar. The prosecution was asking for a twenty-year sentence but lawyer Tigue argued that he wanted only three years as he cited Carlson's spotless criminal record, his health issues and the fact he was convicted of a non-violent drug offense. If any of you people sitting in here today can find any part of that assholes arguments to be valid, get the fuck away from me and get the fuck out of my building! There's an old saying that goes something like, "You are either a part of the solution or your part of the problem." I just deal with solutions. *Capish?*

    That was twelve years ago but those dopers never moved on when Carlson was shut down. And now I will tell you why. It was during that same time that some other fine upstanding lawyers within the city, saw that these pricks didn't work and they couldn't work because of their addictions. The lawyers printed fliers and handbills and had them passed out and plastered all over the city, advertising that they could get those people SSI insurance as to their being disabled. Those slimeball lawyers had lines out in the street full of junkies waiting to get into the offices to be declared disabled to collect SSI insurance. Saint

Louis County is one of the highest paying counties in the nation for welfare. The reason those people never left here is that the liberals made it too easy for them. We gave them everything and they took over our city. Carlson and that maggot lawyer have destroyed the majestic beauty of our entire city. It has been ten years since that store was closed and nothing has changed. There are junkies everywhere, crime rates are through the roof, all because of the greed of a business owner and a handful of slimy lawyers! Are you folks still proud to hold law degrees?

I want the eight of you to go back to the office and I want each of you, one at a time, to copy every page of these case files. Do not ask anyone to do it for you. I want each of you to feel each page in your hands and understand that you are not just touching a piece of copy paper but you are touching the fabric of a human life. A severely damaged human life.

Have you cats ever used or watched someone use a lawn broadcast spreader applying seed or fertilizer? There are settings on those spreaders for breath and volume of discharge. Drug addicts, alcoholics and mentally ill people do not have those types of controls. Their behavior and lifestyle broadcasts to everyone, not just the immediate family. Yes, there are children, spouses, parents, siblings and grandparents that suffer directly but so does our entire society. Think I'm full of shit? Next time you get the sniffles or a common cold, swing by any retail pharmacy and ask for Sudafed. Junkies make speed from it and because of that, you will need to produce an ID with your current address to be copied and sign a waiver that you do not have the intention to make illicit drugs. You are limited to 3.6 grams per day with a monthly limit of 9 grams, you are now being tracked by law enforcement and the DEA for the rest of your life.

Go make those copies and be back here at 12:30 sharp. Each of you is to bring your Banker's Box of identical case files. Those file boxes are now your Binkie and Blankie. Where you go, they go! Make no mistake that you will make enemies in this endeavor. Part of championing a just and rightest cause does two things. One; people with weak egos will try to tear you down, secondly the guilty will attack you for exposing them. I assure each and every one of you that the price of doing the right thing can and will be costly. You will lose friends and even your family may take offense and treat you differently. Your critics will be up your asses with a bazillion candle power flood lights to deflect and minimize their own involvement. I have spoken with all of your bosses, if you don't want to run the risk of being chastised and ostracized you may opt out. No harm no foul. Your jobs are not at risk, however…. your character is.

You are now dismissed.

## Chapter 10
# THE WAR ROOM

I sat in the meeting room for a few minutes after the crew left, trying to gather my thoughts. I left the meeting room and went to get a craft of coffee from the restaurant. I didn't want to waste the time making a pot of coffee upstairs in my office. I didn't want to be bothered with anything other than thinking in developing a plan. When I got upstairs to my office, I opened the drapes and looked out of my glass enclosed, floor to ceiling living area. I found myself laughing while asking myself. "What the fuck am I doing this time?" It seems like every time that I find myself in the middle of something, that I have no experience and no business being in, and today is no different. I looked out into the frozen Bay of Lake Superior. The shipping season is over and all the ships in port are tied up for the freeze and now you could walk across the Ice of the entire Bay all the way to Superior, Wisconsin. Yet my mind visualizes open blue waters. Those same open blue waters that I so often times, saw myself floating in the Bay in a leaky old wooden skiff, with no ores or no motor. I was at the mercy of the winds and the currents as the boat was taking on water. This time there is no boat, there is just me bobbing in the middle of the Bay. No life preserver and I most certainly didn't have the strength to tread water for very long. And as all the many times before, I know that I've done it to myself.

In my thinking, I knew I had to go it alone. This time I couldn't lean on the comfort of my tried-and-true friends. My mind and heart flashed on the Roberts family, then to Woody and Maddie then on to Seth and Mary and finally the Kivis. They all have their own lives to live and none of them have a dog in this fight. God and I know of all that they have done for me in the past. Then the laughter came when I realized that I was 'the dog' in this fight. That laughter didn't last anywhere as long as I needed it to. As the reality of what I've entered into is going to make poor Heather lose her fucking mind. Hell, I may not even tell her for a while. I laid down for a brief nap.

My feet hit the floor at 11:00am and I headed for the shower. I was laughing at myself with thinking, "Who the fuck takes a shower twice in one day and before noon?" It brought me back to memories of the early days, when I was a man of extreme drink, when I would stand in the shower until the hot water ran out as I was trying to remove the stink of alcohol emitting from my booze saturated pores.

I dressed and went out to the lobby to find my favorite, Dorman/Courtesy Van driver, Tim. I said, "Pal, I don't feel like driving right now. How's about we hop in your magical mystery ship and we run me up to my house? I'll be in and out in less than ten minutes.

In less than ten minutes, I was back out with several cases of handguns. I wanted to test the mettle of my new charges. I had Tim then drive to the law office as I made the phone call. When we pulled up to the front of the office building, Cliff came out with a big grin while giving me the finger, as he got into the van. When we arrived back at the Corker Hotel, I sent Tim into the conference room to escort the eight (and perhaps even less now, that they've had time to think about it) to the van, as I went to get a second craft of Folgers coffee. It wasn't that long of a drive to where we were going but I needed my 'Go Juice' to clear my head. I had Tim drive us up to my favorite professional gun shop and indoor shooting range. Some of the group of eight (yes, they all had returned) had never been to an indoor shooting range let alone a gun shop. Of course, those same people had never handled a firearm before. This is the exact distraction that I needed. There were four people working the counters when I arrived. The owner and the chief gunsmith were in the backroom. I asked for them to come out, when they came out it was like, 'old home week'. I hadn't been in the shop for several months due to Covid. These are really good people and they've always been damn good to me. I told them that I needed some help with professional guidance as I have brought some first-time shooters who have never handled a handgun before. The range master took them into the training room normally used to teach Concealed Carry Permit Classes and did a very thorough, thirty-minute gun safety class. Val stayed with me, as she was a former police officer and was well versed in safe gun handling. While the clerks outfitted everyone with proper fitting shooting ear muffs and safety glasses, I could feel their apprehension.

Cliff nodded his head and motioned the gun store owner, Val and myself to follow him to a far corner of the store.

Cliff:   David is about to make some enemies and more than just a few. Those enemies will most certainly splash over on my people. I want my people to all have a concealed carry class, tomorrow if that is feasible. I want my people to become proficient with their new guns. I would like them to spend three, four-hour days here. I will buy eight handguns today, for my people on your recommendations. Cost is of no concern. Shall we go shooting now?

The gun store owner was all grins as started to pull new handgun cases out of the back room.

Once we went into the firing range and I opened each of my gun cases, even the gun store owner and his star second in command gunsmith, grew some wider than average eyes. With both of them saying, "I've never seen stuff like this before. Who the fuck are you, really?" The shop owner grinned as he said, "You have six of the sexist 1911 pistols on the planet. I can see that they have all been hand worked, would $30,000 in cash help you to slide them over my way?

Me:   Does the name Jurgen Wagner ring a bell?

Gun Store owner:   I know of a grand national and world champion shooter by that name, but I've never met him.

Me: I have, Jurgen super tuned these sweethearts for me. We shot together a few weeks ago. Remind me to someday show you how to keep your spent casings from never hitting the floor while practicing side control.

Gun Store owner: I will run to the bank and bring you back $60,000 in the next thirty minutes!

Me: Naw, Jurgen and I are Pals now, I'm sure you understand. I'll make a deal with you guys, bring in two of your clerks and if you four will coach my friends for a while, you can shoot these beauties.

On the way back from the range, Missy asked me what I thought about the news story of a local black child wearing the BLM logo swimsuit in last week's YMCA swimming competition in Superior, Wisconsin, who was temporarily disqualified from the meet. I looked back at her and said, "I'm not going to answer that now, I'll need this distance in travel to control myself before I answer your question, but I'll tell you this much, it pisses me off to no end."

Once we got back to the hotel and into the conference room (after of course another round of coffee) I completed my answer with Missy.

Me: Break out your recorders and turn them on. As far as I'm concerned in reference to that 12-year-old black female swimmer? It is a non-issue, you and the rest of the media made it an issue because the NAACP jumped in with both feet. I won't even ask you how the fuck it became OK for girls to join the

YMCA and participate in a sporting event sponsored by the YMCA. Duluth has a YWCA, can boys join? Same goes for girls being allowed to join the Boy Scouts of America.

Back to your news story, who in the fuck would take such an issue into a children's sporting event and make that even more important than the event itself? I'll tell you who, Assholes! Attention hungry assholes who set this entire thing up to claim fame and a healthy financial settlement for damages. The twelve-year-old's mother claimed that her 6th grade daughter wanted to make a statement about Black Lives Matter in reference to a 22-year-old black male that was fatally shot by Minneapolis police during a no-knock search warrant just a week earlier. The mother claims that her child decided to buy the iron-on letters to put them on her swimsuit as a statement rather than a protest. Someone forwarded a picture to NBC news of the child wearing her black swimsuit with the white letters reading, "BLACK LIVES MATTER." What I found interesting was that the photo only showed the child's body but had a full-face photo of the mother. Before I go any further, the mother identified herself as a, "Diversity Officer" at a local college. Smell a bit fishy? In a matter of a few minutes the mother put her game-plan into play after the child and mother were told by volunteer swim meet officials that she would have to change swimsuits as policy forbids any political statements on swimwear. Somehow the NAACP was notified of the officials ruling just moments later. The contrived story was picked up by

CNN and US News within minutes, as well. Suddenly the president of the Duluth branch of the NAACP gathered twenty or more people from allied special interest groups, who all went to the swim meet to advocate on behalf of the child. Shortly later the YMCA vice president showed up and quickly overturned the disqualification, the volunteer official was fired and never allowed again to attend a swim meet. How's that for a rather large FUCK YOU?

The child is the only black child on the swim team. The mother says, "It's not a political statement, don't read it as an organization. Read it as a person saying their life matters."

Anyone with a brain would read it as nothing more than power and media hungry adult assholes with their own agenda who give no fuck about the event or the other children involved, they had to make it about themselves. It's just another attention grab and more importantly, it's a colossal money grab!

There are rumblings and perhaps even some quiet efforts to look into BLM as a hate group and their misappropriations of funds. BLM used extortion tactics to amass their approximated $200 million dollars or more. One high level person is currently under investigation as to how they were spending that money.

Let's face it, the Clinton and Obama family's still control our federal government along with George Soros and a large basket of other dirty assholes. Everyone has an agenda and believe me when I tell you this, their agenda does not include your wellbeing in any way, shape or form. This is about power and control and nothing more. That twelve-year-old child is just another puppet dangling from the string so the BLM group can attempt to look legitimate and nothing more.

The Clinton/Obama/Soros mob were the ones that implemented their massive divide and conquer plan. The riots of the last two years were being promoted and used as a distraction to cover up their many financial and political crimes. In the matter of the twelve-year-old child being used as a springboard to great wealth, mother dearest fucked up just a bit. Her ego jumped ahead of her intelligence. which of course is greatly in question. Mom broke the story two days before the Super Bowl along with the Olympics opening ceremonies and during the Canada truckers protest along with the "Durham Report" that could put the last three democratic presidents and presidential staffers into Guantanamo Bay prison for their entire lifetimes. Mom was somehow thinking that she would be a special guest on every talk show throughout the land with such a hot button topic. Guess what mommy, the Super Bowl won, the Olympics won, the Truckers strike won and now the Durham Report will help the people win. Mom's plan fizzled like a mega-pack of wet bottle rockets! I'm sure mommy will have her day in the bright lights, but not today. So, let's move on to that young black man that was killed by officers of the Minneapolis police department. He was not the intended person for the search warrant. I believe he was a cousin to the criminal the police were looking for. He was lying on a couch under a blanket with a gun in his hand. Supposedly he has no criminal record or has never been caught for his crimes. Now get a load of this bullshit from Minnesota's Attorney General Keith Ellison, "Amar Locke's life mattered" he said in a statement sent to NPR radio when he went on to say, "He was only 22 years old and had his whole life ahead of him." Now state Attorney General Ellison is having his staff review all the body cam footage frame by frame of the police officers involved in the incident to see if his office will bring criminal charges against the police.

However, Minnesota AG Ellison has had his own dirty laundry that's been aired publicly. It seems as though he likes to beat up on women. He has been accused on numerous occasions and by more than one female of assault and rape but there's never been any charges brought forward. Did I mention that AG Ellison is up for re-election? So, anybody here wanna raise your hand and tell me all about my white privilege? One last thing, fuck the Minnesota Twins and their first base line, outfield wall with George Floyd's name, dates of birth and death on the wall. The Minnesota Twins don't own that stadium, the taxpayers do!

I don't know what it'll take to have a fair and honest Midterm election or for the General election. If the republicans can find a way to stop the cheating to separate all three branches of government now controlled by the democrats, we'll see a different

America. If not, we're just going to become a third world country.

Now enough of that shit, I'm fucking sick of it. I'm sick and fucking tired of it all! I don't want to hear another word about any of that political bullshit, we have bigger fish to fry and we have a just cause and a righteous cause. Let us begin. I invited Cliff to sit in with us this afternoon so you can enjoy his support. Cliff, do you have anything to say?

Cliff: I'm sure some of you, especially my staff people may have stepped into a bit of fear, but fear not. I assure you all that my law practice is well prepared for any push-back and we carry deep resources. You will all be protected for your parts in this action. As time goes on and if you decide for whatever reason to leave the practice, I cannot protect you at that point. You just may suffer some consequences as I understand David has outlined earlier. I believe in this project; we had a man die almost in our own laps and I'll be damned if I'll let his death go unnoticed. David is on the right track; he's got balls bigger than any bull I've ever seen in the pasture. David and now you people, have 100% of my backing. This whole concept makes me feel thirty years younger and I find it extremely exciting.

Me: I am tired and need a nap. Today is Tuesday and you have a half day of shooting ahead of you for the next three days. I don't want to hear from or see any of you until Monday morning. I want each of you to playback your recorders several times each day. When you come in on Monday morning, I want each of you to convince me that you belong on this team. Do not forget your Banker Boxes! You are now dismissed. Val, hang back for a minute.

     Me:  Val honey, I need your help. I need you to go see your parents tonight. I know that your dad is waiting for you in the lobby right now and you heard him promise to use his full weight but I think he needs a bit of reassurance. We are doing a high risk, high cliff-dive and we're coming in hot! We will not be satisfied with any kind of settlement and no one's going to soft play 'Patty Cake' with us. This could get damn ugly and damn dangerous. Val, when you get home tonight let your dog out and change your clothes. Go to your parent's house, crawl up on your daddy's lap like you're six years old but don't show him your pretty polished fingernails. Show him your claws and don't show him your perfectly formed pearl white teeth, show him your fangs! We are now the Warriors for the people who can't or don't know how to fight for themselves. I'm tired of listening about and reading of people who lose their lives and destroy their families to suicide. It is my plan to enact a national law that we can pass to protect the weak and underserved of our society, that new law will be known as, "Heck's Law."

## Chapter 11
# HECK'S LAW

I told myself much earlier that I wasn't going to involve anyone else and I had to do this one alone. Well, my ego got in front (far, far in front) of my better judgment. There's no way that I can do this alone. I need guidance, I need experience and I know that I have to ask for help. Lucky for me, I knew just who to call but I wasn't quite sure how to ask. So, like most everything else I do, it's, "Powder River and Let Her Buck!"

It took me another few cups of coffee to gather myself before I picked up my five-hundred-pound cell phone. I received a very cheery greeting on the other end. Madeline said, "We thought you might have left the country, we haven't seen or heard from you since early December, what's going on?"

Me: What's going on is more than I can handle, where are you two honeymooners? I trust that you are both well?

Maddie: We are in Miami; we've been here since the end of November. Don't you remember that we're snowbirds? We're just packing a few bags to head up for the Daytona 500 race. What's going on with you, my lovely man?

Me:   Well, really nothing all that important that can't wait until the end of the race but since you did ask, how's chances of you two shortening your Florida tanning sessions and returning to Duluth? You do know it's going to be Spring in just another short 26 days and tomorrow's high temperature is supposed to be hovering around -30! What do you say Babe, you ready to turn in your flip-flops for moon boots?

Maddie:   You asshole, only if you're on life support and they are ready to pull the plug.

I could hear Woody laughing in the background. He said, "We have a two-bedroom suite in the grandstands, you and Heather love racing, I'll order a private jet and you two can join us for the race. If you try to smuggle in your 'Lil Smokies' they will bounce you however!"

Of course, now they're both laughing and asked almost in unison, "What did you get yourself into this time?" I gave them what I hoped would be a brief overview but it was more than just brief. I heard the sorrow and the excitement in both their voices as I told them about Heck and the files in the Banker Boxes.

Maddie:   David, I am so sorry for the loss of your friend. Your project is going to be colossal in breadth and scope. I am proud and honored that you would include us!

Woody:   Damn you David. Only you have that innate ability to excite my wife from 1,620 miles away! I think she is panting! My friend, that's not a problem. We'll bring an extra sub-zero suitcase with us to the track and grab a flight to Duluth as soon as the race is over, Sunday night. How about if we do breakfast Monday morning at the same Perkins restaurant when we had our first eye to eye sit down?

Me:   I give you both my word that I will have you guys back in the warm salt air of Miami well before Easter…. of 2026! I need direction from people that I can trust and who won't back down or back off. You two are my go-to crew, I trust you guys implicitly. In the meantime, I'll email you guys a few newspaper clippings and Heck's mortuary memorial book. We'll talk about everything else come Monday morning. Enjoy your race, love you both, bye-bye.

Woody:   If you don't bring Heather to breakfast, I'm not coming! I will need someone to hug on, while my wife slobbers all over you like a St. Bernard.

I poured a cup of coffee and lit my cigarette in the kitchen before I opened the patio door to step outside as the wind was a steady 22mph in the 26 below zero temperature. With the warmth in my belly from that phone call the cold and wind felt like a warm spring day.

I went back into the house and I finally had the nap that I had longed for in the last several days. I woke up with a happy heart and a smile, right up until reality backhanded me on my ass!

Holy shit! I haven't told Heather about any of this. She always cues me with her patented look and smile that tells me she knows that I'm up to something but she lets me run with it until I have everything worked out in my head and ready to talk about it.

I have to cleanse my skull. I've got too much of the left-wing social justice bullshit dancing through my head and it's taking me nowhere. All I'm hearing about is the street gangs slinging drugs and out of control homicide rates, smash-n-grab, welfare fraud and physical assaults are a product of the republican party and no longer prosecutable, all in the name of 'Social Justice'.

Are you fucking kidding me? The federal and local governments along with chicken-shit employers mandate masks and vaccinations but those same people refuse to close our southern borders or keep violent offenders in jail. They will not demand vaccinations or masks for the tens of thousands of illegals pouring into our country with many of them having extensive criminal records and carrying weapons along with huge amounts of deadly drugs!

They won't arrest and turn back these illegals, they give them money, safe passage and housing! I sure as fuck picked a hell of a time to be sober!

Lucky for me (or maybe not) the doorbell rang. It was my buddy Paul the mailman. Paul and I met for the first time in the midsummer two years ago. It was one of the hottest days of the summer and as Paul was walking to the house across the street, I noticed he started to stumble and was actually staggering. To me, it meant only one of two things. Either he was drunk or he was experiencing a heat stroke. I went out to him, took him by his arm and guided him into my house. He had a pale look about himself and acted confused. I could see his body was starting to shut down. I grabbed a hand towel, ran it under cold water and put it over his head. I asked him if he had any existing medical conditions that would warrant an ambulance and emergency room visit.

I pulled out three ice cold bottles of flavored water and pushed Paul to drink them quickly. We had the AC on so it was about twenty degrees cooler in the house than outside. Paul was quite embarrassed over his condition and kept apologizing. I said, "Pal, if we don't look after each other than who's gonna look after us? It is just what we do my friend."

From that day forward I would come to the front door as Paul was coming up my front stairs to put the mail in the mailbox. We always had some fun greeting exchanges that were quite humorous. Paul likes to laugh, much like I do. I got to learn some things about him and his family over the years.

My new book orders were always delivered via USPS and the boxes were caution labeled with 'HEAVY' stickers. I gifted him copies of my different books. Paul seemed to be quite taken by that, to know that he had made friends with a novelist. We always greeted each other with some kind of off-color or dirty joke. Late this last summer, Paul came to the door wearing his uniform shorts with a rather large bandage on his lower leg. When I asked him if he had hurt himself, he said no, he was bitten by a spider and he'd been to the doctor a number of times to have the wound lanced and drained but it just kept getting more and more infected. His calf was noticeably swollen. So, from that day on, I gave him the nickname, "Spider Man" but told him I would call him 'Spidey" for short. Every day after that, I greeted him with, "Hello Spidey" and we would both laugh. He got his revenge shortly afterward. I made the mistake of ordering padded envelopes for my book mailings from a company that loves to send out huge quarterly catalogs for anything to do with the manufacturing and shipping industry. One day a new catalog arrived. I was on a phone call with my publisher so I didn't get to greet Paul that day. When I pulled the mail out of the mailbox there was a catalog with a circle around the address that read, "Chief of Operations of David J Brown Books LLC." Well Paul circled the word chief with an ink pen and a note that read, "I had no idea that you were also a chief!" From that day forward, Paul has called me 'Chief' and I of course, call him 'Spidey' in our daily greetings.

We have a large corner lot, actually four lots. My writing desk is wedged in the corner of my living room with windows facing south and east so I can see traffic on both the avenue and the street. I can always see his mail truck coming. Several times this Winter, I would meet him at the door with a steaming hot cup of coffee, seeing that he was outside all day. He would always step inside and we would insult each other while enjoying our coffee. Of course, I have two Donald Trump inauguration coffee mugs and Paul takes a great deal of pleasure in drinking from them. We have likeminded political and social beliefs. Paul understands my writing obsession and never rings the doorbell if I don't greet him at the door. He just goes on his way but on the days, we receive packages that would be considered, free goods by those fuck-rat porch pirates. Today he did ring the bell and what the package contained was a clinical rapid-test Covid-19 self-test kit.

    Of course, with my not trusting anything from a democratic White House, I cautiously opened the box. Even at the time that I ordered this free test kit, I was suspicious that there's a good chance that those swabs were embedded with the covid virus. My suspicions grew once I opened the box when I saw that this kit was prepared in China! Can you fucking believe it? It came from fucking China, the same fucking China that developed and gave us the disease, is now selling us the material to test to see whether or not we've got the disease that they gave us! Could this swab actually be carrying those disease chemicals? Fuck this, I'm not going to use this bullshit, yeah that's going in the garbage.

    I settled in with a cup of coffee before my shower so I could run up to the grocery store and I hit that all too familiar wall. The wall of rage! Behind the rage comes depression as I start asking myself if what I'm doing is right.

It may sound strange to some of you, but I don't always trust myself. I have found myself interrogating myself as to what my true motivation and intentions are. So now I'm sitting here immobilized and haven't had my shower yet and now knowing it's too late to get to the grocery store to avoid afternoon traffic. Fuck it, I'll go in the morning and this time, I mean it! One of the things I do when I get into this upside-down funk, is I like to open my phone and watch homecoming videos of veterans being greeted by their families. My brain tells me if I can't feel joy at the moment for myself, I can feel joy for other people, so I watch those videos. I also like to watch the videos of America's Got Talent and the X-Factor. I like to watch people when they realize their dreams are coming true. These show contestants are mostly young people who all they've ever known is one dream and that's to be discovered to become an entertainer and hopefully become famous. Some of them are quite young, most in their early teens and yet they have amazing natural and developed talent's that most adults will never hope to achieve. Their dreams excite me, even as much as their performances. To see the judges give them high marks is a very happy time for me because somebody got to realize their dream. I never dared to be much of a dreamer as a child or even as a young man. I was of the belief that dreams were for other people but not for people like me. I had a lifetime of evidence to support those beliefs. Ironic as it may sound, my first book that I wrote and published was, "Daddy Had to

Say Goodbye." When a reader buys my book, I always sign it with the same message lines that read;

"Dreams are worth dreaming, dare to dream my friend and dream big!"

That message speaks of my heart and prayers for them. But yet, I sit here at the moment without dreams. Depression is a dream killer. I think I've made it abundantly clear over the years that I don't believe that any kind of therapy or medicine is going to take me any further than my belief in God will. I lived all of my childhood watching my parents living in their addictions and I will never risk being like either of them with using pharmaceutical or street drugs! So now it's 3:30 pm and I still haven't showered and I'm just sitting around feeling mopey and wanting to eat everything in the house. It took me a bit longer to find my center but it did come and it made me chuckle to myself.

"You dumb fuck, you have to admit to yourself that once again, you allowed your fear to control you! You let it keep you from your game, you were supposed to shower right after Heather left for work and the dogs were loved up on and fed. But no, you just sat there in your fear and let it take over your entire day. I should have been grocery shopping and gone to the meat market and been home for at least the last 3 hours by now. So, pal what are you afraid of on this fine day and isn't it the same as all the other days in the past? I'm the one who tells the world that fear is an acronym, it's not even a word. Don't you

always say that fear stands for; False - Evidence - Appearing - Real?
I go to fear because I feel incompetent, because I feel weak and unworthy. Well, this is where I have to let the big people take over, I've got all these lawyers and heavily experienced investigators and my friends to help me. I have a driving passion in this matter but no experience. I have to allow the experienced people and trust them to do what's necessary. Yes, I must give them guidance but I also must listen and that's going to be the hardest part for me. To listen without my being critical or judgmental has always been my Achilles heel. I don't like listening; I like thinking and I like doing! I have to know that we're all in this for the same reason. I can't allow any of this to be about me, if it's about me, it can only be about my memory of Heck and all those poor souls tucked away in those Banker Boxes. Of course, a big part of me wanted to run away and entertain myself as a distraction but I knew I had a huge task at hand. I spent two long days developing a plan. I would have worked all day Friday as well, except for the clown show that came blasting into town!

## *Chapter 12*
# OVERKILL

Well now it's Friday morning, Heather just left for work and I'm settled in with the dogs to feed them their breakfast when my cell phone rang. There was no caller ID so I'm guessing it's one of those Roberts family, 'ghost phones'. Just the phone number smelled like my old friends in Chicago. The cheery voice on the other end of the line confirmed that with a greeting of, "Are you going to sleep all day?" That voice belonged to one of the sweetest women that I have ever met, she simply said, "David, Paul and I are on vacation at one of our island resorts. I don't want to take a lot of your time. I just want to tell you that you have our backing 100% and you have an open checkbook for anything you need. Don't worry about any of the costs of your latest adventure. We've got it covered. Love you sweetheart, we'll talk to you soon and enjoy your visitors."

Before I could even think about what visitors she was talking about, my cell rang again and of course, it was Amanda Roberts.

Amanda: How do you like our timing, pretty well orchestrated, don't you think from a woman halfway around the world and me being in the dead center of Chicago land?

David, I'll be there tomorrow. I've got a few things to tie up here, but for right now there's some guests who are waiting to see you at the hotel, get your ass down to the Corker Hotel, comb your hair and please brush your teeth. I'll see you tomorrow.

This time I had almost a full minute before the next phone call came in and it was my pal Tim from the Corker Hotel, who is the doorman/courtesy van driver. Tim sounded excited. I could almost see his hands waving in the air like an Italian sandwich maker saying, "No soup for you!"

Tim:   Holy shit David, there's like a dozen or more people here wanting to see you, a couple of them look kind of rough. There are a bunch of other guys wearing work shirts for electrical, plumbing, HVAC, elevator repair and floor polishing services. They are all just pushing service carts around, all with the identical large silver tool boxes on them. I googled these company names and there are no such companies by those names in this entire state! I don't know who the hell they are but they wanted the van keys and they drove all three vans into the underground garage and then they took out those long poles with mirrors on the bottom, like they use at the checkpoints at the borders. They looked at the whole undercarriage of each van and searched the insides. This is a little scary. They have put step ladders in the elevators and locked them out like elevator servicemen but these guys are wearing expensive suits and shoes. Somehow, they got master keys to everything and are opening every door in the joint. I thought you should know. There's a lady with them, she must be famous. She's sitting in the lobby with some other women and the hotel guests keep walking by and keep pointing at her and whispering. I don't know who she is but she's part of that same group of people. They all came in together in muted gray spooky looking vans. I've never seen that color of gray on a van before, but they are all identical with black windows. What's really spooky is that those vans don't have any manufacturer or model badges on them. Even the headlights and taillights designs are like I've never seen before. The front grill is different too. All the license plates read, "Temporary-in-Transit!"

Me: Tim, it's all good, they are the advance team for the Wizard of Oz show. I don't know what's going on either, these are solid people, you don't have to worry about them. I know who they are, they're actually friends of mine.

As directed, I brushed my hair and brushed my teeth, dressed and was on my way down to the Corker Hotel within 20 minutes from the start of this charade.

I picked up a tail almost as soon as I left my driveway. There were two Dodge Charger, SRT's following close enough that if I brake checked them it would make for a rather loud crash. Two more of the identical cars pulled out in front of me at the end of the block. I guess that I was getting a personal escort to the Corker Hotel. I giggled with thinking that it would be fun to cut off onto a side street and take them for a bit of a high speed cruze. Not knowing who these guys are yet, I unsnapped my shoulder holster and drew my Smith & Wesson 45 caliber custom pistol and held it in my lap. Within two minutes my cell phone rang and it was a 'Bill' who I know fairly well. He said, "David, they saw you draw your pistol, they work for me, please holster your weapon and follow them to the rear of the hotel.

 As I parked, the two cars directly behind me pulled up alongside on both sides of me. Each car had three passengers all holding up badges. The passenger of the car at my driver window asked me where my gun was. I told him that it was in my lap, and he asked me to please holster it? I did, he asked me to step out, I did. He asked me to follow him into the back door of the hotel assuring me that my truck would be parked in the garage. Two Bills met us just inside the door and escorted me into the lobby as two other Bills fell in line.

 The first two people I saw were even more Bills. Behind them stood Cat, the martial arts specialist and private bodyguard to the stars. She was standing alongside Norbs, the world-famous novelist and screenwriter.

 When Cat saw me, she came running, she had to have been at least 20' away but I knew she was going to jump in the air and fling herself at me and I'd have to catch her and try not to go over backwards. "Jesus Christ Cat, I'm not a kid anymore!" Cat being the prankster she is, stopped almost toe tip, to toe tip with me. She did not throw herself in the air for me to catch her and I said, "Cute move babe." She just smiled back and said, "I wanted to see if you were going to shy-freeze or hold your ground!"

Me:   Well sweetheart I hope I passed your silly little test, now give me some lovin's!

We had a warm hug with mutual cheek kisses. We walked hand-in-hand over to Norbs and I got another very nice hug from her (that is once) Cat signaled to the massive wall of rippling flesh in high dollar suits that I was, "A friendly." Alongside and a bit over Norbs shoulder was her lady-in-waiting bodyguard, Patty, who over time, I have learned to respect and never want to fuck with. I looked at the two-security lady's and said, "Which of you two Babes are in charge? Who's got the ball, I'm assuming it's you Patsy?" Patty smiled as she said, "Yes David, I have the ball and since you've arrived, I will continue to have the ball, do you understand? It might be your show but I'm the director. Let's all go somewhere where we can sit down in private, and don't fuckin call me Patsy!"

We went into a conference room at the end of the hall that is all but sound proof. Everyone had a seat including the Bills and Norb's people, who I just call, "The numbers" as they identify themselves as to their current physical security positions by the eight compass points.

Patty: Well David the reason we're all here and with more coming is because you pulled a very large trigger. Amanda got a call yesterday afternoon from Maddie and Woody; they are greatly concerned for your safety. From what you told them, you're about to bring the whole fucking nation down around your ears. I like the concept, it's actually quite stimulating, if not a bit crazy.

So, I have some other people here that I want to introduce to you. This lovely lady here answers to the name of Sarah. Sarah was a member of President Donald Trump's forward advance team. She was in charge of the security logistics for the "Secret Service." Sarah is a very nice lady, she is also no one to play with however, she's direct and she won't settle for anything but absolute perfection from everyone, including you! Before you embarrass yourself by asking her what's in her bra, we are all armed, the same as you.

Sarah: David let me use one of your common sayings when facing poor odds, when you speak of, "Wearing pork chop shorts into a lion's den." Well, my friend, that will happen. We have some extra security people here today because they are now assigned to you and your wife Heather. Things could get very hot, very quickly, we're here to keep you both safe and help you develop your plan.

Me: Sarah, what a lovely name you have.... don't fuckin tell me what to do!

The lead Bill jumped in and suggested that everyone go to the restaurant's private dining room while they give me my security briefing. There were six Bills from the Roberts security team and six members from Norbs' security team. These guys were every bit as serious (in posture) as if they were punching in the nuclear launch codes.

Lead Bill:   David, you need to understand the dangers that you are stepping into. Yes, we all know that you have traveled the world and, in some cases, faced great danger but this is going to be different. You're not just a person in the way of someone else's freedom or next breath, now you are a target and believe me when I tell you, there will be X-rings and red laser dots dancing on your head and chest. We will do our very best to keep any of that from happening. From this moment forward, you are in the gravest of all danger. You've kept this thing pretty quiet up until now, so we don't believe there are any leaks currently, but as you so aptly pointed out in your book, "Daddy Had to Say Goodbye" that witnesses and co-conspirators, "Should be exterminated to remain free." However, what is about to take place shortly, puts an X-ring squarely on your forehead and we're prepared for it. As a matter of fact, one of your old friends from Chicago, named Toby, is sending some of his specialists in, to bask in this -30-degree weather. I believe you refer to them as, 'The Gunsmiths'? You had them pegged right from the beginning. We're going to try to stay out of your and Heather's personal lives but we are in charge of your safety. There are three agents currently at Heather's work location. We have two agents currently at your home. As soon as Heather gets out of work she'll be escorted to your home and we will escort you to your home to meet up with her. You two will need to pack several weeks of clothing, including any medications and personal items, our people will be at your home twenty-four hours a day. You're going to stay here at the hotel up in your suite. You of course are going to bring your dogs but you can't return to your house. We can't have either one of you going anywhere without an escort team. To put it in your terms, "This aint our 1st rodeo."

One of the things we're going to be doing immediately is, we will remove all of your firearms from your home. They will be well secured at an undisclosed location. The first thing your adversaries will do is try to deem you to be unstable and a threat to their safety and security. There's a pretty good chance that your concealed carry permits will be revoked as soon as you conclude your first press conference. We all know of the deep respect you carry for law enforcement and that you are friends with both the local Police Chief and the County Sheriff, who however both have bosses. We are all smart enough to understand that loyalties will be stretched and tested. We're going to take you down to your Federal Judge friend and have your retired status changed to active. We're going to do the same thing with Heather, she will be sworn in as United States Deputy Marshal, so you can both be armed without needing a concealed carry permit. There can be and are several layers of threats in this business and some of the more dangerous, who at times look to be the most inert, are the general public. Duluth is no different than any other city. You have local wack jobs who live to do nothing but protest and disrupt the public to get their pictures taken and interviewed on the TV news. These people are very dangerous. You fully know about the people that carry box cutters, sharpened screwdrivers and other weapons who would rush you and try to reorganize your facial features and internal organs. The hotel security team has been instructed to secure all packages that arrive at this facility. We have portable x-ray machines arriving this afternoon along with two drug and explosive sniffing dogs. We will screen all packages and we will open all packages addressed to you and Heather as well as all incoming packages for the hotel and guests. We also have dogs to patrol the grounds, the hallways and public access areas. Your safety takes a much higher priority than your privacy. In short, my friend, you and Heather are effectively, now in lockdown.

## *Chapter 13*
# FOCUS

Whatever was said during the rest of the breakfast meeting, I didn't get any part of it. I was a million miles away and running for my life. I wasn't running for my own wellbeing; I was running from Heather's wrath. She has no clue as to what is going on and the massive machine that is being put in place and she is going to be beyond pissed. I certainly do know that she loves me, but I don't believe there's a woman on this planet that would put up with all these instant adjustments just because of my own selfish desires. She shouldn't have to pay the price for my reckless if not insane ideas and actions.

As my escort team was driving me to my house, my stomach muscles tightened with every block, every traffic light and every stop sign. Shit was about to get ugly and it's all my fault.

There were Jersey block barricades on both corners of the block. So, the streets in front of and alongside our house were effectively closed. That's gotta make the neighbors damn happy! Those ghost cars that escorted me down to the hotel were now parked in the driveway. I was riding in an SUV obviously bulletproof because you can't roll down the fucking windows and the windows were a bit distorted, besides when you hit a pot hole (which Duluth is famous for), it's like there's no bump at all. Where the fuck do they find bulletproof SUVs in Duluth, Minnesota at any time of year, let alone mid-Winter?

As I came into the house there were suits and sport coats standing everywhere and in every room. A lady 'suit' pointed to the kitchen and said, "Sir, your wife is in the kitchen, we will take our leave for a few minutes."

Heather was in the kitchen pouring a cup of coffee into my favorite cup. She had a look of confusion and surrender. It might have even been a look of resignation; I couldn't get a read on her but the cat's tail was swishing in my belly.

Heather:  Baby, I get it, it's just what has to happen. You know that I love you and you know that I support you with everything you do and yes, I'll buckle up to go along on this carnival ride too. Honey, take a breath and get some color back in your face. You look like sun bleached dog shit.

Two of those gray vans arrived with the blacked-out windows and backed into the open garage stalls and closed the doors. I assumed they were here for our guns and ammunition so I headed to go downstairs to give them the combination to the gun vault room door and the gun safes inside. Heather and I both wanted to go down there and watch and make sure nothing got damaged but then again, we're dealing with pros and these people are very respectful, we just have to trust them.

I was stopped by the same 'Bill' lady and Patsy at the top of the staircase. Patsy smiled as she asked, "Going somewhere Mr. Brown?"

My temper started to flare but I was able to choke back my words of, "Who the fuck are you to tell me or ask me where the fuck I'm going in my own goddamn house! I'm about ready to throw all of you fuckers out of a window!" After I cooled down in the next few seconds I said, "Yes, my Lovelies, I'm going downstairs to unlock the door to the gun room. Would you care to join me? Patsy smiled as she said, "Mr. Brown, there's nothing down there for you to see. I'll be happy to show you." Heather came with me. Not only was the heavy steel vault room door standing open to the vault but all of the gun safes were gone, they were fucking gone! Six, 760-pound Liberty FATBOY safes that were all bolted to the floor and back wall, were all fucking gone! Patsy smiled as she said, "Allow me to explain, we had to remove your guns to keep them safe from the 'Others'. You will be briefed on who the "Others" are a bit later this afternoon." Patsy went on to tell us that they couldn't tell us where they're going to be stored so if at some point we are asked, we won't have to lie under oath.

I went to the dog's room to let them out for some daddy lovins. Gibbs tore out of the room and did not return with my command. The two other dogs followed me out of the room to the living room. There was Gibbs in Patsy's arms and he was giving her a doggy facial.

    We packed as earlier directed, for an extended stay at the hotel. We were in-and-out in less than an hour, which most husbands would do backflips and head stands over, with thinking of a woman packing for several weeks, in less than an hour.

    On the way back to the hotel we had plenty of escorts which I found amusing but yet was quite impressive as they had identical SUVs as the one Heather and I were riding in, that kept peeling off the route. Those were obviously decoy cars. Yeah, these people know their business all right. When we got to the hotel they drove around the rear and into the underground 'exhibition' parking garage. There sat both Heathers and my vehicles along with a rather large fleet of dark windowed cars, a few more gray vans and a half dozen more black SUVs. When the fire door was opened to enter the lobby there was no one around and I mean no one! Not even a desk clerk, a doorman or any hotel guests! We were escorted in a tight group to the elevator and whisked up the elevator to our floor and into my suite. I looked at Patty and commented, "I've ridden these elevators hundreds of times, you guys put turbo boosts in these fuckers?

    Patty:  We've made some minor adjustments throughout the property. That elevator is now express only. It cannot stop on any other floor nor will it open for anyone but team members. This elevator only goes to your floor. Everything is now facial recognition and fingerprint access only.

Me:   You removed all of the hotel guests and all the employees?

Patty:   We lodged all of the hotel guests in our top competing hotel properties and comped their stays here as well as their rooms at the new properties. The hotel employees are all being paid their regular wages and all of their benefits will continue.
Only our team members and your guests will be staying here.

My thought was, "These people know something that I don't know. A whole lotta something!"

Patty:   We've swept this place three times now. You will have floor guards here 24-7, we've done a bit of reinforcing in your glass areas. You will still get to enjoy the view but will just be a bit distorted, pretty much the same as in the town cars. Also, your friend's, Madeline and Forest Quinn have just arrived at the airport and they'll be here in the next twenty minutes. Do you wish for me to make accommodations here at the hotel for them?

Me:   That would be swell Patsy, but only if they choose to.

I'm thinking, "What are these guys doing? They have three day passes for the Daytona 500! They have a "In track hotel suite, tickets for the exclusive

'Driver and team owners meet and greet', garage passes and the pit passes. What the fuck are they doing? Has everyone gone nuts? Maybe I'm the only sane one on the whole fucking block, for all I know!"

    Patty:   David, please call me Patty. Not Patsy, I told you about that the last time we met! So, knock that shit off! It's Patty not Patsy!
    Me:   Good copy.... Patsy!

## Chapter 14
# THE OATH

We had only been back to the hotel for twenty minutes. Heather and I were both hanging up our clothes and arranging our clothes in the dresser drawers. There was a knock on the bedroom door and it was Patsy, she asked if I could step out of the room for a moment. I gave Heather a soft kiss and stepped out into the living area. Patsy handed me a headset and said, "Put this on, its wireless and secured." I put the headset on and Patsy said some kind of a fancy codeword that I didn't understand. It was Amanda Roberts and she said, "I know you're busy but this can't wait. I need you to go downstairs with Patty, get in a vehicle and head to the airport. Just you however, Heather will have to stay behind and she will still have a full complement of security agents. It'll all make sense to you in a bit of time. We love you. I'll see you soon."

I told Heather that I had to go to some kind of meeting that I didn't know anything about either, but I wouldn't be too long. I told her if it was going to be more than an hour that I would call her.

Patsy said she would stay with Heather and the rest of the team. I rode the elevator with three Bills and met another three Bills in the garage. The four gray vans that were parked there earlier were now gone. One of the Bills jokingly said, "If you want a disguise, we have a fat suit we could fit you in or you could wear this mask with a hair piece and full beard or if you prefer, we can just do this," as he pressed a button on his key fob and the SUV windows colors kept changing from clear to two shades of gray, to jet black. My sporty response was, "I don't give a fuck what color you make the windows, if these pricks don't roll down, I'm going to smoke in this son of a bitch and everyone's going to choke to death!" We all had a good laugh and we got in the SUV.

I guessed that we're going to the airport. Those ghost cars again, fell in front and behind us. But this time they were all different colors, I thought that to be quite interesting. We got to the international airport and drove to the Executive (private airfield) side. The sliding gate was open and there was no guard at the guard shack. Instead, there were six robust looking gentlemen with white and black camouflage, cold weather suits with face masks. Their custom black, full-auto long guns looked damn serious. I can only guess that this must be a part of the "Gunsmith" crew from Chicago. Our driver surprised me by not pulling up to an aircraft but instead he pulled up to the side of a large commercial size aircraft hangar. There was a large sign over the front of the hangar that read; "Twin Ports Skydiving and Parachute Club." My thoughts were, "Fuck this shit, turn this bitch around and take me home or I'll fuckin walk!" I have done some skydiving in the distant past and I have parachuted more times that I ever wanted to, but with a heavy backpack and some rather elite firearms, but those days are fucking over, they've been long over. I was escorted to a 'man door' on the side of the hangar. There was an empty, small reception area, we went behind the desk and thru a glass windowed door and I almost dropped to my fucking knees. There stood the entire Robert's family, all of them! What the fuck is this? Jane told me yesterday that they were on some exotic private island! What the fuck are they all doing sitting here?

It was handshakes and hugs all around but I wasn't feeling it, I just wasn't feeling the love, not at all like before. This felt dark, this felt scary dark. Paul started off with, "David it's time that we tell you the truth and we're going to tell you all of the truth, then you can make your decision. You can make your choice and if you don't like our truths, we will all walk away and leave you to your life. We only ask that you hold our confidence. Can we agree on that? I'd like to shake your hand on that."

I shook Paul's hand.

Paul:   Well David, let me start from the beginning. This will take some time. We first heard of you through Father Martin. Father got on to you sometime back. Yes, Father Martin was a Catholic Priest who was also the chief of security for Pope John Paul when he came to the United States for, "World Youth Conference Weeks." Father Martin saw what you did that day when you were pulled over alongside the road with hundreds of other cars at, Saint Milos Catholic Retreat in Estes Park, Colorado. When you saw the Pope step out of his vehicle and start walking down the highway greeting people and giving blessings, you came out of your truck with your badge held high in your hand and a handgun held at your side loudly saying and repeating, "Off Duty Denver Metro Police!" Father Martin couldn't help but notice the way you handled yourself and the way you quickly controlled the crowd and ushered them back into their cars. Father Martin knew that at some point, you may become an asset to, "The Company." Here is what I and we want you to know, my friend. Our love for you as well as father Martin's love for you was not fabricated. It's what's in our hearts but everything around that, has in fact been fabricated and now I would like to explain why. David, you will learn of the principles of, "The Company " as we go on. Many of the people in the last few years that we have been friends with, are our coworkers. That's right, we all work for the same company and the name of the company is, "The Company."

    Every nation, since the beginning of time has had dual and opposing political parties of power, oftentimes not liked by the other side. There's more to just Democrats and Republicans and some of those other fringe freak groups. We of, "The Company " are not a party. We are loyal to our founding fathers of our constitution; we like to be known as Patriots. We are a stand-alone government organization who falls under the Constitution of the United States but are not directed by any politician or group including the President of The United States. We cannot be subpoenaed in any matter to testify or to give up any records. Look at, "The Company" as a sovereign nation on a private island. We answer to no one other than God and ourselves. Our mission statement is quite simple. "We defend from within. We fight domestic government corruption on all levels." David, we are the last house on the block, if you will. If our government fails to defend the people of our great nation, we will! You, my friend, have been invited to join up with us. The pay is excellent, the benefits are not, other than we guarantee you a military funeral with high honors. Any questions so far?

Me:   Yeah Pal, I've got a shit-ton of questions! So, all of you guys in, "The Company" are what? You give each other back rubs in the sauna and bake pies together? You're the 'Wizard of Oz, pulling all the levers and whistles and I'm to dance to your fucking tune? Count me out, this is bullshit. All I have been hearing the last day and a half is that I'm in some sort of grave danger. Where the fuck is that coming from?

Paul:   David may I continue?

I nodded my head.

Paul:   Well David the only true secrets, anywhere in this world are the ones that are never spoken or written of. The only secrets that are safe are the ones in your head. I'm sure this will piss you off to no end but you have to know of this. You, along with most other people on this planet, use your computers, cell phones and smart TV's and other electronic devices without safeguards. Yes, many subscribe to security software programs but everything you write, send or post, is there for the taking unless you are encrypted in multiple levels. There's really no need for encrypted computers for the general public other than those sneaky fucks that are data miners, who sell your information to even larger, sneaky fucks. Remember when you could sign up to be placed on the, "no call list" that actually worked? Your political representatives sold you out to data miners and phone solicitors for big bucks!

    Encryption usually has to do with banks, large corporations and of course government offices. Your new HP laptop that Heather gave you for Christmas has been open to us the same as your old Asus computer you had and honestly, I don't know how in the fuck you kept a three-year system alive for eleven years, is a total mystery but congratulations on that. So now you're writing a new book and that title itself is very ballsy. "The Raping of Lady Justice" tells us that this is your time. David, we're on your fighting side, we want to help you make the changes that you've been writing about. Yes, we have read your current writing word-for-word, we read your emails, texts and of course your Facebook posts and comments. It is what we had to do, please understand. We have brought some of the best equipment and personnel to secure all communications along with the latest physical security systems. A word of caution my friend. Your home and property are being outfitted with the same security systems that we will be using in the hotel.

Now, for the flip side of that same coin, someone else has been reading all of your writings, word-for-word also. We don't know who or why (just yet) but they are watching you and what you've been writing, you've been flagged as a potential threat to national security.

David, you are just not someone that bears watching, it goes further than that. There is an 'Order' out on you. You are a target with a hefty price on your head and that is why you are in great peril. You have stepped into something that makes them want to shut you down, permanently!

We have quietly had people embedded in your life for the last four years. You have spoken and written of taking off the lid of Pandora's Box in the past, well buddy boy, that box is now laying in pieces, smoldering at your feet. We want to protect you and we want to help you on your mission. Father Martin told us early on, that you are more than just what we all initially thought. He told us to watch for signs for when you are ready. One of our specialists saw those signs four days ago in your writing. So did our and now your adversaries, almost at the same time. We are not here to direct you in any way, shape or form, we are here to support you. But at the same time, we're here to keep you and Heather safe. David, you are surrounded by people that truly do love the both of you and we will not allow harm to come to either of you. We want to see you complete your mission. You'll be meeting some of the nation's top script and speech writers, press agents and public relations experts, all from the former Trump administration. We will not interfere with your choice of words. All we want to do is make them more palatable. There are times my friend, that your language becomes quite rich and to some, might even be seen as offensive. I believe that you want to make friends, not make enemies. We'll spend more time talking about that later. Are you in so far?

Me:   Well, it's too fucking cold outside to get a tan and I don't care for ice fishing so yeah, let's go ahead and see if I can get my fucking head blown off. It should be fun. They said it should be fun, right?

We all had a good, yet guarded laugh and everyone stood and hugged. Jane took me by the hand as she said, "Sweetheart, this is going to set you back on your heels a bit. If you've ever thought you couldn't pass a treadmill test for your cardiac condition, you're about to climb onto the treadmill machine of a lifetime. You're going to meet some people that you've met from the past, who weren't the people that you thought you knew. They were all put in place by, "The Company." The people that you are about to see, all voted you into, "The Company." We select people by vote and all votes must be unanimous."

One of the Bills opened the door to the hangar and Jane was absolutely right. I couldn't believe who I was looking at! The first person I saw was Ann, the retired Critical Care R.N. who cared for me as a private duty night nurse. She spent countless hours and weeks caring for me until it was found out that she was part of a plot to kill me.

Jane:   David, Ann did not betray you, she is one of us. We had to hold and protect her cover. Please understand, I think Ann would like a hug now.

Ann came into my arms sobbing and apologizing, telling me that it was just her job to watch over me.

Ann:   Those two men who came to kidnap you in your room with a laundry cart with guns, were not of our making; they were actually trying to kidnap you for ransom.

Me:   Ann, honey, we will have dinner soon, I promise. Who else was playing me in the hospital?

Ann:   Do you remember the nurse anesthesiologist, Ken? He is currently on another assignment that he could not break away from but he gives you his best regards. He told us how you taught him the value of his family and the wisdom you shared with him. He wants you to know that he did plant those, "Family Honor Memory Trees" with his children, for generations to come. Ken of course voted yes.

Me:   Anyone else from the hospital in on the voting game?
Jane:   No David, Ann and Ken were the only two of our group. David all of those other relationships that were enjoyed by hospital employees were courtesy of you having a good sense of humor along with your kindness and sensitivity towards them. Nobody was paid to stroke you, you earned that yourself, my friend.

And here comes another surprise. Tim was sitting there, Tim the Doorman/Valet at the fucking Corker Hotel! Tim the car parker is a goddamn federal agent! Jesus Christ, what world have I been living in?
Next of course, there sat that loving couple, "The Quinn's."

Woody:   David, you must know that my and Maddie's affections for you and Heather are as true as true can be. We have been well established in our cover for over twenty years. We are well known throughout the world as rare book collectors, which is true. Neither of us have ever read a writer with such personal honesty, deep passion and conviction as you carry. We fell in love with you long before we ever met you. We were assigned to you as a 'case' an hour after you called us in Miami.
Maddie:   David, I never expected to meet someone like you in Duluth, Mn.
Yes, we do live here and we both adore what you did for Mrs. Johnson, Marge and Axel Kivi, Mary and Seth

and those two lovely girls, Vicky and Missy, you live your life with an extreme and pure poetry of the heart. Of course, we voted yes!

Paul:   The rest of the people in this room work for the company. Again, I want you to know that our friendship is based on your personality and what you stand for, we all love you for that.

Me:   Guys, I'm spent. I do want to sit with each of you during the next week but I am currently out of gas.

We were then let out into the hangar area and there were two very large private jets with four of those gray vans with black windows loading large metal cases from the aircraft.

Gregory had been silent all this time right up until he said, "Hey David, want to see something cool? Check this out." As he pointed and nodded to one of the people that was sitting behind the wheel of the nearest van and gave him some kind of hand signal, as he did, each van changed color and I couldn't fucking believe it! How in the fuck? I get that part where you can change tints on windows, but on a complete metal vehicle? You can change the color of the vehicle with a switch? This is some kinda "Star-Wars" shit going on here. My friends, Eric Bomey and Matthew Wood would wet themselves over this! I think I'm gonna dig this!

Gregory:   David I too, want to say we're not here to change your course of direction, we're not here to put words in your mouth or direct your actions, we are here to simply support you because we think you've got the core of what's necessary for your city, your state and our nation. I know you want to start with your city and county situation leading into the state of course but buddy boy, this thing's getting big and it's getting big in a hurry. This movement will go federal in the next thirty days. We've brought along some highly talented people that will help you establish your platform. Please trust them and us. They have your best interest in name and heart and yes David, we know of Heck. He sounds like a man who had the friend he needed at the time he needed him. Thank you for serving Heck and honoring him and others like him with your current mission. "Heck's Law" will happen, you have my word and the word of everyone in, "The Company."

## *Chapter 15*
# PREGAME

All of this cloak-and-dagger bullshit, put me into a heavy mental overload. I want to grab my go-bag and head out into the woods. Ball freezing cold with blowing snow piled up to a Giraffes ass but who gives a shit, I've got to get away from all this! Of course, there's no way I'm going out with the cold, snow and wind of late February in northern Minnesota. Then it came to me. What I actually needed was to bathe myself in a cloud of spent gunpowder.

I turned to Gregory and asked where the fuck are my EDC's (every day carry guns) were.

Gregory:   Check your book storage room in your suite, we've laid out twelve of your and Heather's favorite custom handguns and rapid-fire carbines, as well as a very fair amount of ammunition. What's on your mind?

Me:   Let's get back to the hotel. I want to grab those guns and Heather and go out to the shooting club. I need to cleanse myself with the smell of burnt gunpowder, kind of like what the natives do when burning sage. You up for that pal? Gregory smiled as he said, "My time is your time, your lordship!"

We ended up with three vans and three SRT pursuit cars along with fourteen people. I was surprised when Gregory dialed a number and I heard him say, "We will be there in sixteen minutes. I will need you to evacuate your building and lock your doors. Unplug and disable all of your exterior security cameras, your gun shop and shooting range cameras as well. Have all of your employees as well as yourself, secure your personal weapons. There must not be any loaded weapons on the premises. Four of our people will enter first to sweep your building, before our party enters your building.

Me: Did you just call the gun shop? You gave them orders as to what they need to do? You told them to evacuate their building, what the fuck is wrong with you?

Gregory smiled as he said, "You really want to be around a group of total strangers who are all carrying loaded firearms? At this stage in your life, I don't think that's a good idea, pal. You better think things through. If you get killed, my mother would never forgive me! Besides, I have arranged to pay the owner a full week's receipts for three hours of privacy. You got a problem with that Skippy?"

Well of course, Gregory was right. When we arrived there were no vehicles in the parking lot, which normally at this time of day has at least a dozen or so vehicles in it. I guess Gregory carries a big stick, even here in Duluth, that and of course a mighty fat checkbook! As we walked in, a number of the Bills and Numbers guys let out a few low whistles with seeing some of the rental guns they had on the back wall, behind the counters. There were eighty running feet of rental guns with a third of them being fully automatic assault weapons.

I said to one of the "Number" guys, "Let's all go on the range and you can show me how fast and accurate you are with those bulges under your jackets." He smiled as he said, "No can-do partner. Our weapons must be duty ready at all times. But if you're paying for this trip, we'll shoot the shit out of those guns on the back wall, as he grinned at the store owner and head armorer and said, "If it's OK with you fellas of course."

The store owner smiled back as he said, "Anything you guys do here is OK with me, as long as somebody pays for it."

Gregory handed the store owner a thick envelope saying, "This should cover the cost for our outing today."

Three store employees heavily loaded several push carts with a variety of ammunition calibers. We had a great time. The smell of burnt gunpowder was intoxicating but was overridden by the smell of hot steel from the smoking barrels. I think we might have to go good on a few new barrels. We did however make lots of noise and covered the entire floor surface with a few inches of brass casings. Most everyone had gunpowder smudges on their faces when we left the store.

    I told Heather on Saturday morning that I needed to be in seclusion. There is a lot at stake and I've got to think all these things through, before Monday morning.
    Even before I can get to that, I've had something nagging at me for the last several days, that I know I have to look at and come to terms with. Of course, it has to do with me giving Heck the council to trust no one in the jail, to avoid any contact and not to speak to staff or inmates. I told him that he had no friends in that entire facility. Inmates will try to befriend him to try to use him for their own gains for an early release, staff will forward everything they hear to further his prosecution for their own gains with hopes for a favor or promotion.
    Part of me wants to think that I pushed him to where he found himself at the point of no return. Was it me who figuratively put that pen in his hand? Why in the fuck didn't I give directions to the lawyers that day, that they were not to take any notes or have any writing instruments on the table? That's SOP in most every case. How did I miss telling them that? And how did they not know that on their own accord?
    I know I had to put that out of my mind for the time being because Monday is for all the marbles. I don't need any attention from anybody as far as a claim to fame. I just want to do what's right in the

name of Heck and those poor souls in the Banker Boxes.

I fully knew that most of those people were lost causes. At this time, they can't be my concern but they are certainly my motivation. There can be little doubt as to how they were failed by the system and how they were failed by design. That design is best described with one word. That one word is, 'corruption.' I know we can't fix those corrupt people but we can fix the system so they cannot do it to us again! When I say us, I mean all of us!

    I started listing the examples of corruption in local government services. But I didn't get very far before my mind went back to the Banker Boxes and I locked onto what I believe to be the only potentially defendable case file in that entire box.

## Chapter 16
# THE MOODY CREW

This case was not all that unusual, strange yes, but not all that unusual. This case has to do with a married couple by the last name of Moody. Bart Moody was in a horrific highway, head-on automobile accident. Moody and the other driver were both drunk. Moody's blood alcohol level was 0.81 just one point over the legal limit. The other driver was three times over the legal limit with a blood alcohol reading of 2.45. The other driver and two of his adult passengers were instantly killed. Moody was hospitalized for five months and went on to a rehabilitation hospital for another four months. The other driver was driving his company supplied pick-up utility truck. His two passengers were his boss and his boss's boss. Moody walked away with large stacks of cash that should have taken care of him, his wife and their two children for his lifetime. The children came from Mrs. (June) Moody's previous marriages. Indications were that Mr. Moody was known as a roaring drunk and bully prior to the accident. After the accident Moody became even worse and was kicked out of most every bar in the city. That is a lot of bars!

Moody tried to buy a bar but after the city looked into his police records, he was denied a liquor license. Moody had no choice so he became a, "Stay at home drunk." June Moody was no better. She too liked to fight, and had a very abrasive personality. They were both sloppy drunks and always in trouble with the law. They lived in a neighborhood of about eight square city blocks. Those eight square blocks were the most visited neighborhood by the police in the entire city. Almost every city has a neighborhood known as, "Asshole Acres" and Duluth is no different. It seemed like the developer built those homes just for those kinds of losers, the kind of people that don't give a shit if their trash is laying all over the street, their dogs running lose and whose yards their dogs shit in, they don't mow their lawns and they are all fucking deaf because their TVs and radios are always at full volume. Domestic assaults are quite common and almost the norm, to the point as if it were a sport, like bowling. The Moody's were in the top three of police service visits for domestic abuse in the entire neighborhood, The Moody's were well known by the police and jail staff along with, of course, the judges.

    Well, one fine and glorious evening, Mrs. Moody told her husband that she was going to go play bingo at the local church bingo hall with her sister. Her sister actually came into the house, said hello and they left to go play bingo together.

    Mr. Moody was drinking beer and watching a high school hockey game on TV. The girls were only gone for a half hour when he got a phone call from one of his drinking buddies who said that he was sitting at the bar at a national chain restaurant and he could clearly see Moody's wife playing lovey-dovey kissy-face games with some fellow in a booth. Moody (who was drunk at the time) jumped into his car and drove to the restaurant. When the husband walked in, his friend pointed out where they were sitting. Bart Moody (a very large and powerful man) walked up to the man sitting with his wife and punched him three hard shots in the chops. For the most part, Mr. Moody obliterated this man's face and knocked him out cold. Mrs. Moody was screaming and swearing as she reached into her purse and pulled out a .38 caliber snub-nosed revolver to shoot her husband for beating up her boyfriend. They struggled over the gun and the gun went off and struck the boyfriend and finished the job on his face. Of course, the bullet blew his brains out and onto several restaurant customers. Several witnesses reported hearing June Moody cursing her husband with words of, "I'm going to kill your broke ass, you fucker, you spent all of our insurance money!" Two witnesses both claimed that only June Moody's finger was on the trigger when the gun discharged.

    Now they are now both in jail and being charged with second degree murder and a laundry list of lesser charges. Some family members are caring for their two children. I have dealt with assholes like that all throughout my police career. Yes, those kinds of pukes are disgusting and despicable but they still should have their day in court with proper representation. I have to keep my mind right and know that everything I do has to be above board. This has to be about Justice not vengeance. Justice is not just about putting away someone that nobody likes to have around. I had been on several domestic violence calls over the years and at times I wish the spouse would have killed the other so we did not have to put up with their bullshit, three or four times each week.

But again, I can't allow my own prejudice to override someone else's right to a fair trial. I get that whole, 'Crime of Passion' thing. Just because these people are dirtbags doesn't mean that they don't deserve Justice. I'll tell Val to staff and move forward with this case.

## *Chapter 17*
# THE LIST

      I, of course, wanted to start with our local service providers. Not the kind that takes care of our gas and water lines, trash service or electrical and cable but the true providers. I'm looking at, of course, the service providers in human services. Those services range anywhere from police, fire, hospital, social services and the courts. To the best of my knowledge, I don't believe that Heck was ever lost in the abyss of social service. I've checked as far as I could go and I don't believe he ever applied, received or was offered anything from social service. He was pretty much a recluse that asked no one for anything.
      But those other criminal cases in that Banker Box have. Most all received some level of attention through social service or the court system on more than one occasion. So, the big question is, are these all-bad people or people that have gotten a raw deal out of life? Of course, people with mental health issues, whether it be drug related or mental illness are still the most neglected people in need of services.

Today's most popular buzzword is, "The Underserved." In most cases that simply means, "I was too busy fucking off and it's almost happy hour or 4:30 and I got shit to do!"

There was a time when 'self-service' meant you pumped your own gas. Today, people serve themselves because it's all about them. Enjoy your cocktails, douche nozzles!

There was just one more thing dancing in my head that's holding me back in designing my strategy. I knew I had to sit with the entire Roberts family to hear the truth. The truth that I had suspected and have been avoiding for some time now. I called Amanda and asked her to gather up the entire family and to come up to my suite. It's time that I hear the truth, the truth I have suspected but tried desperately not to accept.

They were all there in the next ten minutes. I asked Heather to not join us for this conversation. I looked hard, perhaps harder than I needed to at both Amanda and Jane as I said, "Ladies, I've known for many years of my life, that few things are as they first appear. But on this one, you completely blindsided me. I think I know why you did it but I need you to tell me, why you did it. I'm ready to hear those truths. Now that I know all that I want to know, with everything being all about, "The Company" I want to ask you straight up. You know I'm not going to take anything other than the truth, right?

So, there was no publisher or movie studio that bought my books? There is no movie studio who is going to make a movie of any of my books? This was all a product provided by, "The Company." Am I correct ladies?

Jane briefly lowered her head, when she raised her head again, she had tears streaming down each cheek as her eyes begged for my forgiveness.

Jane:   David of course you are right. "The company" bought the rights to your books but the company does not own the rights to the books. You still hold all of the copyrights of your books. We made sure that our lawyers used the right verbiage so you could reprint at any time that you choose. You can reactivate your copyright at any time, we don't own your copyright, we just borrowed them for a little while. David, we bought your copyright for only one reason. You've never received the proper recognition that you so much deserve for your talents. Sadly, you have never received the sales that you deserve as well. You are right in knowing that everything is a setup in the writing and publishing industry. There is no honor or respect from the 'Big Five' publishing houses for independent authors. Very, very few independent authors ever make any kind of a livable wage. Well sweetheart we bought the copyright to give you and Heather some comfort so she could retire. We didn't want her to worry about supporting herself when she leaves her job. We wanted you both to live free of worry with financial independence. So yes David, I am guilty, we are all guilty of loving you to the point of accepting you two as our own family members. We only wanted to give you security and comfort. I hope you understand. There is no question that your books are all stand-alone, high-quality work. I don't believe there's another author, past or present that can match you.

Paul smiled at me and said, "That's all bullshit, I just bought my way into your life
because I knew that you would not have a damn thing to do with me if I were just me!"

I threw a small handful of sugar cubes at him and we all laughed. I said, well who's going to break this to Heather? She needs to know or maybe she doesn't, maybe she doesn't need to know! I'm asking you all, should I tell her or do I go along with this farce? Would I be protecting her or am I trying to save face and protect myself?
Jane:   David, I don't believe you have to be an author to garner Heather's love and respect. You already have that from her, more than most women would ever give a mate. She actually believes in you and loves you for who you are, not for what you do but who you are, and that my friend is called God's loving grace. You want to challenge that Skippy?
Me:   No sweetheart, supposedly true love needs no protection but, in this case, I will follow your lead, it will remain between us. Can you ladies take Heather somewhere and do what girls do for a while? For me, I need a nap. Thank you, guys, for laying the truth out in front of me. I suspected early on that the book deals might have been more than a gift rather

than a business deal. I won't ask if the movie deal is of the same ploy. Now I can move forward and I appreciate everything you've done for Heather and I. If you all don't mind, I need to lay down for a bit and close my eyes. I'll see you all at dinner.

When Heather and I were escorted to the dining room for dinner, everyone was already seated. There were only two open seats, obviously those were for Heather and me. What surprised me was the person who was seated to my right. She is the one person that never quite accepted us as the rest of the Robert's family has. Yet, there she was with her shit eating grin. I thought to myself, "Fuck this! I'm not asking, either she tells me or she doesn't but I'll be damned if I'll ask her."

I said hello to everyone and I sat down. Edna Roberts nudged me in the forearm with her elbow with a smile and said, Nice to see you again, slick! I smiled as I said, "You wanna throw down with me baby? You wanna wrestle right here on the floor, in front of the whole crew? What are you doing sitting next to me? This is reserved for friends only!" She smiled and said, "I asked to sit here, I want to make amends to you. You deserve an apology and that apology must come from me. So here it is and it's the only time you'll ever get me to apologize, that shit I just don't do. David, I misjudged you. I was terribly wrong. I've spent my whole life in government service and I've watched some of the ugliest shit that I can't ever speak about, take place before my very eyes, all by people of great power, great wealth and refinement. I guess when I first met you, I judged you as I do everyone but this time, I have to admit that I was flat-out wrong. I don't like to be wrong but with you I was. I guess I am one of those people who can't handle envy. I was always looking for your angle, I was looking behind you to see where the dirt was and I'll be damned if I could find any! Your only problem is that you're too damn honest and too damn direct, you are the reason that we have all the security here. It is because you are too damn honest even for your own damn good. I'm thoroughly going to enjoy this ride and I want to champion your cause on a federal level. If you will, I'm asking you to help me initiate starting a New York size telephone book of dirty power players. It's not like I don't have enough data and since I've retired from the department, I'm under no obligation to withhold their filthy little secrets. My level of respect for you is as great as any other human being other than my husband of course. With your permission, I would like to call you my big brother.

    Heather smiled and leaned behind me and loudly whispered, "He's mine and you can't have him." Most everyone got a big laugh out of that. Now everyone knows that we are now one cohesive unit and we will not be defeated!

    Gregory, who was on the other side of his wife Edna, mentioned that he would enjoy this meal tonight more than most any other night.

    Even as Edna was making her deep, heartfelt apologies to me, I was seeing and thinking of this sweet but hard bitten small framed woman, who took two bullets into her body as she dove in front of a seated president, that ended her career as a Secret Service agent. If I died next to her in an assault, I know that I would die with honor.

Amanda:  You should enjoy your meal tonight, Skippy, as all of the foodstuffs are fresh, flown-in this afternoon. We donated all of the food stuff, even the dry goods to a food shelter. Not that there was anything wrong with the food that was currently in the restaurant but this is a common security precaution for high level dignitaries. SOP calls for the restocking of all goods, wet, dry and frozen. Everything in the hotel pantry and the pantry in your suit is fresh and has been inspected by our people. So tonight, you're dining on the freshest of the fresh. We of course, brought on our own highly trusted and well vetted kitchen, laundry and maid service staff from our other properties.

I guess that I somehow failed to pay attention, but suddenly (as my eyes were scanning the room) I saw the young married couple (Ricky and Sarah) from the newspaper that went off to work for the Roberts resorts as promotional photographers, to far-away exotic lands and now here they sat. I got up from my chair and walked over to them and asked, "You kids are a part of this deal?"

Ricky:  Sarah and I were just brought into "The Company" two months ago. We had to prove our salt for a period of time but now we are here as your personal photographers, we are going to document everything for a future coffee table book. You know David, those things that you despise and will out sell your work twenty-to-one? Yeah, that kind of book.

They both stood, shook my hand and hugged me and thanked me for the initial opportunity and said their life has never been as exciting and rewarding since they've met me. It didn't seem long before dinner was being served and of course the servers were people I've never seen before, obviously from another restaurant within the Roberts organization. I smelled it before I saw it and when the server lifted the silver tray cover, there it was, my favorite meal of all time, 'Dinty Moore' beef stew!

Amanda smiled as she said, "Yes David, even the 'Dinty Moore' beef stew and Hormel Chili with beans were flown in fresh. They should last for another twenty years if you leave it in the can. We've all come to understand that you have only four loves in your life: your love for Heather, your love for your fur babies, your love for all things that go bang and your love for canned goods.

## Chapter 18
# CLASS IS IN SESSION

    I woke up Sunday morning wishing it was Monday. I felt fresh and I felt ready to stomp some ass. I don't know the last time I felt this excited. I'm ready to slay fire breathing dragons.

    With the Roberts family and "The Company" (of course) behind me, I can't see any viable reason why or even how we could possibly fail. Yeah, we're going to have a fight on our hands but we're only going to show one card at a time. I think by the third time we turn a card face up, we're going to get a lot of people wanting to join up with us and walking away from what they've known to be their accepted normal. It's not so much that they want to join a winning side, it's more like they didn't want the embarrassment of being shown to the public and even themselves and their families of what and who they actually have become. No one likes to be made a fool of, especially fools. Nobody likes to be called a liar and a cheat especially when we can prove that they are liars, liars and cheats.

The late morning shit-show came to visit with a phone call. It was Edna, no greeting of hello, good morning, or I trust you slept well bullshit. "We are waiting for you and Heather, it's time for your mid-day security briefing. We are in the Mariner Room."

A part of me, actually a large part of me, wanted to tell her that I was still in my jammies and I haven't pooped yet. Edna had an edge to her voice and sounded all but dreadfully serious. So, we headed for the door. When I turned the door handle to go out into the hallway it didn't open. I looked at the handle mechanism which showed three red blinking lights, which told me these doors are still locked. I waited a minute and then the lights all turned green and I was able to open the door and step out into the hallway. We were met by two Bills standing directly across from our door. There were another two Bills standing at the elevator and not surprising when the elevator door opened, there stood two more Bills. I was damn glad that I hadn't eaten breakfast yet, that fucking super speed elevator would have caused me to blow breakfast all over the walls and floor of the son of a bitch.

The entire Robert's family were seated. There were six "Bills" lined up along one wall. There was a four-to-five-foot gap and there stood six of the, "Numbers people." Another four-to-five-foot gap between them and there stood five of, "The Gunsmiths."

Me: This is all real cute but we're not doing a reenactment of the OK corral, there's more fucking guns in this room than in most gun shops! What are you guys up to?

Edna: David this is part of your new routine, this is going to be your daily routine. You and Heather both must attend three security briefings each day, mornings before your sessions, mid-day and of course, evenings. These briefings are part of your security dome. You both must be ready to evacuate your room and this building in a moment's notice without hesitation or conversation. You must not stop to gather any personal items. If we do have to move you, there are people assigned to gather your clothing, personal possessions and your sweet baby Papillons. I suggest you both sleep in pajamas to avoid any embarrassment. If we go to "Code Red", (which is an emergency evacuation) we will not call your room, we will enter it, we will put hands on the booth of you and physically remove you with extreme velocity. With that in mind, if either of you feel a forceful hand on your body's pressing on you, follow that person's directions. If you hear a commotion, a gunshot or hear the word 'down', go to the floor immediately. Don't resist, you will feel the body weight of the agents assigned to you, they are shielding you with their body's.

My mind flashed back to the day when Edna was a Secret Service agent assigned to the Presidential Security Detail when she shielded a sitting United States President with her body and was hit two times with bullets intended for him and it gave me the shivers. To think of her willingness to so freely give her life as her dedication to complete her mission is mind boggling. Now that is how you spell, BADASS!

Edna:   I'm running the security end of this operation and as you know, I will not fail you two. Trust me when I say no harm shall fall upon either of you, however your cooperation has everything to do with your safety and security.

Edna walked over and put her hands on two large boxes as she said, "You two must wear these, every moment that you are not in your room. There can and will be no exceptions. These are the very finest and latest of body armor available. They are exclusively used for dignitaries and high-level politicians. They're not anywhere near as uncomfortable and bulky as the body armor you wore back in the old days, David. These are formed fitting and they actually are breathable, they can become your best friends. I will fit you both with your vests back in your suite when today's briefing is concluded. That's right, anytime you leave your room and floor, you must be wearing your vests, the same as we all do.

The nine people from the law firm will be picked up at their homes tomorrow morning and every morning that follows and driven down here. They will also be driven home at the end of each day. There will be no private vehicles allowed on the property at any time. All of the personal property of the law firm's people will be examined and confiscated each morning before they enter the hotel proper. They will be searched for recording devices and hand wanded in the garage. We are issuing each of them a laptop and a printer while they're here. Their systems will be locked-out, they cannot send or receive any communications from outside this building. We will have six to eight of our people who are some of the best attorneys in the nation. Two of them are constitutional specialists, two of them are highly respected prosecutors and the other two are highly respected defense attorneys. They will be guiding your group of nine. Any questions?

    Heather:   I have the utmost confidence that David will do just fine protecting me and himself. Is all of this really necessary?

    Edna:   Heather, if David were to go down, who would protect you or him? You must wear your vests and carry your weapons when you leave your room.

    Me:   Honey this nasty little girl is absolutely right, we have to follow the rules too. Remember when you were a kid and had to eat everything on your plate before you could have desert? In this case the desert means that we get to live.

    Edna:   Heather and David I will try my very best not to stress you or make you uncomfortable but we have rules in place that must be followed with no exceptions. David this is your show but I'm the director, you must understand and accept that!

Gregory:   David she is the best of the very best and you two deserve nothing less. Following her directions will keep us all safe and secure.

Me:   I've got no problem with any of that. If we're done here, what do you say we grab lunch, I will buy since it's "The Company's" money and I have to tell you all that this whole "The Company" thing with air quotes, is total bullshit and it doesn't sit well with me. It's kind of like some super power up in the sky that's going to throw lightning bolts at us if we don't go along with whatever, "The Company's" desires are. I don't care for that crap at all. Can we find another name for, "The Company"? All of this 'Star- Wars' stuff is for children. How about if we refer to, "The Company" as, "Karen"? You know the Karen type who is the bitch of the block. She's the most hated bitch on the planet that seems to run every HOA in the nation and wants to write you a ticket for breathing out when you should have been breathing in, yeah that kind of Karen.

Paul:   That's a firm and hard no David, stay in your lane. Woody, I believe you and Maddie are now up to bat.

Woody:   David, when you called us and asked us to dawn our Michelin Tire Man winter suits in exchange for our speedos it set off alarms in our heads and here is why.

First, you have never asked us for anything other than for us to join you for a meal and wonderful fellowship. Since we all know you as a man who speaks as he writes, it caused Maddie and I to look at your current online activities and before you ask, yes, we have access to your computers and phone logs.

We at first, were a bit baffled as we didn't find anything to provoke your urgent request. We read your latest novel in-progress and found nothing to elicit our attention. By the way, while reading your last novel, "Brothers of The Tattered Cloth" I almost pissed myself when you were ripping into Norby as to how she was so rigid that you couldn't understand how she ever got her legs far enough apart to conceive her children let alone to give birth to them. David, that was the richest humor that I've ever had the pleasure to read! It still makes me chuckle. When Maddie and I see a too tightly wound woman like the 'Karen' you earlier described, we look at each other and softly say, 'Norbs'. We could both see the grin on your face as you wrote those few lines.

Me:   Woody, can we wrap this up, say before the race starts?

Woody:   Again David, we found nothing that brought us to suspect that you were in trouble. That is until we started checking on the people who were watching you from the other team. We realized that you were on to something once we took a closer look at your current search history along with the IP addresses of your watchers.

Maddie:   David this is not easy for me to speak of but it carries a level of importance that can't be ignored. Do you remember the plane crash of senator Paul Wellstone from Minnesota who died in the crash on October 25th 2002 in Eveleth, MN along with his wife, one of his daughters, three staffers and two pilots?

    Me:   I wasn't living here in Minnesota at the time but yes, I do recall the news stories.

    Maddie:   Well, if you were to believe the NTSB reports and how they blamed the two pilots for not lowering their landing gears soon enough to break their air speed which caused the crash, you have to be an idiot or someone who heavily smokes the devil's lettuce.

    David, we believe that the plane crash was no accident. The debris field was far too large for anything other than a bomb or a missile. We believe that the Wellstone's were assassinated. David they were personal friends of ours, we've spent many evenings and weekends with them over a ten-year period, we dined together almost monthly. As you know, Woody and I are staunch Republicans and Paul was a staunch Liberal Democrat. Yes, he was one of those fiery, fist shaking liberals fighting for all people, not just his party but for all people. That was the beauty of Paul Wellstone, he fought for all people, not just for his people as most all other political party members do. Paul was a straight up, no nonsense guy. He and his family and those other people on board that aircraft did not deserve to be murdered. At the time of the crash the upcoming election was only 11 days away and was one of the most closely watched races in the nation as it would determine control of the U.S. Senate. David, you're a smart fellow and I'm most certain that you know who killed both JFK and his brother Bobby, of course it was his own party. We think Paul was murdered by his own party; they couldn't control him. He was too honest, they needed someone who they could bend over and be willing to take it in the ass. They wanted total ownership of him. Paul was not that man.

    Woody:   David, it may seem that we went off track with speaking of Paul but we want you to fully grasp the threat. Here is the deal; similar IP addresses belong to some of the same political strategists that we believe had Paul killed. We further believe that Paul was about to drop a bombshell on the Minnesota Democrat party, exposing the corruption and bribe taking through all levels of his party. Whatever it is that you know David, is viewed by the opposition as dangerous. That's why we think you're at risk, if they'll kill a seated U.S. Senator and his family, they sure as hell will kill a novelist from Duluth.

    Me:   In truth I know damn little, I suspect a great deal however and I think everyone understands that to simply have suspicions, will not bring a conviction. We have to be able to prove our case. This whole gig is about proving our case! *Capish?*

    Let's go eat. The race comes on in two hours and I'm not going to miss the start of it. I think they are running in Daytona this weekend, right Woody?

Lunch was no different than sitting in a restaurant with a bunch of people. Other than the only thing you heard were knives and forks being scraped on fine China and coffee cups going back on the saucers. I didn't hear any conversation amongst what, the thirty-five people seated? Yeah, these folks are serious alright.

We went to our room. Loved up on our fur babies and got comfortable to watch the race. We both fell asleep at some point but woke up for the last 30 laps. After our 'race naps' we showered and went down and enjoyed dinner. The conversation was light and enjoyable. Heather and I both slept well and I woke up at 4:00 AM ready to meet the day. Even the dogs didn't want to get up that early.

Edna, Gregory, Paul and Jane along with Phil, were waiting in the hallway outside of the Mariner Room. It was the only meeting room in the entire hotel without any windows. I smiled at Phil and asked, "Are you ready for this? Phil smiled back and said, "I've never been more ready, this is going to be fun. Thank you for looking after my people and keeping them all safe. We are all in it to win it, my friend!"

## Chapter 19
# GAME TIME

I took a deep breath, leaned over and kissed Heather and nodded to the two Bills in front of the closed doors. We walked into the room to see several of the firm's attorneys and research people, with questioning faces. I smiled and said, "Edna, I believe some of these people have a question or two for you."

Edna introduced eight of "The Company's" staff and asked each of the law firm's people to introduce themselves. There was one female that obviously felt that we all needed to know of her many, many excellent academic achievements. As I was listening to her dribble on and on, I glanced over to Edna and smiled with a head nod, as I telegraphed, "Well played my lady, thank you for allowing the weakest link in the group to expose herself so early on."

Edna gave a protocol briefing and laid out as to what security measures were necessary for each and every moment that they are in the building, firmly admonishing them all to not speak of any conversations or documents they will see.

I could hear and see that she was leading up to a crescendo with a starburst ending.

Edna:   No one is to leave this facility until the day is declared complete. We will not have established quitting hours; we will be done when I say we are done! No one is to leave this building with anything that they personally did not bring with them. You are to speak to no one of the work that is taking place here. You are all now effectively in quarantine, if you violate any of the rules in the contract in front of you, your status of quarantine will advance to, "In custody!" You will not make any public statements or give any interviews to anyone. If any of you violate the contract rules you will be prosecuted and disbarred from ever practicing law again. Please read and sign your contract for our witnesses and notary to sign.

Edna pointed to a large framed painting of a World War II battleship at sea, hanging on the back wall as she said, "Loose lips sink ships."

The only female attorney (other than Val) of the firm's group that was present looked pissed-off and appeared to be ready for some level of confrontation. I walked over and stood in front of her and nodded to Edna as though I was going to take this. I smiled at the young lady and asked, "What's your name Miss? And what kind of bug do you have crawling up your ass this fine and lovely morning?" She reeled back in her chair and I could see she was already about to surrender. I said, "No Babe, you got something on your mind. Put it all out here for everyone to hear. That's how we operate. There are no secrets, no other agendas other than the one I'm about to present to you, so what's eating at you?"

Before she started to speak, I opened my briefcase and pulled out her personal file and another sheet of paper. I started with, "OK young lady, it says here that you graduated at the very top of your law class and your undergrad work was in the humanities. I see that you also did campus and community theater. This paper in my hand shows that you googled me. You scrolled through my Facebook and my website for 57 minutes and 14 seconds and you also tried to hack into my emails.

Me: Nancy girl, all you had to do is ask. My friends here have computer systems that can tell me what you're thinking before you even think it! You're out of your league doll face. I will answer your question and perhaps some of your colleagues' questions at the same time. I believe your question has to do with, "Who the fuck does this, 'nobody prick' think he is? Why is he running this project? He talks hard to everyone and acts all-knowing like he is superior to everyone! I don't and I won't fucking work for this arrogant, narcissistic bastard!"

Does that pretty much sum it up, Nancy girl? I will fucking tell you exactly who I am. I am the man who can give you cause to brush up your resume before this morning's coffee break. Still love me babe?

I am the only person in this room without a sheepskin hanging on their wall. I have a high school diploma and I graduated 14th from the bottom of a class of 453 kids. I have never entered a college campus except to speak in a packed auditorium for a shit-ton of money. I don't have a trade. I truly don't have any level of education. I am a generalist; I know a little about a lot of things but I don't know a lot about any one thing. I have slept with more women than attend your Sunday church services for an entire month. I have been married and divorced five times. I am an alcoholic with thirty-one years of continuous sobriety. I have authored and published seven novels. I am a man of honor and dignity. I am American Patriot and pro Police through-and-through. Other than my shirt size, you know all that I'm going to tell you. Make no mistake sweetheart, this is my show and I will run it my way. If you take exception to either my filthy language or my unorthodox ways, feel free to leave this room at any time.

I will say this to all of you at once. I don't give a fuck about your personal lives, who or what you identify as, who you sleep with or what your political affiliation is. None of your bullshit belongs here in this room or in this fucking building. So back to you Nance, what is it young lady? What is it that is about to get you sent home if not for the day, perhaps for a lifetime? Do you need to find another law firm to represent?

Nancy:   Well, it was nice to get a ride for work today in a really nice car. But when they photographed me, took my fingerprints then took my cell phone, my purse and my briefcase and told me they would be secured in another area for the day it pissed me off! That's my property, they have no business taking my property from me!

Me: Oh, that's damn cute Nance, maybe you could find a slime-ball lawyer and file a lawsuit and crush us all? Shut the fuck up. There is something else even deeper, let's have it Nance.

Nancy: Well, those men at the gun shop were rude and oppressive. I didn't like any of them!

Me: Nancy girl, I'm sensing a bit of a pattern here. Is it all men that you dislike or just certain types of men you dislike?

Nancy: The man at the gun shop who was showing me how to shoot my gun was laughing at me and called me mean names. I got to like him later on but he was a hard driven asshole. He obviously likes pushing women around!

Me: Nance, put your feelers away. No one here gives a fat flying fuck how you may feel, we just want to know what you're going to do about it.

There's more to it Nancy girl, so what did the mean man do to you, that makes your teeth grind at night and pout like an eight-year-old, at this glorious moment? I'm suspecting he may have put you in your place and removed your wonder woman powers. Now you want to power stomp around like a flag flapping in a gale force wind. That's too fuckin bad about your Nance, deal with it. Before we go any further, I want you to know that those people at the gun shop are all dear friends of mine. What did Matt do to you that has your skirts in flames?

Nancy:   He kept calling me names from the very first time I tried to shoot the gun. When it went off, it scared me so bad that it jumped out of my hand and it dropped on the floor.

Me:   Nance, what you just said is indicative of your generation and your profession of the, "Don't blame me" crowd. You and your kind (of which there are many) take no responsibility for anything that is your fault but take credit for shit and broadcast your success of which you had little, if anything at all to do with. You are the type of country gal that rakes her leaves in the fall into a huge pile and sets them on fire although there are heavy winds at the time. You say to yourself, "It should be fine." You start a massive grassland fire that takes several fire crews and several days to extinguish. The phrase, "It should be fine" falls from the lips of you and your entire generation. "It should be fine" is a phrase that actually means, "I don't give a fuck about anyone or anything because I want to do it!" You and me along with your people are not the same. You dropped that fucking gun; it didn't jump from your hands. Take some responsibility for yourself for the fuck's sake! If I see another look on your face like I just did, you are gone. Children pout not adults. Try adulting and see if that works.

Nancy:   I'm sorry but Matt told me that I was 'limp-wristing' the gun and that I needed to hold it like it was a man's dick! I couldn't hold it right to please him. It just felt funny to me, so do you know what he did to me David? He took a roll of that self-adhesive medical bandaging and wrapped my hand to the gun. Every time I shot, he called me a "Limp wristed Googan!" Which really pissed me off because I didn't know what a Googan was so I went to the ladies' room with my hand still taped around the gun and googled it and that really pissed me off!

Me:   Nancy girl, I do know what a Googan is. It has to do with lowlife boaters or fisherman who have little or no regard for regulations, shows no interest for anyone's safety and act stupidly. A Googan is simply someone who doesn't belong somewhere, someone who's intruding in someone else's space, comfort, and security. Lighten up babe. So, you had three days of four-hour sessions each day. How did you feel at the end of the third day?

Nancy:   Well, I hate to admit it but I became a pretty good shot but I was still pissed off at Matt for mistreating me.

Me:   See if this fits, honey try to match what you get, with what you give. You don't show a whole bunch of respect to anyone because you believe you are superior to them. Would you like to leave now? We can get you into a car in the next three minutes and whisk you away to your home and your new career. Nance, shut the fuck up for the final time. Nancy girl, you're no better than anyone else in this room and many here are far superior to you in the practice of law, humility and maturity.

I looked over at Phil and I said, "Phil, kindly nod your head in approval of what I just said to Nancy, please." Phil nodded his head as he stated, "There will be no further questions from my people. Would you like to start now David?"

Me:   Phil, I think I'll let your people digest what just transpired between Nancy and me. Why don't you join me for a cup of coffee in my private garden and by the way everybody, my enclosed garden is my private place. No one is to enter without my personal invitation. Of course, the Roberts family and associates are welcome to join us. Anyone who dares to try to come in there without an invitation from me, will be quickly turned around and sent home. Who knows, maybe even shot!

Phil and I each grabbed a cup of coffee along with a cookie from the snack bar and went out into the garden and sat down. I first said, "I wanted to shock her because I think she will be the fiercest fighter of them all. Well, what's she made of, do you think she can take it? Phil smiled and said, "David she is a fucking she-devil.
Your interaction with her was brilliant. Be assured my friend that nobody is wondering now, who the fuck you are and no one wants to take you on. That exchange was masterful, I loved the way you kept setting her up and teeing off, you want a job? All of my lawyers are strong and they won't back down

either, but if you're asking which of the four of them is the top 'go to' person, yep, I would go with Nancy.

Me: Don't forget that there were three of your people (including your daughter) who sat with Heck just minutes before he killed himself. How are they doing?

Phil: Well, my daughter, who you like to call Val, has had trouble sleeping. Her mother has taken her back to her apartment several times to pick up fresh clothes but ever since Heck died, she has stayed at our house. Some nights I hear her sobbing and it breaks my heart. She is convinced that he used her ink pen to kill himself. She has been seeing a grief counselor and a psychiatrist and taking some low-level anti-depressants.

Me: Do you think she can handle all of this shit storm that is about to make landfall?

Phil: David, you damn well know she can and will. I know you are asking that only to give me and her mother an out. With what you're about to step into, will give her purpose and drive like she has never known before. But you already know that, you sly bastard.

Me: Is your staff truly aware of the potential risks?

Phil: I've spent quite a while talking with them about it and the people at the gun shop helped us greatly. Yes, they're up for the task.

Me: As long as they all understand that this task could get messy, real messy.

Phil:   David, I've been assured by the people of "The Company" that no harm shall fall upon my business or my people. We too are in it to win it.

Phil and I shook hands and we returned to the Mariner Conference Room.

*Chapter 20*
# GAME TIME

Me: So, everyone, let's start over. Good morning, everyone. I trust everyone slept well? Snacks as you can see are provided here in this room, lunch will be served at 11:30 and an afternoon snack if you so choose, will be available in this room. If we have to go past 5pm (which is rather likely) you can order dinner off the menu and you can eat at your workstations. Do we have any smokers who will need breaks? I see no hands are raised but if any of you are closet smokers you can take a break at any time. No one is to leave this room to go anywhere without a professional escort. No exceptions! Well kids, let's get down to business.

Now listen tight, none of you are to accept any gifts of any kind, from anyone! You are now in social quarantine. You are not to be out in public or even attend family functions, not even your immediate family. The only family you may entertain are the people that live under your roof and no others. You are not to have conversations with your neighbors or even your associates at the law firm as to this project. We can only hold the element of surprise if we remain silent. Yes folks (as I pointed to the beautifully framed photo of a US Battleship) loose lips do sink ships!

In short, we are going to rock some people's worlds for the greater good of all men, women and children. What we're going to do is we're going to do a full-out assault on corruption within government offices, services and of course, the filth of politics. We are going to afflict the comfortable and comfort the afflicted. We will define the true term of bipartisanship. We will expose the dirt of these scumbags regardless of their political affiliations.

I'm sure that you all fully understand what corruption is and that has been taught all during your law school classes. But yet let me ask you this, why do lawyers have to take an oath? Because many can't be trusted, is that why the oath is in place? And no, you can't argue any part of that with me. I win, my house, my rules!

I win and why in the fuck do they even attempt to teach ethics in law school when lawyers are of the most unethical, lying, thieving mother fuckers that ever crept the face of the earth. That's right my friends, I've got a real hard-on for lawyers, yet I have several friends who are lawyers. Today I'm going to learn to love lawyers. But only if you do what I say, do that and I will learn to love you deeply.

It is now the time that we release the beast and let her feed. Just so we are clear, crystal clear actually, I will read the many definitions of corruption from my dear friends of Wikipedia.

Wikipedia's definition of corruption is: "Corruption is a form of dishonesty or a criminal offense which is undertaken by a person or an organization which is interested with the position of authority in order to acquire illicit benefits or abuse power for one's personal gain. Corruption may involve many activities which include bribery and embezzlement, and it may also involve practices which are legal in many countries. Political corruption occurs when an office-holder or other governmental employee acts in an official capacity for personal gain. Corruption is most common in kleptocracies, oligarchies, narco-states and mafia states. Corruption and crime are epidemic sociological occurrences which appear with regular frequencies in virtually all countries on the global scale and in varying degrees and proportions. Each individual nation allocates domestic resources for the control and regulation of corruption and the deterrence of crime. Strategies which are undertaken in order to counter corruption are often summarized under the umbrella term, 'anti-corruption'.

Additionally, global initiatives like the, "United Nations Sustainable Development Goal 16" also have a targeted goal, which is supposed to substantially reduce corruption in all of its many forms."

I won't bore you guys with the many definitions and scales and causes of these slimy pukes that steal and lie their way into wealth with our money.

OK, that's pretty much it but we're not going after the world, we're not even going after our nation, at least not quite yet. We are however going to deeply touch upon our state servants' professional and personal lives. Our main focus will be on this city and this county's trusted servants.

I'm pretty sure that at some point we have all said or at least have heard someone say several times that, "You can't fix stupid." Well, that's true enough, we can't fix stupid but we can fix its stupid policies. Stupid policies that allow dysfunctional people to hide behind the rules that they make to protect themselves, with the assistance of their unions and PAC's. Criticizing politicians or department heads is of little or no value, that bullshit happens all day long every day. Facebook blows up with this political bullshit on a constant basis. So how do we present something that they can't lie about or deflect? As that wack job, talking head, Jen Psaki likes to say, "We'll have to circle back on that." Politicians are not listening even when you're looking them in the eye because they're already working up the answer as you are still asking your question. Not all, but the great majority of politicians are of course, lawyers and well-practiced professional liars.

The way we're going to come at these people is we're going to recruit them. We're not going to throw stones, we're not going to directly confront, we're going to recruit. How do you recruit a hostile and protected politician?

Believe it or not, the answer is quite simple. What we're going to do is we are going to publicize their records of function and failures. We will play on every bureaucrat's greatest fears. The fear of being discovered and found out!

Now you guys are going to have to hunker down and do that whole "Freedom of Information Act" stuff. I don't know where the power of subpoena comes from but you'll all figure it out. We've got some great minds in this room and some are heavily experienced. Let's start with our illustrious governor of Minnesota. This ass-clown Governor, Mr. Tim Walz suddenly came up with a budget surplus of 9.6 billion Dollars! That's right, Billion with a big fuckin B! Three weeks prior, our state auditor announced that it was a 7.7-billion-dollar budget surplus and now they found even more free money, how exciting! Where does this surplus come from when our state's economy is on its ass? Unemployment is at an all-time high and few people are willing to work, so where does this surplus come from? The working taxpayer of course! Hell, Minnesota is just one of fifteen states that taxes social security payments for retirees. It doesn't take a genius to understand that the supposed surplus came from federal and state allocated program funds that existed in name only. I've talked to you earlier about the underserved citizens of this area. The governor had no intention of releasing funds to his party's ghost social services programs. That budget was designed to allocate funds to be siphoned off and somehow that money ended up locked in someone's back room and they were the only ones with the key. So once again the underserved become the victims of their servers, isn't that fuckin sweet? We have junkies and mentally ill people dying every day at their own hands, because nobody can get to them because there's no funds to put anybody in play to get to them, yet they have a surplus of 9.6 billion dollars to fuck around with? That's not surplus money that's fucking blood money!

Now the shit slinger, Governor Walz is proposing that "HE" will give every Minnesota resident $500.00 from the budget surplus. We have midterm elections coming up. Governor Walz is running for re-election. That shit heel is holding those funds to be released just prior to the midterm elections on Tuesday, November 8th. This maggot is buying votes using our own fucking money! He fucked up so badly with allowing the rioters and looters to destroy several private businesses along with major retail stores all throughout the state that he is using our money to throw a 'Hail Mary' to win the election.

Sadly, former President Obama placed the bulk of the U.S. Somali immigrant population smack dab into the middle of one of the very few of the Republican strongholds in the Minneapolis area, which changed the entire voting districts boundaries. As of 2018 there were approximately 94,000 Somalis in Minnesota. Not to be out-done by the Somalis, the nation's largest Hmong population is also nestled in the Minneapolis area with an estimated population of 66,000. The state of Minnesota's budget is inappropriately spent on welfare services over mental health and human service's needs. I won't even comment on the state's shitty roadway systems. Minnesota has always been known as the 'Gimme State'. There are 3rd and 4th generation immigrant welfare recipients who have never held a job in this country. None of you need to comment on or argue with what I've just said. Call me any name you want, but just not to my face. Speaking the truth is neither bigoted or racist.

Let me share a quote by Kid Rock that was quoted when he answered a reporter's question early today, March 21st, 2022. Kid Rock was asked if, "He fears the cancel mob?" Kid Rock responded with, "I am un-cancellable, because I don't give a fuck!" This man is singing my song, because I don't give a fuck either.

There are three people in this room that had a horrible experience just a few days back. Hopefully not crippling but it is guaranteed to be life changing in varying degrees. Most of you will hopefully never see that kind of thing but they did. None of these three will ever be able to fully describe those moments of looking into Heck's eyes without knowing what was about to take place. That's something you just can't forget about, you can't pretend it didn't happen, because it did. Those memories, questions and self-blame will come. Those memories won't simply just swing by to visit them from time to time on a normal day. Those memories will wait, they will patiently wait to come storming in on their lowest of low days. The days that they can't escape it, the day's that will all but consume them.

The reason I'm telling you all this is because I'm looking at you guys and I see indifference in some of your body language and on your faces. Most of you didn't have the personal interaction that our three had. I suspect you don't carry the passion and the drive that I need you to carry into our mission, so I'm going to give you some passion and drive because we are not going to fail, I won't allow it!

Today I am going to set your bellies on fire with horrific true stories that hopefully will cause you to engage your minds, hearts and souls as our three friends here have experienced.

The Mariner conference room had wall to wall drapes with white grease boards behind the drapes. I walked over and opened the drapes to expose four of the 4x6 foot grease boards. I stood in the center of the four boards.

Me:   Everyone turn your chairs and look at me. Who here has the best penmanship with a grease pen and who can write using the long forgotten cursive writing technique?

I was surprised to see one of the males from the law office research department raise his hand. His name was Peter. I had Peter come up and stand next to me and introduce himself. I stepped aside and told him to use the top four inches and centered in the two grease boards framed in teak wood.

Me:   Peter, you will be writing our mission statement that I hope will become each of your life's mission statements. Please write these four words, "Least we ever forget!"

What totally surprised me was that he was left-handed and had the most beautiful flowing cursive handwriting that I have ever seen. He read the approval on my face as he sheepishly shrugged his shoulders and said, "My Mom was an English teacher, she insisted that all of us kids not just use cursive but we had to master it as an art form."

Me:   Peter your mom rocks! Thank your mother for me, please. Now Peter, you will please write the following thirteen names. I want each name to be two inches high. I want seven names on the first board and six names on the second board, so even an old geezer like me with vision problems can clearly read them from across the room.

# *Chapter 21*
# UNDISPUTED PURPOSE

Me: Peter, please write each of the following names on each line.

Cassie Bernall, 17
Steven Curnow, 14
Corey DePooter, 17
Kelly Fleming, 16
Matthew Kechter, 16
Daniel Mauser, 15
Daniel Rohrbough, 15
Rache Scott, 17
Isaiah Shoels, 18
John Tomlin, 16
Lauren Townsend, 18
Kyle Velasques, 16
William "Dave" Sanders, 47

Once Peter was finished, I had to turn away and lower my head in silence, to gather myself.

Me:   Thank you everyone for your attention and your silence. As you can see that twelve of those names belong to teenagers and to one adult. There is one great commonality within this group of thirteen. Peter, please bracket all of those names. The great commonality amongst the thirteen is that they all share the same date of death,
April 20, 1999. It was the day of the Columbine High School Massacre in Littleton, Colorado.

There were two other males that died in the school on that day as well. I will not have their names placed on this board, it would dishonor the memories of the children and their teacher, because those two who are not listed, are the shooters. I think we all need a break.

I left the room and headed to my private garden. Kat fell in alongside me and matched me stride for stride. I (now, we) went into the restaurant for a craft of coffee each and headed to my garden sanctuary. Patty and Sarah were standing inside the secured garden.

Patty:   Damn you David, you can't just go waltzing around here like you're at Disneyland, the danger here is real. Yes, I have been fully briefed on your keen skills of observation and situational awareness. I know that you have engaged in gun fights as a police officer when the odds were not in your favor. David, that was twenty-five years ago and you just admitted that your eyesight is failing you. Please do your job and let us do ours. Besides, a lot of us have grown to be quite fond of you. May we join you for coffee now?

Kat:   Hey stud, we almost got to see you cry a few minutes ago. Us gals were about to rush you to get to see who of us would get to hold you first. Heather signaled us with a slight head shake to give you your time. That woman loves you like no other could.

Me:   I'm here to smoke several cigarettes and enjoy my Folgers coffee, did you just say something sweetheart?

After revitalizing my lungs with several cigarettes and splashing some cold water on my mug, I returned to the Mariner conference room. I now saw the interest in the eyes that I had hoped to see.

Me:   I want to take you back to April 20th 1999. Most of you legal beagles were still eating boogers and messing your diapers. On April 20th, 1999 the "Columbine High School Massacre" took place. At the time this was the worst school shooting in U.S. history. What's my connection to it? I was driving in the far southern part of metro Denver, actually it was in the city of Littleton, a suburb of Denver metro. I was driving north on South Pierce Street. South Pierce is a six lane north-south, 45 mph speed zone.

DAVID J. BROWN

I came to a red traffic light at 62nd street. I saw nothing but a wall of bumper to bumper, emergency lights coming over a long hill in the southbound lanes towards me. Two city blocks to my right was Columbine High School. All I could see was the upper roof line of the school through the trees. (Columbine is a public high school located 11 miles Southwest of Denver proper and runs grades 9 through 12 The student body enrollment was approximately 1,697 at the time of the incident.) Three Littleton police vehicles turned in front of me and blocked all three northbound lanes. I was the 1st car at the traffic light in the far-right lane. It almost looked to be a parade, but it was at quite a high rate of speed.

I knew something was terribly wrong as the police cars screamed and streamed in front of me going towards the high school. I had my truck radio on a local talk show station. I knew there must be a shit storm that was about to break if not already in progress. The steady stream of fire rescue and ambulances occupied the left and middle lanes that left nothing to my imagination. The talk show broadcaster broke-in with a helicopter traffic report that was reporting that there are active shooters outside and inside Columbine High School using high caliber semi-automatic rifles and bombs were suspected to have been planted in the school. The helicopter pilot reported seeing six people laying on the ground and not moving on the school entrance sidewalk.

From my experience as a former metro police officer, I knew that there were going to be a lot of problems with this response. I saw squad cars from several different departments from all over the entire metro area and several suburbs and even cities from twenty miles or more away. I could foresee what was about to unfold as the shit storm of the decade was brewing. I turned off my truck's ignition and sat for the next twenty minutes. During that time, there was not one ambulance (from the dozens that went in) that came out from the school.

At that time, every city police department, EMS and fire departments in the metro area all had their own radio frequencies. There were no universal emergency frequencies, so the responding police departments could not talk to the other departments, they could only talk with their departments and dispatchers. Dispatchers had to call by phone the other departments and relay the officer's messages back and forth. Cell phone towers had to be blocked so command officers could communicate with other command officers via their cell phones.

There were no established multi-department tactical protocols for command and response at that time. One department wanted to charge into the school to take down the shooters and another department wanted to enter and rescue the wounded, and another wanted to directly engage the shooters and so on. There was a lot of arguing going on, some of the arguing of course, was ego driven but it appeared that no one was clearly in charge. There was a lengthy delay until entry was made due to fear that the bombs were remote control, trip wired or were on timers. That and the fear of the hostages would be killed if officers engaged with the shooters. At the time the number of shooters were thought to be six or more.

Well, there were fifteen deaths that day, twenty-four injuries, twenty-one received bullet wounds and the other three injuries came from the children diving out of classroom windows of the school to escape the shooters. There was one teacher that used his body to shield some children hiding in a small closet that was shot to death. The killers were Dylan Klebold age 17 and Eric Harris age 18. Earlier that day they had planted two bombs in the cafeteria using two twenty-pound LP tanks (like the ones you have for your BBQ grill) they had the tanks hidden in large duffel bags and they had duct taped long nails all around the exterior of the tanks (to cause additional injuries and death) and set timers to blow up the school with hopes of killing several hundred children and staff members.

They then retreated from the school to their cars waiting for the bombs to go off. The timers failed to set off the bombs so they got out of their cars and started shooting people in the parking lot then entered the school to do what they hoped the LP tanks would have done.

Those chicken-shit little pricks turned their guns on themselves when their work was complete and they ended their own lives. That's the only good news in this entire fucking story. What role did their parents play? Who else knew about what they were planning to do? Supposedly they both had been planning the assault for the last year and a half and were active members of what was a loose knit internet group of freaks that refer to themselves as the, "Trench Coat Posse" or the "Duster Mafia." They were both heavily involved in the Goth Movement as well. Those punks were just a couple of losers that didn't fit in anywhere and they wanted to punish the entire world because they were nobody pukes. They targeted Athletes, Minorities and Christians that day. It was initially reported that one student by the name of Cassie Bernall was asked by one of the gunmen if she is a Christian, she responded, "Yes" and she was immediately shot in the head and died. Her parents later wrote a book titled, "She said yes."

In the aftermath of the massacre the public wanted justice. Well, they didn't have those two little shitheads to go after so they went after the man who sold a gun to Harris, Mr. Mark Manes who also sold Harris one-hundred rounds of ammunition the day before the murders. He was sentenced to 6 years in prison. Another man, Mr. Philip Duran who introduced Harris and Klebold to Mr. Manes was also sentenced to a minimum of prison time. Some of the victims and their families of the children killed or injured filed lawsuits against the school and the police. The parents contended that the police should have entered the school immediately and perhaps some of the children may not have bleed to death. Most of those lawsuits were later dismissed in court. And of course, then came all the liberals throughout the country along with Colorado's gutless gun control lobby, with lawsuits and demands that we redesign or completely abolish the 2nd amendment because after all, the guns killed those children and that one teacher. It was most certainly not the fault of those two poor misguided young boys, it was the guns that murdered these people. And some of you wonder why I have a great distaste for lawyers? Some of the students' families filed lawsuits against both the school and the police. For what reason, for not getting there sooner? How about parents not raising their kids properly, shouldn't they be sued?

Let's take a break. There is more to come that will blow your hair back like you are straddling a rocket. See you back here in twenty minutes and remember, no one is to leave this room without a professional escort.

## *Chapter 22*
# THERE CAN BE NO HOLIDAY

Even before I left the room, I knew I hadn't convinced them yet. There were too many people sitting there looking relaxed as if they were thinking, "Yeah well, that was there.... this is here, that was then.... this is now." I have to go deeper with them. I know the stories that I must tell that would do that very thing but I also knew that I would have to pay a deep, personal price in my gut. I wasn't even done with my second cigarette and I was ready to go back in the room. I had to hook their passion and I was ready to go to war within myself to do it.

Me:   I hope you all enjoyed your break. I want to tell you a story that is still taking place in Pueblo, Colorado and the reason I mention Colorado is that I lived there for forty years and it's still deep in my heart. The politics there suck monkey butt, but the state's mountains and the 'Real people' of Colorado, make living there palatable. There are two types of people in Colorado. First you have the freak imports from California who claimed that they wanted to get away from the insanity of the drug culture and crime and the high cost of living along with their East Coast counterparts who claimed the very same reasons to invade Colorado. The only problem with those folks is that they brought their same liberal bullshit politics along with them! There is a broad divide between the 'Real People' of Colorado and the, 'Coasties'.

Pueblo, Colorado is a high desert town in the southeastern part of the state. That area is well known for some of the best melons and vegetables in the entire nation. Pueblo County is a rather poor part of the state. There is a steel mill there that I believe has shut down in the last few years, so the economy isn't what it should be. I think the population of Pueblo is around 110,841 people. So on to the story.

There was a significant increase in homicides in 2021 from 2020 which were allegedly committed by well known, (to law enforcement and the courts) violent felons that left local people scratching their heads as to why these criminals are free to commit these homicides. In 2020 the city of Pueblo had a reported 14 homicides throughout the year, while that number itself is high enough, 2021 brought a 117% increase by rising to 29 homicides! Twenty-nine homicides in one calendar year with that population and that size drew some unwanted publicity into the area. I read some interviews that were done by local news stations with the Pueblo Police Department. The Pueblo Police Chief Chris Noeller, revealed the criminal history of backgrounds of those who he believes are responsible for the bulk of the murders in their city. Most of the people that are suspected of committing many of these murders are seemingly repeat criminal offenders. The majority of the homicides were committed by 13 known gang members, some who were previously deported illegal aliens that have snuck back into the country. Nine of those killers who were arrested have five or more felony arrests on their files, two of the suspects had ten or more felony arrests and one of them had fifteen or more felony arrests. Three of the murder suspects were out on a no-bail bond at the time, or were on parole or probation or early releases before the homicides were committed. A Pueblo Police Sergeant, Frank Ortega, had the courage to say, "There are quite a few of these thugs that if they weren't locked up, they would be out killing people right now."

    While that statement from sergeant Ortega is obvious, what he is seemingly referring to is a broken Criminal Justice System. Repeat felony offenders should be in jail, common sense tells us they would have never had the opportunity to commit the current murders that they are now charged with. The police chief then allowed that, "If the alleged criminals are going to be allowed to bond out of jail or if they are going to be released out of prison and back into the streets of Pueblo there's only so much, we can do. We are repeatedly arresting the same violent offenders who are carrying weapons and using those weapons to commit more crimes." The chief went on to say, "Homicide is one of the hardest crimes to prevent because it's usually an emotionally based assault or decision that is based on a prior relationship. People are being released repeatedly on 'No-Bail Bond' after they have committed violent crimes or the courts are not interested in punishing people when they violate their parole. Those kinds of things are putting them in a position where they can commit more violent crimes." The problem that Chief Miller is highlighting is not just central to the Pueblo area but seemingly everywhere throughout the United States. Some judges have swung largely to the left in terms of Criminal Justice reform. Those judges are typically allowing defendants to simply walk out of court after they've been arrested for a new offense or have violated the terms of their probation without any further consequences.

Some areas like California and Chicago are mandating that offenders that are being released wear ankle monitors, however the courts leave it up to the suspects to make those arrangements.

Stepping away from Pueblo, Colorado, my friends at 'LET' (Law Enforcement Today network), reports that the far-left acting Oregon Governor Kate Brown was furious after a judge blocked her from a mass prison release of criminals, so now she's got a new plan. One of her powers is the right to grant commutations of prison sentences. Governor Kate Brown decided to hand over that decision making process to the state parole board. This issue wound up in court after a group, "Common Sense for

Oregon" sued the state governor for the attempted expansion of the state parole board's power. If Governor Brown's efforts had been allowed to pass, there would have been numerous juvenile convicts in front of those decision makers seeking early release. Citing roughly 250 cases would have been in front of the parole board. A circuit court judge decided Governor Brown could not transfer her constitutional authority to grant communications and clemency to the parole board's discretion. The move would have expanded the parole board's authority, which the judge says is not allowed under law. Another part of that same lawsuit is the court upheld nearly 1,200 commutations.

Her office said of that decision: "The governor is pleased with the court's letter opinion and has affirmed that her use of clemency powers was within her authority and upheld every single communication granted to date impacting almost 1,200 individuals." Governor Kate Brown believes that her clemency authority can and should be used, "To address systemic failures in our Criminal Justice System while we work to make lasting change."

Apparently, she also believes that her authority should be exercised by a group of people who are not granted said authority by the state's lawmakers. One of the clemency requests she was looking at was from Ms. Lynley Rayburn.

Here my friends, is where things get ghastly stupid.

This is a homicide case which is referred to as the, "Oregon Christmas Killers." On December 23rd of 2005, two people entered the home of Dale Rost the 3rd, who resided in Sheridan, Oregon. The two suspects Gerald 'AJ' Smith, twenty years old and his twenty-nine-year-old girlfriend, Ms. Lynley Janet Rayburn, kidnapped Mr. Rost outside of his home as he was walking his dog, late at night. They stripped him naked, bound his wrists and ankles, slapped him around until he gave up his bank and credit card pin numbers and then shot him in the eye with a 22-caliber rifle. Mr. Rost died instantly. The suspects opened all of the wrapped Christmas gifts and took several of them as well as ransacked the house. The only defense presented by the accused was the fact that they were both high on meth, so if you're high on meth it should be OK to kill people, right? Are you fuckin kidding me?!?!

Mr. Rost's body was found the following evening by his daughter who went to check on him after he failed to appear at his daughter's home for Christmas Eve early dinner and gift exchange. He didn't answer her several phone calls. Can any of you imagine, entering your parents' home and finding your father stark naked and bound, laying in a pool of his blood with his brains splattered everywhere?

The killers, Smith and Rayburn were apprehended driving the victim's car. Both pled guilty to the murder of Mr. Rost. The Yamhill District Attorney, Brad Berry prosecuted both cases. The

DA's claim was that Ms. Rayburn was involved in the planning of it, she stripped Mr. Rost naked and tied him up. She was involved in ransacking the house looking for credit cards and other valuables.

After serving fourteen years in prison, Ms. Rayburn submitted a Clemency Application to Oregon Governor Kate Brown's office petitioning for an early release. In the petition, she argued that she accepts responsibility and wants to do better with her life and that she wasn't even in the house when Mr. Rost was murdered. However, the DA disputes that and told one reporter that the petitioner changed the facts of the case. In his own letter to Governor Brown, D.A. Berry states, "To portray herself as she does in a clemency application as, "Well I was kind of there and then I went outside whenever everything happened" is just a lie."

Well that governor is a total piece of shit. She made the statements that she believes that granting clemency is an extraordinary act that should be reserved for individuals who have made incredible changes and who are dedicated to making their communities better. So, I guess this bitch will now stop humiliating and killing people if she is released?

As I understand it, Mr. Rosts' daughters hope the governor takes their family into consideration. The one daughter says, "If Ms. Rayburn gets released from jail it's not like our dad is going to show up at our door and it's all over with," said Olsen. "He's gone forever, he's not here to be a grandfather to our kids, he wasn't here to walk me down the aisle, he's not here to call with exciting news. We don't get any of those things back." Ms. Olson went on to say, "The Lewis and Clark report is all based on opinion but no facts from the case."

Both killers, Mr. Smith and Ms. Rayburn were both sentenced to 25 years to life with an automatic clemency hearing after serving fifteen years.

The aforementioned petition appears to have been the work of a group of students at the Criminal Justice Reform Clinic at Lewis and Clark Law School in Portland. They sent a 112-page letter to the governor describing Rayburn's troubled childhood and alleged attempts to improve her life behind bars and helped her file an April 2021 application for executive clemency. It just so happens that the good old governor Brown, also attended Lewis and Clark law school.

Part of the student's clemency application stated, "Ms. Rayburn is polite and soft spoken, she likes to see the positive in life and is grateful for the program she has participated in while incarcerated to work on herself and do good in the Coffee Creek Correctional Facility. She accepts responsibility for her actions that led to her incarceration and wants to change to do better with her life outside of prison."

That is one hell of a reach from Ms. Rayburns statements given to police detectives at the time of her arrest. She told detectives, "I fucking did it, and I fucking killed him," She continued with, "I had to kill Rost so he couldn't identify me because I have kids!"

What was such a sweet mommy of three darling babies doing out at 1:30 am and high on meth?

It's no secret that Gov. Brown is a flaming liberal that blames society for people's many life's ills. She is, of course, a leading warrior in the movement to defund police.

## Chapter 23
## *CHARITY CASH COW SCAMS*

Now let's turn our attention much closer to home. We will now visit Saint Anthony, Minnesota as a matter of fact. Saint Anthony is 148.4 driving miles from Duluth. Saint Anthony is a small bedroom community with a land mass of only 2.37 square miles with a population of approx 9,030 people. Two counties run through that tiny city. The city is four miles from the heart of downtown Minneapolis.

St. Anthony's largest money producing industry is a charitable group named, "Feeding Our Future." They have a gorgeous website adorned with photos of healthy foods and uplifting explanations how nonprofits help to feed Minnesota's hungry children and seniors. All through their website, the group slips in multiple requests for donations, telling the viewers how every little bit counts towards paving the path for a better tomorrow. The trouble is that, "Feeding Our Future" does not feed starving children or seniors. These fuck-rats are only feeding their bankrolls to the tune of $197,000,000 to support their personal luxury lifestyles, rather than putting food on the tables of the under privileged. According to the FBI, tens of millions of federal dollars meant for, after school and adult day care programs funded the Saint Anthony based nonprofit which instead, used the donations to buy 14 properties, numerous vehicles, high end travel and expensive goods.

FBI agent Travis Wilmer stated in an affidavit: "The companies and their owners receive tens of millions of dollars in federal funds for use in providing nutritious meals to underprivileged children and adults. Almost none of this money was used to feed children or seniors; instead, the participants in this scheme misappropriated the money and used it to purchase real estate, cars, and many other luxury items.

The website of this group's mission statement is; "We are driven by a single goal: making participation in the USDA child and adult care food program safe and easy for community partners. We ensure programs are easily able to receive funding to purchase nutritious meals."

The FBI thinks, "Feeding Our Future" whose reimbursements for the food program grew from $3.5 million in 2019 and 2020 and leapt to $197.9 million last year (2021) FOF worked with food distributors to file false claims for huge amounts of food that was never delivered to needy clients."

I'm sure no one will be shocked that, "Feeding Our Future" (FOF) went on the offensive and called in a pre-paid marker from Judge John Guthmann of Ramsey County District Court ($197 million bucks can easily buy a Judge or two) and sued the Minnesota Department of Education (MDE). Of course, the bought and paid for Judge Guthmann ruled and ordered that MDE pay FOF $35,750 in damages and their attorneys fees of $11,750 for failing to follow through on an earlier agreement, finding the MDE in contempt of court. This slimeball puke Judge, went on to write that because the MDE failed to obey his orders to act on pending applications could cause "irreparable harm and accompanying collateral consequences to the children it serves."

You folks still believe in the righteousness of jurisprudence?

I personally would rather tell my grandma that I was a piano player in a whorehouse before I'd admit to being a lawyer. You should find this rather rich. The very moment that the Judge's ruling came out in favor of the FOF, the FOF Director, Aimee Bock made a statement that read;
"During this time of high need, the Minnesota Department of Education failed to process applications as required by law. MDE not only violated federal regulations and also violated a previous court order even after being found in contempt of court, The MDE continued to take the position that it is above the law and the children in Minnesota do not deserve access to precious meals and snacks."

The lovely Miss Bock has asserted that the group hasn't participated in any illegal or money laundering schemes.

Can anyone in this room tell me why a District Court Judge would take on and damage the credibility of the State of Minnesota Department of Education and the FBI in this matter? It clearly is his lame and dangerous attempt to silence them before he is found out. This prick needs to be looked at, charged, prosecuted and do some serious, quality prison time.

Before the FBI investigations findings and criminal charges of corruption and bribery are leveled and goes public, I suggest you all take a highly accelerated piano playing class to avoid disappointing your grandmother's!

No charges have been filed so far as of January of 2022. The FBI claims the conspirators have stolen millions of dollars of federal funds and the scheme is ongoing. Minnesota Republican state senator Roger Chamberlain called the alleged massive fraud outrageous. "It's simply outrageous that nearly $200 million dollars of money provided to feed children and seniors in need, was abused in this way. It's imperative that government agencies ensure every dollar is going to the programs with robust track records, so we could know that not a single dime is wasted."

I think you'll love this, a federal government decision in 2020 paved the way for the fraud on the United States Department of Agriculture eased its rules to allow restaurants and other places to distribute food, including multi-day meals consumed offsite, mainly because adult day care and in person teaching at schools have been shut down to mitigate covid-19. Low-income families are supported through meal programs with these institutions and changes had to be made to continue feeding the needy.

    The Minnesota Department of Education, which reimburses local organizations with federal funding, began examining the FOF because suppliers reported the nonprofit to the USDA office of the inspector general in October of 2020 and tried to stop payments because FOF couldn't explain the drastic increase in meals served. At some point the FBI did an investigation and seized a great deal of records. One of their findings was that an unnamed business partner used a $386,000 cashier's check to buy a four-unit apartment building in South Minneapolis. The documents state that $200,000 of that amount was traceable to the fraud and money laundering scheme involving the FOF. Attorney General Keith Eliason said he's investigating FOF for alleged violations of state nonprofit law and filed a petition in Dakota County District Court for a court-supervised dissolution of the group. Acting on the FBI investigation, the US attorney's office listed 14 properties, 12 in Minnesota and two in Kentucky, that are connected to the alleged fraud.

    On January 20th more than 200 law enforcement personnel searched more than a dozen Twin Cities sites linked to the probe. No arrests were made at the time. The F.B.I. said several FOF employees and multiple business owners, operated shell companies to conceal the stolen funds.

Afterward, MDE moved to terminate the contract and issued an order to stop payment to the organization, effectively freezing its funds. One official ensnared in the investigation was Abdi Nur Salah, who had been a senior policy aide in the office of Minneapolis Mayor Jacob Frey before being fired when the alleged fraud became public.

If the fraud goes deep into the mayor's office, how much deeper does it go in the other state offices or even the federal offices? Yeah, this shit needs to be looked at.

Just like those assholes that fast talk commercials always say; "But wait... there's more!"

There is more, but after lunch, see you all back here at 1:15. Before you leave this room you get to be addressed by our top security director. If any of you break any of her rules or try to push the envelope just a tiny fucking bit, you will be escorted off the property. Your employer will have a courier deliver your final paycheck and personal items from your office. *Capeesh?*

I knew it was time to help Heather break out of her Covid bubble. Neither of us have been sick or did we take the jab. We have not been out anywhere in public for the last two-plus years during the covid situation. It was time, I think we all could use a change of scenery after being locked down for the last five days. I asked our drivers to take us to Grandma's Saloon and Deli, up on the hill. It's time for a, 'Steak Cheese French' and to see a smile back on her lovely youthful face. She was hesitant at first but I assured her that because we have yet to be found out as to our project, that we are relatively safe. "Besides baby, we got some bad ass guns with us, not to mention our own. Lunch was quite enjoyable. There was some good-hearted ribbing and banter back-and-forth but you could also cut the air with a knife. We intentionally returned back to the hotel before one o'clock because I wanted to have a private conversation with both our security team and all of our principals, minus the law firm people. I had an idea of a strategy for when they returned but I wanted to run it by the Roberts group first.

Amanda sat there and looked at me like I'd lost my mind and perhaps I have. When the law firm team came back into the room, I smiled at each of them and stated that I hope they enjoyed their lunch and this would be a rather brief afternoon session, brief but not easy.

Me: Here is what I'd like you all to do. I want you to each and individually write a letter of discharge for a person in your law firm who is underperforming their assigned duties. As a matter of fact, their work is so sloppy along with their aggressively foolish and cruel demeanor to both staff and clients, that they have become a dangerous financial and image liability. That person's name is David J. Brown. Remember that you are attorneys and that person has worked in your firm who's also an attorney.

Nobody that works for this company of yours is stupid, so you've got to make this thing iron clad and bulletproof so the company can't be taken to court and that none of you can be held financially responsible, in fact you are betting your homes, your wealth and your family's futures! You are to work in silence, there will be no collaboration of any kind. When you are done you will turn in your, "Unsatisfactory Employee" discharge letter to Phil. I'm going for a nap; you have 90 minutes. Y'all best get to writing.

    There were suddenly several deer standing in the middle of the road, staring at the headlights of a speeding vehicle while sitting in that room, along with a couple of sheepish grins and one with a wolfish, teeth mashing snarl. You could almost read their minds.

## *Chapter 24*
# *THE IMMEASURABLE DEPTHS*

Heather giggled in the elevator, all the way up to our suite with her saying, "I'm sure glad that you love me. The mind-fuck that you just threw on those poor people was sweet poetry. That, "Piano player in a whorehouse" statement was signaturely you. You are a hard but lovely man Mr. Brown!"

I looked at our six-security people that were riding in the elevator with us as I said, "Ladies and Gentleman, you may now laugh." They did laugh, they laughed like college kids after an hour of playing beer pong.

Although our nap was brief, it was quite refreshing. We rode down the elevator with the same security team that rode up with us, there were still a few snickers and giggles with smiling eyes. Myself and Heather included.

As we entered the Mariner Room everyone was seated. Val stood up and raised both arms like a choir director would do and everyone stood and started to applaud and shouted out a few cat calls here and there.

Me:  OK Princess, what's this shit all about?

Val:  You effectively showed us how to lose our jobs in less than 90 minutes. You're right David, Mr. Rick Warren, is a Baptist Pastor and author who wrote a quote that reads, "A lie doesn't become the truth, wrong doesn't become right, and evil doesn't become good, just because it's accepted by a majority."

You have taught us that, "You can't fight what's right and you can't bend the truth. At some point those untruths will bend you." That was a brilliant life lesson that none of us will ever forget. Where do we go from here?

Me:   Anyone remember those cheesy "but wait…there's more" commercials? Oh, there is more all right, we're not ready to jump into the meat of it all quite yet. Tomorrow morning, I am going to broaden your horizons even further. However, I think we need to catch our collective breaths. We will now go to an early dinner, unless some of you have a piano lesson scheduled.

Phil:   You are one slick devil. Some of my people didn't like you this morning. Now they are all wishing that you were their law professor. I am personally convinced that you could take the Detroit Lions or the Cleveland Browns (worst teams in the NFL) to the fucking Super Bowl! You say that you have no education…no education my ass! I gotta go with Father Martin's observations, "You have suffered well."

## Chapter 25
# GET WOKE - GET BROKE

Heather and I slept well. We thoroughly enjoyed our dinner guests and our meals.

Heather:   Now my love, that you showed your powers of teaching, what is your next act? It will be tough to follow yesterday's performance.

Me:   Well babes, I'm thinking that more than a few of our associates are entertaining that very question as you have. Hopefully a few missed a bit of sleep last night. The yawning and tired looking ones will also show us that they are the ones with the truest passion for honesty and right living. Remember dear heart, that if someone claims to be what they are not, they will involuntarily tattle on themselves without saying a word. Watch the head movements and the eyes. Fibbers can't help not getting caught.

We enjoyed a lite breakfast with the entire Roberts clan, along with Woody and Mattie.

Me:   Don't you Robert's people have a multi-huge fuckin conglomerate operation to oversee? You cat's still slumming it? What gives?

Paul:   We are here to observe the master.

Me:   Cute sport, have I passed muster?

Paul:   I guess we will see the grand finale by 10:00 am? You still haven't declared yourself as to whether you're with us.

Me:   You all may want to hold back on your invitation until after 10:00 am. No professional baseball pitcher can survive with just throwing a fastball. Wait until you see my sidearm sinking curveball!

I intentionally did not include Val or her people, along with my newspaper pals and my doorman friend Tim to breakfast. If they were a part of everything that is going on they may become mentally lazy. I want them hungry for more, I want them thinking.

I felt a bit silly having an entourage of security escort me to the Mariner Room.

Me:   Good morning, everyone, I trust you are all rested and ready to work this fine morning. We are going to get right to it. In the next three hours we are going to finish this up and I'll turn this project over to you once I tell you what this project is truly about. Peter, I need you to join me at the center section of the grease boards please. Peter, I need your lovely handwriting on board #3. Please write these three sentences and number them please. I want them centered from top to bottom and side to side. Like the last two panels you did yesterday, none of these boards are to be wiped clean.

I hope you thanked your mom for me last night. Please write these three lines.

## Number one: "Rocks are hard."
## Number two: "Water is wet."
## Number three: "People lie."

So, we're just going to focus on why people lie. I think the rocks and the water pretty much explain themselves. Who are the biggest liars? Well, they're normally men, they're normally white and normally straight. So why do I highlight this group? Simple, they are the biggest liars. The number one reason that any of us lie is to protect ourselves, the number two reason we lie is to protect others. Oftentimes the people we try to protect are people we don't even know. So why would we lie? Well, that's pretty simple. We lie for acceptance. We like to become a part of something that we're not currently a part of and oftentimes we lie about being a part of that same something that we're not a part of. Please follow closely, stay with me on this.

Let's start with our country's gay population. The percentage of gay people in the United States comes out to a little over 7% according to my pals at Google. Yet we have gay pride month, we have gay pride parades, gay pride marches, gay pride concerts, we have gay pride almost everything. So why this national and international celebration for less than 7% of our population? Simple, non-gay people need to feel righteous and valued. Yes, some are family members or friends of gays that want to show their support. Granted, I have never attended a gay-pride event but have seen them on television. I dare say that the gay events have a crowd in attendance far greater than 7% of the population. I don't know who set the power curve in the minority groups but if you own a business you don't want to cross them.

We don't have a month-long celebration for veterans. We don't have a month-long celebration for first responders or a month-long celebration for white or straight people.

Let's move on to our country's black population. We have a national holiday for Martin Luther King, we have black history month, we have a number of black television networks, we have black music and acting awards, we have the NAACP, the BLM, the ANTIFA and a number of exclusive black private colleges. We have all kinds of spokespersons for people of color, what do we have for white people? Oh, that's right, we don't have anything, thank you. White males don't fall under the protection of the, "Equal Opportunity Laws."

So, the question that demands an answer is; is racism systemic or is it created and if so, by who? Who by color groups are the most racist? Who are the most bigoted? Is it the white population? Is it the people of color? My answer doesn't matter and neither does yours, especially if you're a white male. I have four separate things to present this morning before I release the beast and let her feed.

Let's look at the BLACK LIVES MATTER (BLM) movement. Remember that we are fighting our nation's greatest foe, corruption. Corruption is the greatest threat to the free world. BLM has proven that a supposed movement to advance black people is actually an organized crime syndicate, who does not serve the black masses, they only serve the few top tier. We are talking about billions of dollars! BLM is nothing more than a shakedown operation that is typically directed at all levels of businesses. There are constant articles about BLM using the funds raised for executives' personal use which is a simple microcosm of an international mob. The controversy surrounding BLM's finances pivots around the CEO and co-founder, Patrisse Cullors, who suddenly amassed a rather impressive financial and real estate portfolio. Ms. Cullors stepped down as CEO after her financial holdings came to light along with her four real estate properties valued at $3.2 million.

The crown jewel of her properties is a custom ranch property in rural Georgia that has a private airplane runway. There is over $60 million dollars missing (or more) according to the IRS.

Ms. Cullors is also involved with a number of other social justice groups along with her husband, Janaya Khan. A few of the groups they led were, "Dignity and Power Now", "JusticeLA" and "Justice Teams Network." The feds are also investigating a series of red flags in those groups.

When the federal government started multiple investigations of BLM finances, Ms. Cullors reportedly appointed two active, senior directors to take over management of the funds following her resignation, as she slithered away from BLM in hopes of dodging prosecution. Both of the recently appointed directors quietly announced that they never took the jobs they were appointed to because of disagreements with the BLM finances and movement. They even stated they don't know who leads the nation's most influential social justice organization. Washington D.C. ordered BLM to immediately cease its fundraising activities and were quickly joined by New Jersey, North Carolina, Maryland and Virginia, who all banned the group from raising money. Even Amazon has suspended BLM from using their charity platforms. Now this is quite interesting, more concerns were raised this past week when BLM sent a message to supporters asking for financial support for Supreme Court nominee, Catanji Brown Jackson. The message includes a button to donate to the charity to support the judge's confirmation. This would seem to be a violation of IRS rules which mandate that nonprofits are supposed to be non-political. Once you press their donate button, you're directed to a Black Lives Matter group's affiliated Political Action Committee. The Western journal reports that the BLM PAC is preparing for the most critical mid-term election yet, every single election race is an opportunity to build greater black political power. The fundraising page linked to the messenger site said, "If you are ready to continue the electoral fight for Black Lives Matter, please chip into our efforts to start building for the 2022 midterms."

So, Joe Biden has openly stated that he 'WILL' seat a black female on the Supreme Court. What is this bullshit? We don't have any white male or female candidates for the Supreme Court? Doesn't this scream racism in and of itself? This current administration is the epitome of organized crime. Bribery, collusion, deceit, and lying are the hallmarks of the Democratic party.

The "National Legal and Policy Center" noted that the appeal for political funds appears to be a clear violation of IRS rules prohibiting charities from soliciting contributions to a political action committee. BLM came over the top with a power shot that now includes the gay and transgendered community. This bullshit just never seems to stop. Check this out, this is from, "Fireside Campaigns" which again is just another cash loaded, heavily secured closet door.

A recent email sent by Brad Bauman, the CEO and managing partner of "Fireside Campaigns" claimed that they (not he) inadvertently included a fundraising link to a non-fundraising email. "We take full responsibility for this error."

Bullshit, he got caught and as all cowards do, he blamed, "They!"

Our friend's at "Charity Watch" made the statement that the Black Lives Matter foundation presents a conundrum because much of what they claim to do with their funds cannot be verified."

Well, no shit! Here's an example and it's, '20 impact report'. BLMGNF States that it has committed funds to thirty local organizations and BLM chapters, for approximately $21.7 million dollars. There are currently no records of distribution of those funds however.

A Boston couple who are Black Lives Matter paid activists, are facing federal fraud charges and conspiracy charges after allegedly using a nonprofit they founded to scam at least $185,000 from BLM donations. Ms. Monica Cannon-Grant and her husband Clark Grant, allegedly used money from their nonprofit, "Violence in Boston" to pay for their rent, shopping sprees, hotels, car rentals, auto repairs, meal deliveries and a summer vacation trip to Maryland. They are currently facing an eighteen-count indictment along with two counts of wire fraud conspiracy, one count of conspiracy, 13 counts of wire fraud and 1 count of making false statements to a mortgage-lending business. The husband was also charged with one count of mail fraud. They were arrested a few weeks back; both were released without bail. She'll be allowed to continue working at the nonprofit twice a week but cannot handle the group's finances. This gets even better, in October the husband was arrested by the FBI, charging him with lying on a mortgage statement and collecting pandemic unemployment benefits illegally. The couple first founded "Violence in Boston" in 2017 with a mission statement that reads; "To improve the quality of life and life outcomes of individuals from underserved communities and reduce the prevalence of violence and the impact associated trauma in social injustices through advocacy and direct services." According to their website, Mrs. Grant was later named, "Best Social Justice Advocate" by Boston Magazine and was one of the 'Boston Globes' "Bostonians of The Year!" She is a prominent Black Lives Matter leader in the city according to Fox News.

    This even gets better, in 2019 The Grant crew used a $6,000 Grant from Suffolk County District Attorney's office which they used for a three-day violence prevention retreat in Philadelphia. The next year they collected donations of up to $50,000 per month. The couple withdrew some of the money in cash from ATMs or transferred the donations to their private investment accounts at the Robinhood and E*TRADE websites according to the indictments. Mrs. Grant and her husband also illegally collected $100,000 in federal pandemic related unemployment benefits. The pair collected state unemployment benefits while Cannon-Grant allegedly earned more than $27,000 in consulting fees for working with a media company on its diversity equality and inclusion training. She took home $2,788 weekly from their other group, "Violence in Boston." Her husband, Clark Grant, was also employed full time with a commuter service company. That's right, they collected all these funds and yet pulled in unemployment.

    Just three days ago, the 'Daily Reporter' broke the story that Ms. Cullors was using BLM funds to purchase a mansion in California. An investigative reporter from the 'New York Magazine' Mr. Sean Campbell, reported that Ms. Patrisse Cullors bought a mansion in Los Angeles for the tidy sum of Six Million Dollars! Ms. Cullors immediately went on the defense calling the news reports and Mr. Campbell by name as, "racist and sexist" attack against her and BLM.

Well, that is becoming an all too often played tune when thieves get caught. Of course, today's dirty players have changed the phrase from theft to 'misappropriation of funds'. This brings us back to the supposed, "Servers", screwing over the "Underserved."

For me personally, I have withdrawn my life-long support of The Salvation Army when they announced that they have become WOKE. I won't support any charity for any cause ever again. I will only spend my money on putting out bird houses and feeding stations for the birds during the winter months.

You must know that there are dozens and dozens if not hundreds of people involved in all this scamming. It just boggles my mind and personally, it greatly sickens me.

## Chapter 26
# NO END IN SIGHT

BLM uses intimidation and fear to pressure major corporations to donate to their cause. They obviously learned that from the Mafia and much like the Mafia, BLM uses threats to get what they want. The threats run the gamut from negative press to ruining reputations to physical harm to arson and to death, but not just for the big corporation executives but their entire families. They operate without boundaries or penalties. The top BLM leaders use the threat of exposure even with our nation's leading politicians. Anyone remember seeing the entire House of Representatives along with the house speaker and president Biden and his rag-doll, giggling VP kneeling in the United States Capitol Rotunda with their fist's raised in salute of solidarity with black power? Anyone remember during the democratic debates when Camilla Harris called Joe Biden a "Sexist and Racist"?

The Rotunda of the Capitol building is supposed to symbolize the physical heart of our nation. Are you fucking kidding me? They used the heart of our nation to kneel in solidarity with killers, rapists, thugs, thieves and gangsters? That's how fucked up this country is and that's how fucked up the democrat leadership is. If any private business doesn't fall in line to their demands they are boycotted and picketed. Of course, the pickets block entry to the business and will assault anyone that insists on any attempts to enter into the business. Delivery agencies are turned away as well as mail service. The picketers will block all access to non-political, non-corporate types that don't fall in line, and are called bad names in the media. Social media is full of name calling by people that claim to be enlightened but are complete strangers. When a white Democrat liberal realizes they are losing any argument they call you racist even in non-racial conversations. The liberal democrats have transitioned to be nothing more than Marxist thugs, while being led like Lemmings by the socialist regime of fear mongers. You had to have watched at least some of the national sponsored marches and riots on television. Anyone take notice of the majority of the mostly peaceful protesters being fueled by white people? There were plenty of news reporters who shot footage of beatings and lootings. What was the color of the overwhelming majority of the looters who were supposedly fighting for social justice? The four major targets of the looters were, big box stores, liquor stores, jewelry stores and of course, running shoe stores. How in the holy fuck does stealing flat screen Tv's, expensive liquor and cigarettes, gold and diamonds and armfuls stacked high with high dollar sneakers, improve their long-term goals to achieve social justice for all? These losers are just low-life hood rats, they're fucking criminals whose only agenda is their own personal greed. Better yet, how in the fuck is this overlooked by law enforcement and accepted as a new normal? People are tearing down historical monuments all over the nation without any fear of repercussions. How does destroying historical markers make way for their New World Order agenda? What time will the book burnings start? Will they be televised? Local college students who have zero real life experience are currently removing any books that make the slightest reference to offend the woke and college administration gives their full support. News networks no longer report the news, they only give you their slant on the news and avoid stories that don't jell with their twisted agendas.

Many of those supposed reporters create the news rather than report the news as it is. It seems that it is just more creative bullshit to promote the reporters' careers and the networks ratings. Which is no different than the failing 'Oscar Awards' earlier this week. I don't even think Will Smith actually made contact with Chris Rock. If he did, why wasn't he arrested? Once again there are different rules for the minority population as well as the money power people. As a side note; the word minority will apply to the white population in just a few short few years with our borders flung wide open. Obama's goals have always been to turn the United States into a 'Brown' non-white population. If any of you sitting here don't think Obama and the Clintons still run the show, you have not been paying attention.

So, let's move on to our next group of lovely American citizens. These are the good folks of Antifa. Supposedly they are a decentralized, leaderless movement composed of loose collections of groups and networks. Antifa is nothing more than a fringe group of persistent assholes that try to distort the public perception of their movement. What the fuck kind of movement burns down people's buildings and assaults people, men women and even children. Antifa has professed their sole purpose is, "To vigorously oppose fascism while some extreme actors who claim to be affiliated with Antifa do engage in violence or vandalism at rallies and events, this is not the norm." However according of course to Antifa, they claim that they're there to weed out the fascists including the white supremacist and other extremists as well as conservatives or supporters of former President Trump. I'm not going to go any further with that bullshit. They're fucking losers that are paid to disrupt the supposed, "mostly peaceful protest."

So, to wrap this up and get busy with what's in front of us, there are two more items that are not only close to home but are at the doorstep of our own homes.

Duluth's "Hills" is a treatment center for disturbed children and their families (which is formerly known as Woodland Hills), made a panic announcement last year that they were going to close its doors in two weeks. This report came from Fox 21 local news, dateline June 15th 2021 Duluth Minnesota. "A local Duluth youth treatment center that has helped children and families for 112 years must close its doors. The Hill Center has served as a juvenile residential treatment facility for over 100 years but in less than a month they must shut down their operations permanently, on July 2nd."

    The Hills group opened a mental health facility in East Bethel, Minnesota in April of 2020 and had to close it last week, which was more bad news for their Duluth facility.

    The Hills leadership reports that funding issues and impacts from COVID as to what is causing these operations to come to a heartbreaking close. "The state of Minnesota is losing 110 beds for kids with mental health issues and behavioral problems and there is such a tremendous need for these services that to have to close down because of financial issues it's very disheartening," Leslie Chaplin the president and CEO of the Hill's said.

    Beside the impact from COVID, funding issues were a huge obstacle, and a partnership could have been the answer to all of their problems, "We could have done a lot to save things here, it needed true partnership from the, State Department of Human Services and that simply has not been there, there has been no partnership at all!" Chaplin said, "Even though the residential help will no longer be available for some programs, the Hills will remain open as the Neighborhood Youth Services free after school program, and various day treatment sites open around the county.

There are some resources available so that families will still be able to access on a prevention basis, this will be a loss but there are still community services available that will be able to support children and families," Paula Stocke, the Deputy Director for Public Health & Human Services, said:

"The Hill's hopes to leave behind a legacy of success, as they have helped so many members of the community to a better place. Plans for employee relocation for their nearly 100 employees in Duluth are still in the works."

Well, isn't that fuckin swell! The director and CEO of the Hills, is concerned about the financial stability of their laid-off nearly 100 workers but not the 110 residential client children! There is some kind of fuckery going on and we are going to find it. Oh, and wait even this gets better, stand by one.

Northwood children's services again, located in Duluth, is Minnesota's oldest child caring agency, has stepped in to fill the critical gap in day treatment for forty young people that was caused by last week's closing of, "The Hills Youth and Family Services" in Duluth. While a spokesman for Northwood Children's Services President and CEO, Richard Wolleat said they wanted to step in and help out.

But here is what grinds my gears, there was no mention of the one-hundred and ten deeply troubled children who lived there. Where did those children go to live?
Wolleat Went on to say, "The children we treat will see that short time off as a mini-break, and their families are enthusiastic about having us now lead the day treatment program.

Again, no mention of the 110 residential kids who were what, just tossed to the four winds? Are you fucking kidding me? These court ordered, deeply troubled and oftentimes violent children simply vanished while the administration tries to gather their own shit together? In the last few months of operation of the 'Hill', there have been several assaults on staff and client-on-client fights, where police from multiple police agencies had to be called in to quell the all but riotous conditions.
Hopefully there's no graft or corruption involved in this story. I'll be extremely disappointed if that's the case but then again, here you have social workers managing businesses and damn little social work is taking place. You can clearly place a lot of the 'Hills' financial failures on the social workers backs because of their poor management skills. Like all other failed social service programs, they blame the government and take no responsibility for their personal and professional failures.

Peter, please meet me at board # 4.

Me:   Peter, please write in four-inch-high letters, the title that reads,
        "Why failure is acceptable."
Below that please write this standard phrase that has a two-line, earth-shattering statement;

    "Either you are part of the solution...OR...you are part of the problem!"

Thank you, Peter, please take your seat.

    Failure comes from egos with people thinking they're more than they are, thinking they're smarter than they are and trying to convince others of the same. That is a true recipe for failure, overinflated egos bring catastrophic failures. Surely you must all remember the name of Sears and Roebuck company stores? Today they are in name only. They have fallen off the grid, no different than Montgomery Wards and K-mart. At one point they were each huge standalone corporations which were located in every mid-sized and larger cities in the entire United States! And now they are all gone. Jesus Christ, back in the forties and fifties Sears retail stores sold prefab homes! Factory built homes! Those homes today are but a memory of the years gone by.

    Now Val, please act as our scribe in this exercise. Class, I want your input, I want only one-word entries.

Peter, please join me in the front of the room. I would like you to use these four boards as one for the title. Please write, "A snapshot of a true American." across the top four inches of these four boards. Now write these four capitalized words as the headers on each of the four boards and center them please.

Board #1    DISCIPLINE
Board #2    SACRIFICE
Board #3    HUMILITY
Board #4    LOYALTY

    Val, please write these same four words, on four separate sheets of paper so we don't miss anything as people are calling out their words while Peter is writing.
    Class, I want you as a group to come up with the synonyms of these four words.
These words should define what a true American is or should be. I'm sure or at least I am hopeful that most all of you have heard about, "The Greatest Generation?"
    Allow me to once again reference my swell pals at Google.

"The Greatest Generation" is the term used to describe those Americans who grew up during the 'Great Depression' and fought in World War I and II and whose labor helped win it. The term, 'The

Greatest Generation' is thought to have been coined by former NBC Nightly News anchor and author, Tom Brokaw and his book by that same name.

Sixteen million Americans died in World War II. That is twice the entire population of New York City! I can't and I doubt very much if any of you can put that into some kind of perspective. Sixteen million Americans gave their lives so we are free to sit here as we are today. Sixteen million total strangers died on foreign soil so we could have the life that we live today. Young men and women left high school, left their jobs, left their families to fight the wars a half a world away. Sixteen million of those people did not return home. The numbers of wounded and disabled are crushing! It just boggles my mind and it should yours as well.

A gentleman by the name of John Warner wrote an article that was published in, "Trend Magazine." In 2018. Mr. John Warner wrote the, 'all but perfect' article on, 'The Greatest Generation' in my opinion. This article is worthy of quoting.

From Mr. John Warner: "Like many of my contemporaries, I left high school straight for the military. It was during World War II, late in 1944. There was optimism about a positive outcome, but the Battle of the Bulge had just been fought—a setback that left America wondering how long the war could go on in Europe and in the Pacific.

Despite this, we went forward with a strong, continuing sense of duty and of devotion to our nation, to the men and women fighting, and to the folks back home who were sacrificing for the war effort with food and gas rationing.

"The Greatest Generation", Tom Brokaw's fine book, tells an accurate story. His words: "These men and women came of age in the Great Depression, when economic despair hovered over the land like a plague. They had watched their parents lose their businesses, their farms, their jobs, their hopes. They had learned to accept a future that played out one day at a time. Then just as there was a glimmer of economic recovery, war exploded across Europe and Asia...they gave up their place on assembly lines in Detroit and in the ranks of Wall Street, they quit school or went from cap and gown directly into uniform."

Tom Brokaw's powerful statement is: "We must remember that we are more alike than different, that how we act toward one another is as important as anything else we aspire to do."

John Warner went on to write; "The lesson for my generation remains the same: Discipline, Responsibility, Humility, Loyalty.

Well gang, here comes the great takeaway for you guys. John Warner wasn't just somebody who served in the military and wrote an article for some nondescript publication. Mr. John William Warner III, just so happens to have been a five term U.S. Senator and the United States Secretary of The Navy! Now do I have your attention?

Senator Warner writes; "I remain a creature of the US senate but let me explain what I mean. When I began serving in 1979, 3/4 of my colleagues were military veterans. We had political disagreements and often fought on the senate floor which was our battlefield but at day's end we shared a drink, talked as friendly rivals and even friends and we found common cause solving problems and serving the American public. Our shared respect for each other largely flourished from military experience. We had learned to respect and to have confidence in the person serving with us, knowing that they're very lives depended on each other, that is a very strong bond! We all are capable of nurturing within ourselves the self-discipline, sense of responsibility and desire for humility and loyalty to one another that leads to finding a common good. I cannot help but think that all of us today have lived through the 2nd greatest economic crisis this nation has faced since I was a child and we continue to combat evil forces in this world that wish to kill and destroy and can shake us to our very roots. These times are shaping who we are today and the hardships and lessons from those events are not all of the different than they were nearly a century ago. I could only hope that we all learned from these times. That we learn that sacrifice can be good for us, that discipline is required of us, humility is necessary for us, and loyalty must guide us. We must always remember that we are more alike than different but how we act towards one another is as important as anything else we aspire to do. If we do, there is no reason why any generation could not be called, "The Greatest Generation!"

To me the greatest generation were the people willing to sacrifice and give of themselves and of their possessions for the greater good of all Americans. There were gasoline and food ration stamps issued to every American to keep people from hoarding, so everyone got what they needed.

The greatest generation came from World War I and World War II and The Korean War. Somewhere in the middle were the everyday common people who were not serving our country in uniform. The majority of non-uniform Americans served our country with all but heroic efforts. People reverted back to making their own soaps, growing and processing their own foods, all for the war effort so the foods would go to our troops. Women and their children would work on weekends (after working all week) on dairy and vegetable farms from sun-up to last light to earn a gallon of milk, a dozen eggs and hopefully a chicken or a pound of hamburger. People saved foil and made huge, huge balls of foil and balls of string and balls of rubber bands for the war effort. We were fighting as a nation, not as a military but as a nation for our freedom and the freedoms of others who are like minded and have the same desires. I suggest you ask your grandparents and if you're fortunate enough to still have them, ask your great grandparents. They most certainly will know! If not, crack a couple of books.

Before any of you break out in applause, slow down a bit. Yes, it was a joint effort of all Americans. Most women were homemakers pre-war. When the men went off to war there was a huge vacuum, it was the women that kept our nation and economy going. Many women went to work in the factories, many never had a job before but they knew they had to fill the positions that the men had to leave. Women worked in factories producing munitions, building ships, airplanes and heavy equipment. These hero women learned to do all the trades and they of course worked as nurses. I suggest you all Google, 'Rosie the Riveter'. Rosie was a government poster program, to encourage women to step into the traditional male roles. The poster was captioned, "We Can Do It! It showed a woman with a bandana tied around her hair; her denim long sleeved work shirt was rolled up to expose her flexing a rather large bicep. Make no mistake people, without our female civilian workers the outcome of those wars could have had a much, much different outcome.

Yes, women workers were every bit as necessary as men were in winning these wars, there can be no doubt about that, ever! What I found interesting was that, that very determined looking woman in the poster was wearing makeup! Can you imagine a woman holding a welding torch burning at 3,200 degrees with welding smoke lofting into her welding hood with her makeup running down her face? I have to guess that it was a subliminal message that was saying, "Ladies, regardless of your work assignments you are all, still beautiful women,"

I'm going for a break, when I return, I want to see just what you brainiacs came up with under each of the four topics. We are about to get down to the nut cuttin. Shitz about to get real kids and I hope you're all on board with it. You, young lady, come with me.

## Chapter 27
# NANCY PANTS

I reached my open palm out to Nancy. I nodded to Phil to come along with us. As always, I headed towards the restaurant for my craft of coffee and maybe a donut or two. I couldn't help but laugh a bit thinking that if anybody wanted to take me out that all they had to do was to wait in the restaurant when I went in for my Folgers. I escorted my two pals to the garden and intentionally sat where we were covered by the trees and bushes so no one could see where we were sitting. There's about to be a bit of a dressing down to take place and I wanted privacy with comfort at the same time. Luckily for me, our fur babies needed their mommy's attention this morning. They were reluctant to eat. I think they need a home fix. Dogs are no different than people. We do our best with our routine and draw our comfort from that routine. I enjoyed the questioning looks on Nancy's face, as I continued to sit quietly and look at her. I want to take her off balance. She needs to be in a neutral gear before any of this will make sense to her.

Me:  Well Babe, it's just us three fellas sitting here now. So, tell me, what are you actually about? And more importantly, what's wrong with you? I want to know about your greatest weakness. You spend a great deal of time posturing and speaking of your strengths and your accomplishments. Where have you failed? I want specifics, we all fuck up in our lives, you're no different, tell me about your greatest fuck ups? That's right babe, as in plural.

And honey just so you know, these next twenty minutes or so will decide your future, not just your future within this company but your future throughout your lifetime. Just a heads-up sweetheart, I already know some of your secrets so in case you haven't figured it out yet, I have people who have people who have other people. Lie to us and you are gone

I knew that I had to break her, if I continued to let her run wild, she would be lost to us. It's time I run her to ground, maybe even saddle break her. Of course, Nancy shifted in her chair several times, lowered her head, raised her head and looked left and right. It's as though she was trying to figure out an escape route but you can't run from your mind, you can't run from your belly and you can't ever run from your past. Your truths will follow you wherever you go. You can't close your door tight enough to keep your truths out, you may hide them for a time but not from yourself at least not for very long.

Me:   So, Nancy, you have been referred to (by your boss) how was that again Phil, "The She Devil from Hell?"

Yes baby, you've been vetted, you've been deeply vetted. I know about your entire family structure. I know of all of the blood-line players and their in-laws and I know that some of them didn't play at all fair with you. I also know of others in your crew that made foolish and costly decisions, both financially and legally. You hide your shame, not for what they did, but what you did due to family pressures to defend them. Because of your family, you were just one vote away from being disbarred. I have to wonder what kind of deal you swung to get that life and carrier saving vote. However, my lady, you have not moved off your perch of unwarranted self-rightness. You're far more guarded than you need to be, you're not posing for an artist who's trying to sculpt you from clay into a bronze statue that you believe is so greatly deserved. A part of you, (just a small part) tells me that you hope that I catch you, the major part of you tells me that you will either try to destroy me or yourself if your true truths are found out. I've been watching you sweetie and I'm of the thoughts that you actually do have a soul. Well-guarded, but you do have a soul, you say you can't lie to me and you can't lie to me because you can't lie to yourself, which tells me you have character and a person with character is a person with purpose. Tell me about the person with purpose.

Nancy: David no one's ever asked me these kinds of questions or made these kinds of statements in front of me. Part of me wants to fight you, part of me wants to surrender. I don't know which way to turn at the moment.

Me: Yeah, honey the fear of becoming vulnerable to others with them knowing your truths (which of course equals your weaknesses) is a huge risk but that risk is only in your mind. Nobody can hurt you unless you allow it. It's like going into a bad relationship knowing you're going to be abused. Who the fuck does that? I'll tell you who the fuck does that, people without purpose! So why are we sitting here now? You need to ask me that. I'm not going to tell you until you ask me why you're sitting here at this moment.

Nancy: David I don't know how to answer you. I've always been rigid and well controlled. That way there's no surprises. So, I try not to expect anything so I don't get disappointed and hurt. Yes, I have walls, I have walls that reach to the moon and back but it's how I feel safe.

Me: You're not willing to risk people getting to know you but people judge you and the results of that judging aren't very favorable for you. Why do you have to be a habitual bitch, you may ask? That's your armor, that's your protection! Jesus Christ woman, your boss here, bought you a fucking gun and had paid for your lessons to learn how to handle it and how to defend yourself! You're afraid of the fuckin boogie man? There's no such thing as a boogie man unless of course you're into the Keanu Reeves, 'John Wick' flicks. Now there's a fucking bogeyman right there, but he's not the actual boogie man, he's the guy that's going to hunt and kill the boogie man! You need to be more like John Wick. You need to go on a hunt and you need to hunt down and kill your boogie man, your boogie man of course are your unsubstantiated fears! *Capish?*

Well, here it is cutie-pie; none of us are children, so I'm not going to ask to poke each person's finger with a knife tip and do a mixer blood thing, like we are all blood brothers and sisters as some kids do. Nor are we going to do a pinky promise either, but I want you each to give me your words, your absolute words that this conversation will never be repeated anywhere with anyone, ever! I don't need you to nod your heads, I need you to boldly say the words, "I promise you David."

They both gave their promise as I poured another cup of coffee and took a couple bites of my donut. I sat looking at the two of them in silence.

Me: So, here's the truth, my truth. You are the only two that are going to hear it at this time, at least from me. I will make a full group announcement later but for now, you two are being told for a very specific reason.

Nancy honey, I think you got game, I think you have a deeper strength but it's not in your glaring looks, it's not sitting with your shoulders rolled back and your neck held high like you're trying to climb out of a turtle's shell. I believe you have a tremendous

strength of heart and that scares the holy hell from you. Well, we're going into your hell baby, and we're going to dig it out of you. Your hell is just your fear and nothing more. Fear is not real. Fear is an acronym that stands for;
False...Evidence...Appearing...Real. Trust your heart, trust your faith and your fear will dissipate like a harmless cloud in the sky.

Now, listen tight, here's the deal, I'm signing out of this project. I'm going to gather up my own life and celebrate my many blessings. You people however are just starting your journey and yes, I assure you, it will be the journey of your lifetime, a journey of millions of people's lifetime's because that's who you're going to serve, millions of people. Phil, you get to play grandpa to this lovely young doll over here. She will be your deeply loved and protected grandchild. You will give her encouragement; you will give her comfort and security. She will trust and know that she can always come to you.

Nancy, I'm putting you in charge of this entire operation. I want you to lead these people. I want you to gently nudge but not push them to win. I want you to support them but not to lord over them. You will need to garner their confidence and trust, just like you're getting from your Grandpa Phil sitting here. Can you dig it? Yeah, you get to play boss! Until I am ready to release this information, you are both to say nothing.

Phil, yes, you're right, your sweet, sweet little Val might be a bit overwhelmed by this, she doesn't have the fight that Nancy has, she also doesn't have the personal problems Nancy has, so that's a blessing.

I want to keep Val clean from all of this. Let's remember what her goals are. None of us can demand that she switches teams just because we have a need or a desire. We have to respect and honor her desires. I so much want her to sit on the Judge's bench. If ever you want to please me with a gift, I want a framed 18 by 24 painting of your lovely daughter Val, in a black robe sitting behind a bench with a gavel raised in her hand. That my friend will complete my heart.

So, Nancy, it's time that you commit. I made a big production out of Peter with his fine, fine cursive handwriting skills as he worked over the grease pencils on those boards. Those words, those writings are your purpose Sweetheart. Do not stray from our purpose, our purpose is our mission and from that we shall not waver!

Remember babe you're the coach now, you're not a player, you don't have to catch a ball to win the game, you have to help others to catch the ball to win the game. You need to learn the fine art of gentle massaging with your hands still in your pockets. That's right, if you want to win, you've got to pull people to your side, you've got to allow them to play their best game. What's the difference between you and me Nancy? That's quite simple, the people back in that room would march into hell with me. They would probably even fight to see who gets to go first, ahead of me. Be who you know you are and who you think you need to be, to champion your people, your people will become champions. You will all become champions.

Now I would like you two to go back to the conference room and relax. Believe it or not, I'm breaking out of this pop-stand. I'm going to go for a stroll outside. Rules apply to you, not to me, you see, I make the rules.

## Chapter 28
# GETTING FIRED

    I pretty much had a map worked out in my head of how I was going to give my glorified babysitters with big guns the slip. I was going to make a break for it. But rather than fuck with everyone's head and put them into a panic, I knew I had to play nice. I went up to the closest Bill as I said, "Walk with me."

    Me: Bill, I have not drawn a breath of fresh air for six days now. The only outside I see is thru reinforced bulletproof glass. I have not smelled the air, tasted the air, felt and not even seen the air! But it's time, I'm going to go outside now, I need some air therapy. You certainly may join me but I don't want a crowd. How about it pal, just you and me? If you can pull that off you are the top guy in my book.

Bill:   David, I think you are a class guy but you know I work for the Roberts family. I fully understand what you want but I can't in good conscience put you at risk by allowing you to go outside.

Me:   So, what now? I'm in fuckin custody? I carry a federal badge that could charge you all with kidnapping! Eat a dick! No sir, I'm going outside with or without you! You may join me, you can be either friend or foe but you God damn well better know, that I will fight you and I don't fight to a draw, I fight to win!

Bill:   Yeah, I get it pal and no, I don't want to fight you. I don't want you to get hurt, not by me but by the dangers that lurk all around us. How about if you give me ten minutes? We'll work up a plan but it will take a handful of agents to work it out. Please don't try to break out, can you agree with that? David, I have three kids all going into braces and one will be going off to college this summer. I can't lose my job. I need your word that you're not going to break out before we're ready. I smiled as I said "Yeah, I'll wait, I'm just being a selfish prick."

I held to my word and didn't try to make a break for any of the doors. I had to laugh when four of the team members escorted me out a backdoor that was in an alcove that's blocked on three sides with eight feet high concrete blocks for the hotel's dumpsters. The open access for the trash trucks was blocked by four of the SUVs. So here I'm standing outside, while trying to enjoy the fresh air with the smell of fresh trash and no sunlight. Now there's a fuckin bonus plan!

I couldn't help but start to laugh as my brain took me back to that ass wagon, Chris Christie, the New Jersey Governor. Do you remember back in 2017 on the 4th of July weekend when he closed all the beaches because the state didn't have the funding for police officers and life guards to patrol the beaches or to have the sanitation department to clean them? I remember seeing the overhead drone pictures of him as he sat in a lawn chair on the beach at the water's edge with his family and friends with miles of empty beach as far as the eye could see. Yeah, that's kind of what I was feeling like standing here right now. I almost asked for a lawn chair. I quickly thought better of it but I would have been funny as shit. Who knows maybe we could have an overhead picture taken of us like CNN did? What was so funny with Chris Christie was that he held a press conference to give his annual 4th of July message the following day of his beach visit. A reporter asked him, (actually confronted him) by asking him if he enjoyed the sunlight of the beach. Christie answered with a very curt, "I wasn't in the sun." Later that day when his press secretary was shown the overhead drone photograph, the press secretary commented, "Yeah well, he didn't get any sun because he was wearing a baseball cap!"

I guess that's how you do it, no different than that 'love child' of 'Chuckie' and 'Peppermint Patty', Ms. Jen Psaki, the press secretary for Joe Biden who has brought lying to an all-time high, she has set a benchmark that will never be repeated and of course her specialty is, "circling back!" Now that phony trash talker claims that she's going to retire from that position and become a news correspondent! Oh, that's got to be a fucking thrill for the laptop warriors.

I slightly heard something coming from the earpiece of one of the security agents closest to me. He walked over to open the door and out came Norbes with two fresh cups of coffee.

Me:  Hey lady, this is a secured area, you're not cleared to be in this area!

Norbs:  See this smile on my face Skippy? These people are my team members, on my payroll. At this moment, I've got more clearance than you'll ever have. I could have you tossed into one of those dumpsters with a snap of my fingers. Drink this coffee then we gotta go.

Me:  "We" gotta go? Who the fuck is "we" and where the fuck do "we" gotta go?

Norbs:  Well, you asked to breathe, Heather has informed me that you have not been doing AA meetings since our last outing, four months ago. I know it's been her who hasn't wanted you to be around other people with the Covid threat.

You're long past due and your attitude sucks, you need a fucking meeting! We're going to an AA meeting, now finish your coffee.

I know all the cities AA meeting locations and schedules. There are hundreds of meetings every week but there's no meeting at this time of day anywhere in the city. Well, we piled into the vehicles and of all places, they took me to my house. The front door was opened for us as we came up the stairs and there were several suits all around the property and inside the front door of my home. One of the Bills gestured that I go to the basement. Why the fuck am I going to the basement, are these fuckers going to whack me? Is this a reenactment of the movie, 'Goodfellas', where Joe Pesci thinks, he is going to get 'made' to be a full-time, 'Wise Guy' and takes a round in the back of the head? Yeah, that's cute, I don't think I'm gonna play that game.

    That was right up until I heard a familiar voice coming from the basement that said, "Hey fucker, we're down here." Yup, that was my pal David from my Monday night AA meetings. I went down into the basement and there were six of my bestest pals from that group, people I greatly respect with long term sobriety and know how to live life.

    I looked at Norbs and said, "Heather's going to beat your ass and eat your bloody liver. I can't be around these people." Norbs smiled and said, "It is Heather's idea, she is on her way and it's been cleared. All of these gentlemen were tested yesterday and again this morning, open your big book, sit down, shut up and listen!"

    I heard the front door open and in came Heather and Amanda. Heather grinned and said, "Surprise, surprise!" I said, "We'll talk later, thank you baby, yeah, you're right, I'm in dire need of a meeting.

However, my love, it looks to me like you've joined the other side. I remember back, not so very long ago, how we don't keep secrets from each other, you know how that works, it's worked for about ten years now. Maybe you should review that?"

Heather: Maybe you should clean up your attitude and get downstairs and close the door behind you!

Without question that meeting was needed more than I could even realize, it was great to see those guys again. I could feel my center returning, while I was sitting with them. You don't have to know somebody all that well to trust them. This whole AA thing is quite interesting. A group of strangers come together (who normally wouldn't mix) as a unit for the single purpose of learning to live alcohol free. Anonymity is the spiritual foundation of AA. For the most part, you don't know anyone's last name because of the anonymity thing. You don't know where they work, what their job is, you don't know where they live, you don't know what color their house is, all you know about them is from what they speak at a meeting and what kind of car they arrive and leave in. Over time, you learn about their heart and you learn about their commitment to live a better life while helping others along the way.

Amanda: David, when we get back to the hotel, mother and I want to sit with you in private.

Me: OK yeah, be sure to shave your legs please.

I got a swat on the back of the head from her. It kind of felt like I was being called to the principal's office. When the AA meeting was over and the fellows left, I took a stroll through the house. I went into the garage and something was telling me that something wasn't quite right. Everything in the garage was just as I had left it, other than one item. It took me a few minutes to zero in on it. That one item was my air tight, waterproof heavy gauge canister that I keep my gun cleaning solutions and oils in. It's all but impregnable. Someone had turned it with the handles facing away from the front.

I went upstairs and asked who was on house duty. Four Bills raised their hands. I asked, "Which one of you four were fucking with my shit in the garage? I got blank looks as I said, "Gentlemen, in the future, before you disturb something, take pictures before & after to make sure you put them back just the way you found them. My gun cleaning solutions and oils were turned to the left rather than dead on center. Again, who's been fucking with my shit?

Lead Bill: We all have David, that's all part of our security sweep. We have to know what is in every container in your garage and yes, we opened your bullet safe too.

Me: So, I suppose you slimy bastards went through my wife's underwear drawer, didn't you? As I started to laugh, then we all laughed. I shook their hands and thanked them for their many efforts to keep us safe.

## *Chapter 29*
# THE REWARDS of EXILE

Heather and I were allowed to sit on the love seat on the deck while we enjoyed the view of the bay of Lake Superior and a full cup of Folgers coffee and two cigarettes each. Patty came out on the deck and with the sweetest smile as she said, "Ok children, it's time to come inside and warm up."

We were back in a vehicle heading back down to the hotel in minutes. The hotel was about the last place I wanted to go right now but I get it. I don't like it, but I get it.

When we got back to the hotel Amanda took my hand as we walked to a different elevator and said, "We're going to mother's room. I'm sorry Heather but this has to be a private meeting. It won't take very long and then we'll have you come in as well. Come with me David.

As always, Jane met me with a warm embrace and a kiss on each cheek. She said, "Have a seat my friend, we need to speak. David, I'm pulling you off this project. It has nothing to do with you being capable, you are extremely capable, but I see how this has worn on you, I see the concern in your eyes, I can see the fatigue in your face and I can see the worry of Heather's entire being. You two have been through enough. You have a room full of Warriors downstairs that you've taken to a bootcamp like no other could in just six short days. They're ready to fight your war. All there is left for you to do is to give them the parameters of the war that they are about to fight. A true leader is one who trains their people to no longer need their leadership. That's you David, you gave them your all, but it's time for you and Heather to regain your personal lives. David, you have worn a uniform and badge of protection most of your life, you have laid in our nation's streets bleeding on more than one occasion, you have given enough. Using one of your favorite sentences my friend, "I am pulling your dance card" and yes, if you want me to say it, I'll say it, you're fired. Fired with the greatest of affections and the deepest of love."

My tears came quickly. Jane was right and I felt that same way but I was fearful of letting other people down. I know I'm not the total answer man, I'm just a guy with a passion for decency and honor and that's all I am. Other people have their own passions and yes, it's time I trust them. It's the hardest thing for me to do is to let go of something I feel so passionately about.

I got up from my chair and went over and sat on the couch between Amanda and Jane and put my arms around their shoulders, drew them close and we all had a good cry.

After a few minutes of eye dabbing and sniffling nose wipes, Amanda said, "Mother, I think it's time that we include Heather now." Jane made a call and simply said, "Please bring Heather to my suite and bring along the dogs too, would you? I need some doggy lovins time."

The entire family came in along with Heather and our three fur babies. You know it's sad to say, but I'm getting used to Heather's shocked look on her face and the way she rolls with it, every time. It tells me that I've got a true mate in my life.

Paul:   Heather, David, it's time we bring this project to full circle. David will be announcing his retirement from this project and you two will return to your normal lives. We fully knew that David had the ability to rally these people and you did a most excellent job, my friend. Your people are now well versed in knowing what's important in this project. In an hour we will all go downstairs and David will lay out the perimeters of the project. After that you two are free to leave as a matter of fact, you can even drive your own vehicle's home. Gregory, my boy, you're up.

Gregory:   Well guys, I'm certain that you both know about fear. You, David, have the best take and understanding of fear as anyone that any of us have ever met before. And now our friends, it is time for our truths. We have been a bit devious with you two.

We've actually been devious with everyone. Let me tell you why. No one, at any time, has been in any danger. We created that cloud of danger to force people to face their fears and embrace their true values. We wanted them to be off balance. So yes, this entire 'grave danger' thing has been a production to motivate your people downstairs. After we announce our true intentions they'll have no cause for any level of fear, they can also work without the pressure of what others may think.

     Me:   I've never been snookered like this in my entire life. That was brilliant you guys, but I expect nothing less of any of you. Congratulations!

     I am a bit miffed however with the idea that you felt you had to shock me like I don't already have that shit coursing through my veins.

     Amanda:   We knew that you would catch us at some point David. We had to put on the show. We had to convince the people in the conference room. We didn't and don't believe that anyone is going to be in physical harm, although there will be some name calling of course and finger pointing and people deflecting, but that's to be expected that's what politics is; "Take no blame, cast it upon others." We've sent your staff from the conference room home for the day. I think we all need to have a nice relaxing nap and start fresh in the morning. David this is still your show and you can lead it anyway you'd like but after tomorrow you need to walk away and we will all do the same. We are leaving behind our PR people and yes, a handful of security to help your team design their approaches, but how you lay it out, is entirely up to you.

Edna:   We will have dinner together tonight as a family. Because we are a family. We are a family of purpose and commitment. We will sit in on your final briefing but as soon as you're done tomorrow, we're going wheels up.

Me:   So, what's it like to operate with an unlimited budget? I can't believe you people used four airplanes, twelve specialty vehicles, flew people and a shit-ton of computers and electronics were transported, you sent your entire hotel staff home and paid them their regular wages, turned away hotel guests, relocated registered guests and paid your competition to lodge them. The cost factors for this escapade must go on forever. You sent your guests to other hotels and paid for their lodging, you closed down this entire operation, you shut down events in the ballroom, whether it be an anniversary celebration or a wedding or whatever the occasion, just for this operation? You did all this just to convince ten lawyers and Heather and I of the importance of your mission?

One of the old AA sayings that is used when a member falls off the wagon and goes back out drinking because they want to believe that they can't possibly be an alcoholic because they are just a social drinker that only on rare occasions, may have a drink or two too many. When somebody goes back out to try to see if they can become a social drinker again, we say that they are out on a "Convincer."

Well, this was a convincer of the most epic of proportions! I applaud you all and I understand, yes Heather and I had to feel it too. It's the only way you could sell the entire package. Yeah, I get it, I don't like it but I get it. Jane, I very much appreciate you releasing Heather and I from the insanity of all of this and wanting for us to have a normal life. Jane, my sweets, I've never lived a normal life, I cannot even spell normal. I can't smell it; I can't see it and I can't taste it. No honey, I'm not retiring from this project. In this town yes, but it's time we take this show on the road. Tell me when and where the next show is and we will be there. I will do this whole same thing all over again You asked me earlier Paul if I was in. Yes sir, I am most definitely in. After tomorrow we're taking this show on the road!

    I sat in total amazement and somewhat even amused. I have never been conned like this, ever before! This was a massive hustle on a most grand scale, this is what movies are made of! This my friends, is one con-job that I'll remember forever. Heather gave me the look and taped three fingers on her forearm which means, "I'm ready to leave Babe, I'm ready to leave now!" We thanked everyone, excused ourselves and said we'll see you at dinner. It was strange to walk out of the Roberts suite without a security escort. We got to walk and get on the elevator alone and the ride up was smooth, as they obviously had already removed their turbo chargers on the son of a bitch. All of a sudden everything in my world was bland. And the world had once again become beautiful. Except the part that I was lying to myself, no I can't do bland, it's just not the way I'm put together. I have fought all of my life to be where I am today. It's the life I choose and it's a life I enjoy. It's the life I was born for.

There were no more escorted brisk movements, we moved at our own pace and when we got to our floor, I put my key in the elevator panel and the door opened and there was nobody with bulging suit coats in the hallway. We went to the door of our suite and it opened with a simple key turn. The light buttons on the door handle had been removed. We're not remotely locked in any longer, fucking weird, fucking great! The first thing I checked when we went into our suite were the windows. They still hadn't removed the shields but I'm sure that'll happen shortly, probably while we're at dinner tonight. Heather and I laid down together, her eyes were still mega wide. In just a few minutes, Heather sprung from the bed as she was laughing and began to unbutton her blouse saying, "Baby I don't think that we need to wear these anymore, as she removed her bullet-proof vest. I stood up and removed my vest saying, "We are not going to throw these away. We have both seen some folks at the gun club terribly miss handling firearms. These will be the uniform of the day when we go shooting."

We talked about the fuckery the Roberts crew put us through with this monstrous charade and we both got the giggles. I asked, "Baby you wanna make a list of all the shenanigans these clowns have pulled on us. Where do you want to start honey?"

Heather: How about those three monkeys that came to my job and told me that they were going to, "handle me?" You're going to handle me? Yeah, let's start with that bullshit! If I wasn't such a lady, I would have punched them all in the balls.

Then we can move on to the crazy car ride back to our house, our house full of agents, and we were told that we couldn't go to our own fucking basement, our vault door had been opened, our safes had been removed, they really worked hard at trying to convince us, didn't they? But as an off-handed compliment to them, they knew we were both too smart to get schooled like rookies. This production was as much for us as for the lawyers. They wanted us to believe that this whole dog and pony show was for the lawyers. No, it wasn't, that's bullshit! They knew that if they didn't convince us we wouldn't be able to convince them.

Me: I'll take that as an extreme compliment. It's nice not to be discounted for a change, you know how I like to switch things up, so just whenever someone thinks they have you figured out, you show them they don't have anything figured out. For me it's just good sport. I only wish that I was forty years younger cause I would go shoulder and shoulder with these guys no matter where they went. There's a lot of heart and intelligence involved here.

Heather started laughing by saying, "What do you want to bet that when we go downstairs tonight, the lobby will be buzzing with hotel guests and the regular wait staff will undoubtedly be happy to serve your dinner. The desk clerks will be at full speed with check-ins and reservations. It's kind of like we entered into the Twilight Zone last week and now just stepped back out. It's kind of a rush to know that I'm 17 years younger than you again. Maybe I'll give this whole survivor thing a spin and go on a bunch of talk shows and talk about the aliens that captured us. What do you say honey?" We both had a good laugh laid on our backs holding hands and quickly fell asleep.

    The clock on the nightstand told me that I've been sleeping for only twenty minutes. Heather was still in a deep slumber. I didn't want to get off the bed and disturb her so I just laid there thinking. Thinking about this journey, how it began and what transpired. This is nothing more than God's work, it's a beautiful blessing but something has been bothering me for some time now. I guess I'd better give it some deeper thought.

    I am troubled about the wooden cross necklace that I was given by the Roberts family that belonged to Father Martin. I was deeply honored to receive it but it never felt right to me. Yes, I have worn it every day but it just didn't feel right. It didn't feel like it was mine, I felt that I didn't deserve it. It just felt like it was on loan and I knew at some point that I would have to return it. But now I don't know how to return it or to whom. Part of that truth lies in all of my personal property. Heather and I have been together for less than ten years. I have a lot of property from the past that means nothing to no one other than to me and in truth, I don't know that it means all that much to me either. It represents a time long past and nothing more. If anything, that property represents an entire lifetime of heartbreaking failures. Of course, Father Martin's cross is different, much different. The tail or long end of the cross is worn thin from his caressing it several times a day, in prayer for almost forty years. I don't know who to pass it on to. Do I just take it off my neck and dangle it in front of Jane and say, "I don't need this any longer, please pass it on to somebody younger than me who will enjoy it and speak of it for years to come, because once I die it's just an old worn out wooden cross laying in my jewelry box?" The significance behind it will be lost in time, just as the memories of my time on earth will also be lost. Well, except for my seven books in the United States Library of Congress but they still won't know anything about the man that wrote them. They'll just know that they're written by a man of my name. Hopefully my books speak of my passion as though I'm still a living being. Yeah, I guess I need to talk to Jane about that and I guess it's no different than the Parson's bench that the Roberts family gifted to Heather. The Roberts family told us that Father Martin wanted Heather to have his Parsons bench that he sat on during Mass from the first day he was ordained until the day he took ill and died shortly afterwards. When Heather passes, no one will know the significance of the story behind the Parsons bench. I must find a way to preserve Father Martin's memory with the wooden cross necklace and the Parsons bench.

## Chapter 30
# THE LAST DANCE

It was almost strange to leave our room again without armed escorts. We didn't have to wait for the door lock on our room to light from red to green before the lock opened. For the first time in six days there were not two Bills standing directly in front of us as we opened the door, nor were there two Bills at the elevator and another two Bills in the lobby as the elevator doors opened. The elevator rode at a normal speed. As we exited the elevator the desk clerks were back behind the registration desk. Tim was there as the doorman and there was a slight amount of movement with hotel guests. I guess it takes a while to bring them all back in.

We went into the restaurant and of course the Roberts family was there looking quite fresh and ready for the day. For me, I wasn't so sure. There were only a few people in the restaurant but nothing like on normal days. I'm sure all that will come back in time. We joined the Roberts family and had a comfortable breakfast together. As I was sitting at the table, I looked at each person and realized that I may not ever see some of those people ever again. There were still a few Bills around and of course Norb's security team but the rest had all gone home or so I hoped. I still can't imagine what it took to put this all together. But then again, I have to remember that we have a young lady in our presence who choreographed the entire secret service operations on presidential visits throughout the country, so I guess I can't be surprised at all. She was just doing what she does.

Norb's walked over and said, "Cat and I are staying behind and would like to spend some private time with you after this morning. I'm hoping you'll have time for us before your next assignment, yes, we know you're back in the game and we're very proud of you, we definitely need you in our game."

I took my deepest of deep breaths before we entered the Mariner room for our last hurrah. I am looking forward to wrapping this thing up and catching my breath.

I greeted everyone and noticed that the four grease boards were now filled-in with the acronyms of each board title. There were twelve to fourteen entries per board, so I knew that this team was in fact now a team but it's no longer my team. After our greetings I stood in front of the room.

Me:   Ladies and gentlemen before we start, I have an announcement to make. I will no longer be heading up this project. I'm turning this project directorship over to Nancy. Nancy will be your 'go-to' person. Phil will be your ultimate supervisor no different than when he is in the office. Phil is the boss and he'll run this crew. So, let's get started.

We have spent parts of a week together. Some of the things that have taken place in this last week, we're not as they appeared. There was some Hollywood activity going on and the reason for that was that we wanted you to feel. We wanted you to feel in the deepest recesses of your minds and hearts as one of your clients may feel when facing the shock of insurmountable odds and a life crushing future of incarceration and poverty.

During this exercise, and yes, it was just that, an exercise. You were intentionally denied access to your private property, you were denied freedom of choice, you were denied freedom of movement. You were escorted everywhere you went but not without you first requesting permission. I won't bother to ask anyone of you how you felt during those moments but now you had only a brief taste of the lives of the, forgotten and the "underserved" with not knowing where and when your next meal is coming from, where you can find warmth and shelter and what harm could come at any given moment. I would like to see the hands of those who've been scared shitless for the last several days now.

Of course, all hands were in the air.

Me: Now please understand that you just had a taste, a very slight taste, just the very tip of your tongue, taste of what your client's victims may have to taste, eat and swallow for their entire lifetime. That victim did not get just a simple tip of the tongue taste, they had to swallow it, all of it and they can never digest or pass it. They can't brush the taste out of their mouth, tooth paste, mouthwash or breath mints will not neutralize or cleanse their palates. You see, the crime victim does not ever get to walk away. The memory of that taste on the very tip of their tongue will never leave them. Our currently twisted criminal justice system will not allow it. At some point the victim will have to appear in court to testify and will be forced to relive those moments of their worst days. But it's never about the victim's day in court, it's just about the perpetrator's day in court. That same crime victim will have to live with the fear that their perpetrator will be released from custody someday, and the violator may want to extract their pound of flesh, because criminals never blame themselves for their activities, they only place blame on those that stop them from their activities, so they hate. The accused hate the court system, they hate the entire fucking world and everyone in it including innocent children. Most all criminals carry the same slogan of, "Fuck the World!" They've had nothing but time to think about the day that they can settle the score. Well, that's what the "underserved" look like in part, but just a small part.

If you're still not convinced of how fucked up our state system is, here's the very latest from yesterday's Duluth newspaper.

"Minnesota prisons are going to hire professional tattoo artists for a new program. The state wants to hire licensed tattoo artists with at least three years of experience and a strong well-rounded portfolio, to start a 'legal' body art program."

Now the taxpayers get to also pay for the inmates' body art? Most prisons throughout the country (including Minnesota) don't allow tattoos, yet inmates, many inmates, have tattoos done in prison and for some reason that's not punishable, although it's against the rules. So, this new prison system program is about establishing a tattoo program in hopes of giving inmates new skills and curbing the spread of bloodborne disease from illegal body art. The article goes on to say that prisoners are known to create their own tattoo equipment using small electric motors and ballpoint pens. Without proper sterilization, the tools can lead to the transmission of diseases such as Hepatitis C and HIV from using contaminated needles.

Hey, state of Minnesota, it's against the fucking law! So now we're going to overlook the law to make prison tattoos safer? Supposedly Hepatitis treatments can cost anywhere between $20,000 up to $75,000. The state prison system treats 80 to 100 inmates each year. As of January 2022, there were 7,511 people incarcerated in Minnesota prisons and past estimates placed the number of infected inmates at anywhere from 1,200 to 3,500. Once again, these silly gooses claim, "By reducing the potential for a transmission of bloodborne diseases we are creating a safer environment for everyone including our staff and also being more prudent with taxpayer dollars."

Yeah, let's do that, what a swell fucking idea! The douche nozzles at Minnesota Corrections have spoken. How fucking ridiculous!

Why doesn't the state hire some professional Dermatologists to remove the neck and facial tattoos so when the inmate is released, they won't look like anti-social assholes and can get a job and pay their own way in life?

Now let's move beyond that silliness and get to what this is really all about. Who we are really about and what purpose are we going to serve? Well, here it is in a very large fuckin nutshell. Again, as I stated earlier, you can't fix stupid but you can expose it. We have to look no further than our local and state court systems. Hell, I get almost weekly bulletins from the Duluth Police Department warning Duluthians that a sexual predator who is, "Highly Likely" to reoffend, is being released back into the community as they have served their time. Have they really served their time? I have heard that same bullshit from convicts for several years as to how they did their time and paid their debt to society.

What debt did they pay to society?
How did they pay it?

Did they pay for their meals in prison?
No, we did!

Did they pay for their clothes and bedding?
No, we did!

Did they pay rent?
No, we did!

Did they pay for medical care?
No, we did!

Did they pay for security?
No, we did!

Did they pay legal fees?
No, we did!

Did they pay court costs?
No, we did!

Did they pay restitution?
No, we did!

    Who paid to support their spouses and children while they were, "Paying their debt to society?" That's right kids, we did!
    One of my hopes is that the entire nation, without exclusion, enact a hardline mandatory sentencing law that can't be challenged or overridden,

not even executive orders can interfere with mandatory sentencing.

Want to shut down crime? Shut down the sweetheart deals between Defense Attorneys and Judges. How do you do that? Mandatory sentencing! It's that simple! Set it up like a breakfast menu at Denny's. You do this certain crime you do this amount of time. Sorry, no substitutes!

I have never denied that I don't like lawyers and I also don't like politicians. Oftentimes politicians are also lawyers and they use the law, they don't apply it, they use it as a tool, and they use it for their own personal gain, not caring where the chips may fall. Clients are looked upon as nothing more than a necessity to gain greater wealth and positions. Family law lawyers make a fortune by playing one parent against the other and they stretch out these proceedings and hearings so that each side's attorneys can bill for every hour or part of an hour, even every minute they write, research, copy and for every phone call, taken or made. They don't care about the children involved; they don't care who the better custodial parent of the two parents would be. They only care about taking care of their own families, the vehicles they drive, the houses they own and the vacation trips that they are about to take. It's just a game, it's an ugly fucking, filthy, nasty game with the only winners being the lawyers. The kids from that slimy game, oftentimes end up being so badly emotionally torn, that they grow to be damaged adults and fall into the waiting arms of the same attorneys and judges of the criminal justice system. The circle is never ending. What's the answer? We need to become the umpires of that game. That's right, we are the only ones that can break that circle. And here's how we're going to do it.

Our city, our county, our state and national elected leaders all need to be dumped on their collective asses! We as a nation, we as a people, are imploding. It's more than just a bit obvious that our current administration has sold us out. We are on the cusp of becoming a 3rd world nation with all of this woke liberal bullshit!

We are only six months away from the November Midterms. That's the only way we can turn this country around. You've all heard the saying of, 'let the record speak for itself'? Well, we are going to do exactly that! We are going to use hard cold numbers, we will use their own numbers, no explanations, just irrefutable numbers. Fabricated numbers are mostly used by liars to lie, but numbers can also be used to tell the truth and we are going to be the truth! The truth my friend's, will set us all as a nation free! How are we few, going to save an entire nation? The silent majority of our nation, states and cities have been looking for a way and a purpose to speak up and be heard and we few will build a City, County, State and National platform to stand on, for all decent and loyal Americans.

So now this whole thing is about you using your training, your knowledge and your experience to rescue our nation. Our city, our state and our nation are your clients, our American way of living is your client, your hopes, your dreams are your client and the hopes and dreams of all other Americans (including your children and grandchildren) are all in your hands and you are all capable.

How does a small group of young attorneys in northern Minnesota take on the power players of the entire country? Check this out kids.

Do you know that just one single snowflake can start an avalanche that can and oftentimes will destroy an entire forest or village? Many people (including myself) call liberals, sissys, whiners, and snowflakes. We are going to become the first snowflakes of an unprecedented avalanche that will expose and destroy those politicians that pray on and steal from the good people of our beloved nation.

Let's face it, we will never be able to create and implement enough laws to control evil. Evil does not obey the laws. So how do we get to them? We go after those who overlook and ignore the laws. For starters we are going to expose the people that underserve the people of need. We're going to start with the Mayor of The City of Duluth and the Commissioners of St. Louis County. The Governor of The State of Minnesota along with all the elected and appointed persons on a state level, we will take them head-on and all at the same time! We will be exposing all of the voting records of all the elected officials in the entire state! Those hidden numbers will expose the losers and the liars who sold us out.

Sadly, the Minnesota Governor, the Attorney General and the Chief Justice of the Minnesota Supreme Court decide the prison releases of inmates. We are going to insist that there be a parole board system. The politicians will no longer be able to sell pardons and paroles to the highest bidder. Early releases for inmates who earn 'Good time' releases, will be abolished. If you do the crime, you will serve the time, all of it! Again, we're only about protecting those who cannot protect themselves and removing the leaders who will not protect America's neglected and forgotten souls.

We are going to mess with the governor's office and all elected state officials. Hopefully when people see their voting records, they will think twice.

Minnesota is not known to be a free-thinking state. I guess I was a bit presumptuous in saying they may think twice, when most Minnesota voters don't even think once! If your parents are democrats, so are you. You have no choice and you most definitely have no voice. If you don't follow your family's political structure in the way you conduct yourself, you become an outcast. If you don't follow the demands of your employer or your Union as to how you vote, you are shunned and most assuredly, you will lose your job in very short order. No free thinker dares to press that issue. Everybody is owned by their own device and the reason they're owned is because they spent money that they didn't have. The Unions have a beautiful game going on. They promise you life-long, guaranteed wages, benefits, and employment, so now you can gauge what you can afford before you buy anything and of course everything is bought on credit and you know that you can pay this off in so many months or years with this amount of income. So, everyone is encouraged to overspend, so you have to stay with that employer and you have to stay with that Union, which means you are paying Union dues even after retirement. Unions are a stand-alone business, they don't give a fat fiddler's fuck about who you are, or what your family needs are. All they want from you is for you to pay your dues and do as you're told, and the greatest part of being a good union member is voting for and feeding the democratic machine. They use the American flag and national holidays as nothing more than propaganda to further their agenda of total control over our nation. Yeah, free thinkers are not a well sought-after commodity in this part of the country and especially in this part of the northern end of the state. I don't know why they just don't give every household at least a snowmobile, a side-by-side, a bass boat, a canoe, a shotgun, a deer hunting rifle because they are all going to buy that shit anyway. Every time you buy anything with credit you are selling your vote and you become indebted to your employer and your union. It couldn't be any simpler than that, kids.

We are going to demand that the State of Minnesota enact a new law (which you people sitting here will put in the pipeline) that demands the voting records along with all sponsored bills be published on all platforms of social media, including local newspapers like the Duluth News Tribune does. This new law will be known as, "Heck's Law. " Heck's Law will hold elected and appointed government officials on all levels, responsible for their acts and non-involvement. Let's visit the corruption of the Duluth News Tribune for a few minutes. They have for several decades published people's misfortunes under the banner of, "Matters of Records."

    This, of course, was long before your time and the internet was not on the horizon for several years to come. The newspaper's release of public records was used in fact, to warn businesses away from extending people credit who had filed for divorce, bankruptcy, had a lien or repossession, who got traffic tickets and DUI's or had been arrested for domestic violence, drunk or fighting in public and or sentenced. This was the newspapers attempt to "Black List" people who were struggling in life. The names of these people (and their home addresses) were published as they were thought to be a risk to the businesses but it had nothing to do with anything. The Duluth News Tribune would periodically announce that they published, "As a Matter of Record" as part of its obligations of service as the keepers of the local historical record." What a bunch of bullshit! Local auto insurance agents studied, "As a Matter of Record " as a bible. They raised their rates on a traffic violation before the ink was dry on the traffic ticket. They show everyone in town who's going through a divorce or separation so they can further be besmirched by the community. It's just a bunch of tattletales vying for attention.

I can't help but laugh thinking back to listening to my parents reading the paper together and my mother or dad would make a comment about, "That dumb son of a bitch, I told him he shouldn't be driving drunk!" My dad told the guy that in the bar, while my dad was sitting there next to him, drunk! How did my dad get home? That's right, he drove home drunk! My dad drove home drunk every night of the week but there they both sat, in the privacy of their own home with a newspaper open, while criticizing someone that had the misfortune of getting caught driving drunk. Yeah sadly, that's the way of it. Yup, condemn people that get caught but never take responsibility for yourself and of course until you get caught, and then of course it's the cop's fault, not your fault, a cat ran out in front of you and made you swerve into an entire city block of parked cars at a high rate of speed! It's of course not your fault, hell you weren't really all that drunk!

That is how pathetic our society has become. But it's also going to be one of the largest tools in our toolbox. We are going to ram our entire toolbox right up their collective asses!

As it states on board #3 over here: "If you're not a part of the solution, you are therefore a part of the problem." Well, there it is, there are no solutions anywhere in this democratic run state, so for my nickel (and I hope for yours as well) I want all incumbents to be removed from their offices through informing the voting public of how these political people choose themselves over serving the public that they are sworn to serve! Are they all thieves? No, I wouldn't say that, I wouldn't say that they are all lazy lying bastards but most of them are. I would say that some people (if not many) are in politics just for the glory of the position and for all of the power and attention, which is a whole different kind of corrupt sickness. Here is the "how" of it my friends.

I believe that I mentioned earlier, how we're going to have the very people that we will be investigating actually want to volunteer to work with us. Well, we'll call it voluntary but they're about to get a nudge of a lifetime, perhaps out the door or into a jail cell! So, gang, here is the nuts and bolts of it all.

We are going to demand the necessary records with court orders and search warrants. The 'WE' are you people sitting here now and the other attorneys from the Roberts group. 'WE' are not going to request records; we are going to demand records! WE are going to demand every office holder, whether elected or appointed and every department head of services categories in the entire state, counties, and cities in all of Minnesota. Remember how the Mafia top leaders were taken down? That's right, the IRS put them away using tax evasion laws. As you all should know, in 1970 the "RICO Act" came to life that put away the 'Top Guns' of the organized crime families. Only a fool would believe that the Mafia died in 1970, the vacuum from imprisoned crime bosses was instantly filled by business leaders and politicians who were far smarter and much less flamboyant. We are going to use the Government's own play books.

First, we will review and then expose their corruption through their personal tax fillings, then quickly on to their office expenditures, that's right where we're going to slam the lid down on the cookie jar! Politicians and department directors love to list the bribes they receive as de minimis benefits. Vacations, golf outings and gifts are not de minimis benefits. WE will expose their fraud, thefts and deceit. Our sharpest tools from our tool box will be their credit card expenditures, both private and public. We are going to comb through every department's expenses as well as any department that may have a petty cash fund. Of course, the elected officials campaign funds donations and expenditures will be a mighty tasty morsel!

WE want full accountability. They won't be able to give full accountability because there's too many of them stealing in the same offices. We're going to examine receipts, receipts from petty cash, receipts from credit cards and especially where expenditures are listed as entertainment, any level of entertainment.

Yes, we're going to catch them and then we're going to expose them and they will be the very first ones in line to raise their hands and volunteer to take control of any potential corruption in their offices. Notice that I said potential, aint that fuckin cute!

Everybody in politics wants to be the shiniest and brightest star prior to the Midterms and of course during the general elections. In the next thirty days, their reputations will be so badly tarnished that a fifty-five-gallon drum of Brasso and a dozen high speed buffers will not bring their imaginary golden shine back. We can bury these lying, thieving bastards long before they can gather themselves for a reply, if we're diligent and if we have the hearts of the lions that I know you all have.

We will review every state judge, every circuit and municipal judge, in the entire state for their sentencing records. I don't even know how that shit works but you guys do. That's not my specialty but we're going to review every one of their findings we're going to review every one of those sentences and you're going to see by the numbers without an explanation, but just by the numbers as to how many people have reoffended since release. If you go to the Saint Louis County Jail roster right now, you'll see that there are 190 inmates in the Duluth Jail, with the vast majority of those inmates charged with committing multiple crimes along with 70+% charged with probation or parole violations. They violated their probation or parole agreements to commit their most recent crimes and many had outstanding violation warrants when they were given those agreements due to jail overcrowding. Catch and release on summons or just a stern warning by the police officer should stop them from committing further crimes. Chances are that these inmates are career criminals who need to become career inmates! Can you dig it?

# THE JUDICIAL SYSTEM IS GUILTY

We're going to take it to every level of government services that have anything to do with public safety. I don't want to know why people are in jail, I want to know why they were let out of jail, prior to committing their latest crimes! Jesus Christ kids, just the other day Obama's pick (that's right, Biden has been in office for over a year now, but Obama and Clinton make the calls) for the Supreme Court Justice took the oath of office. Her only criteria is that she's a female and she's a black and she's a flaming fucking racist liberal. She has all but stated that she hates white people and law enforcement. Well, that should sure as hell bode well for our nation. She wants to abolish prisons and is super soft on crime, especially sexual predators! She has no stance on anything other than her wanting to take charge of the entire criminal justice system as it pertains to the people of color. She's fighting the entire white population, and it won't be long before she promotes reparations for people who were never held as slaves. If you want to examine what a true racist looks like, you need to look no further.

Oh, by the way, let me ask you all? How did you like driving your own cars to this hotel today? How was it walking in the front doors of this building without having to climb over those Jersey barricades and with the dump trucks no longer blocking every door and ground floor windows? What was it like to not have that hand wand rubbed all over your entire body like you're being butter basted for the oven? Who enjoyed not having your cell phones confiscated or your briefcases and purse's taken from you this morning?

That's the way it should always be, but not so much with crime victims. As attorneys, you all have very keen minds and none of you have done anything to show me that any of you are dummies. What you have shown me is that you got the goods to do the deal. The Roberts family has been extremely gracious in leaving behind the 'A- team' of absolute experts in the field of media. Once again, no one here is to make a public statement of any type or do any interviews. This will be handled by our media professionals. I want the full report of every criminal court judge's finding and sentencings. I want the same thing for any divorce court judge and family court judge. I want the numbers. I want to see what the Da's office does with charges handed to them by an arresting police officer and I want to see how those charges are amended. I want to see how those charges are prosecuted. Again, our goal is to expose the weak and soft sentencing that failed to protect us. *Capish?*

By now you have all heard of the murders in Duluth from yesterday morning. A family of four were shot to death in their sleep, along with the family dog. A 47-year-old father, a 44-year-old mother and 2 children ages 12 and 9. They were all killed by the wife's cousin, 29-year-old Brandon Taylor Cole-Skogstad. After killing his four family members he turned his gun to himself and took his life. Of course, all the reports are quite preliminary but it is understood that he did a Facebook post earlier that day praying for relief for the family members that he was about to kill. Nothing can be eviller than intentionally and knowingly planning to kill babies. As far as I'm concerned, nine and twelve-year-old children are still babies. What kind of evil does that? And of course, the question begs to be asked long before it will be, if it's ever asked, "Where did we as a society go wrong? Was the killer just another number of the underserved and ignored? I would like to see his rap sheet. How many times in the past, was he contacted by law enforcement? Was he ever arrested? How many times was he jailed? How many times did he stand before a judge and was given a soft handed jail sentence and put on some kind of supposed self-probation? Or if there have been social workers involved in his life and to what degree? Somebody failed somewhere and the end result is a family of four wiped from the face of our Earth! Who wants to defend that bullshit?

The questions are never ending and those questions go on in several towns in all of our states almost every day.

Let's go on to a federal level. How about Hillary's emails, Anthony Weiner's laptop, Hunter's hard drive? There is nothing on Epstein's probable cause for his arrest or the investigations that led to his arrest. So, the cameras were not working in his cell and the guards were sleeping or playing cards while the prisoner was on suicide watch? His girlfriend and top pimp, Ghislaine Maxwell who was found guilty of Transporting a minor for child sex trafficking and a bunch of other sex related charges with several minors. She was found guilty over six months ago but still not sentenced! But we get snippets of the Johnny Depp trial several times a day and the Maxwell trial was not televised? Who is being protected? Justice is only for those who can afford it! Prove me wrong, please?

What exactly has the FBI and other federal agencies been doing? Why during the trial of Epstein's former girlfriend hasn't there been any mention of the parties involved in child trafficking and children's rapes? Who is hiding this information and why? It must be a government official or several, high level government officials. If all of this does not sicken and anger you, then you do not have a pulse… nor should you.

It is absolutely impossible to go just one day without hearing something about Black Lives Matter and the number of killings throughout the country. There has been a massive increase in black Americans murdered which is directly a result of defunding the police movement that Black Lives Matters promotes. And who is killing all these black people? Other blacks for the most part, yes black on black murders outweigh any other race in the nation. So, what part of any of that murder rate is Black Lives Matter protesting?

The FBI data shows murders across-the-board spiked by 32% and in 2020 compared to the year prior marking the largest single-year increase in killings since the FBI began tracking the crimes. For black Americans the murders have spiked disproportionately. At least 7,484 black Americans were murdered in 2019 according to the FBI and yet, the Black Lives Matter organization was silent when approached for comment on 2020's skyrocketing number of black murders.

Anybody in the right fucking mind who defends BLM as an organization for the people of color are the problem. BLM is a crime syndicate of liars and thieves and nothing more. It is more than a bit apparent that Black Lives Matter is a syndicate of organized crime that operates on fear and extortion. The leaders of each group are quite well-to-do as we spoke of earlier, but for the people that they supposedly represent, nothing has changed for them other than more of them being murdered.

Nice job BLM!

## Chapter 31
# THE CORONATION

Your task is simple but it will take a great deal of courage, so at this point, I'm done. If anyone would like to come up and shake my hand and even give me some lovin's, I would be deeply honored.

Phil:   Before everyone slobbers all over you David with well wishes, hugs, kisses or whatever else you all might feel appropriate, I have a request and an announcement. With your permission David, I would like to take each one of these grease boards and have an art museum curator either spray a protective coating or just encase them in a glass frame to protect them so they can never fade or be erased. And again, with your permission, I would like to remove them and install them in my building meeting rooms and hallways. To coin one of your favorite phrases David; "Least We Ever Forget."

Me:   Yes Phil, I would like them to be protected as well, however I don't want them to leave this room until this entire project is complete. Send in your people to do what needs to be done here, to protect these boards, they cannot leave this building with these boards! If anybody wants to argue that, kindly remind them that I carry a gun and it is always in, "Condition One" with several loaded magazines topped off with 220 grain Hornady Critical Duty rounds that can stop a city bus engine.

Heather:   Ladies and gentleman, I have never spoken for David in all the years that we have been together, until this moment. We are done for the day. I am taking my husband home. Don't any of you expect to see him for the next few days, you may not see him ever again. Norbs, you and Kat will be sleeping in our home tonight. You may bring two of your security people but no more than two. You two asked for a private audience with David and I will grant that but I won't allow you to keep him up all night. At precisely 2:00 PM tomorrow you ladies will be leaving our home and our lives.

Tomorrow is May 1st, and your security people will open our storage shed and carry our patio table and chairs up on our deck and set our shade umbrella up before you leave. David will be sitting at that table basking in the morning sun while editing his newly completed novel for the next six weeks prior to publication.

Now if the Roberts family will give us ten minutes, we would love to lunch with you before you return to Chicago.

Heather took my hand and led me out of the room and toward the elevators, she called out to Tim, the doorman (and undercover) Federal Agent to join us. Tim of course looked puzzled as we three entered the elevator but he sensed that Heather was in charge and he should remain quiet. I took out my special keys for the elevator and our suite.

I placed my key in the control panel and unlocked the auto-stop to go to our private floor. Before the elevator door opened on our floor, Heather held her hand open and firmly said, "Give."

Heather opened the outer door to our suite and stood back as she gestured for Tim and I to enter ahead of her. She then stepped around us with, "Gentleman, follow me." As she walked into the study area and opened the floor to ceiling drapes. I saw that the bullet-proof window shields had been removed.

Heather:  Tim, do you like the view?

Tim:  Yes Ma'am, I do.

Heather:  Glad to know it, our friend. Tim, you have been a wonderful friend and guardian even when we didn't know you were our guardian. Catch!

Heather flipped my keys to Tim as she smiled, saying, "It's all yours young man, we will have no further use for this suite. David will sign the papers right after lunch, won't you please join us and the Roberts family for lunch now?"

Heather took my hand and said, "Sweetheart, our bags are being delivered to the house, we have nothing here to pack, our cars are in our garage, so we will need a lift. Tim, would you mind giving us a ride home after lunch?"

## THE END

### BOOKS BY DAVID J. BROWN

Daddy Had to Say Goodbye

Flesh of a Fraud

Harvest Season: Body Parts

Altered Egos: The Killers In Us All

Brothers of the Tattered Cloth

The Judicial System is Guilty: The Raping of Lady Justice

Betrayed: My Body is Killing Me

*Co-Author of*
#BeLikeEd


To contact the author; David J. Brown please visit: djbrownbooks@gmail.com

Please visit David's Website: davidjbrownbooks.com

You may also make a request for David to speak at your upcoming events at: dbrown624@gmail.com

Watch for David's seven novels to be released in audiobooks in the summer of 2022

Printed in the United States of America

GOD BLESS AMERICA

Made in the USA
Monee, IL
01 March 2024